**SARAH BENNETT** has been re_____
reme_____. Raised in a f_mily of b_____
books of all genres has culminate_____
After: getting to write her own sto_____ _____ with others.

Born and raised in a military family, she is happily married to her own Officer (who is sometimes even A Gentleman). Home is wherever he lays his hat, and life has taught them both that the best family is the one you create from friends as well as relatives.

When not reading or writing, Sarah is a devotee of afternoon naps and sailing the high seas, but only on vessels large enough to accommodate a casino and a choice of restaurants.

You can connect with her via twitter @Sarahlou_writes or on Facebook www.facebook.com/SarahBennettAuthor

# Spring Skies Over Bluebell Castle

## SARAH BENNETT

ONE PLACE. MANY STORIES

This novel is entirely a work of fiction. The names, characters
and incidents portrayed in it are the work of the author's
imagination. Any resemblance to actual persons, living or
dead, events or localities is entirely coincidental.

HQ
An imprint of HarperCollins*Publishers* Ltd
1 London Bridge Street
London SE1 9GF

This edition 2019

First published in Great Britain by
HQ, an imprint of HarperCollins*Publishers* Ltd 2019

Copyright © Sarah Bennett 2019

Sarah Bennett asserts the moral right to be
identified as the author of this work.
A catalogue record for this book is
available from the British Library.

ISBN: PB: 978-0-00-833078-1
EB: 978-0-00-831480-4

**MIX**
Paper from
responsible sources
FSC
www.fsc.org        **FSC˚ C007454**

This book is produced from independently certified FSC™ paper
to ensure responsible forest management.

For more information visit: www.harpercollins.co.uk/green

Printed and bound in Great Britain by
CPI Group (UK) Ltd, Croydon CR0 4YY

All rights reserved. No part of this publication may be reproduced,
stored in a retrieval system, or transmitted, in any form or by any means,
electronic, mechanical, photocopying, recording or otherwise,
without the prior permission of the publishers.

This book is sold subject to the condition that it shall not, by way of trade
or otherwise, be lent, re-sold, hired out or otherwise circulated without
the publisher's prior consent in any form of binding or cover other than
that in which it is published and without a similar condition including this
condition being imposed on the subsequent purchaser.

*For Phillipa – always an inspiration x*

# CHAPTER ONE

'Arthur? Arthur!'

The bellowing of his name roused Arthur Ludworth from a most pleasant snooze in front of the fireplace in the family room. Giving several of the castle's mob of unruly dogs a gentle shove, he fought his way free from the cosy depths of one of the matching burgundy leather sofas and stood. Scrubbing a hand across his eyes, he frowned as Lancelot yelled his name once more. His normally placid-tempered uncle sounded furious.

'Lord, what's he shouting about?' Tristan, Arthur's younger brother by a matter of minutes, protested from the opposite sofa, one arm draped over his eyes, the other holding a brandy balloon which was in serious danger of spilling its precious contents onto the worn and faded Aubusson rug stretched out before the fire. Pippin, Tristan's scruffy little border terrier, raised his head briefly from his master's chest to grumble about being disturbed before settling back down again.

'Mrs W's probably hidden the whisky from him again,' Igraine, the eldest of the three Ludworth triplets, said from her cross-legged position next to the fire, eyes still fixed on the screen of her e-reader. Thanks to an ancestor's obsession with the Knights of the Round Table, it had become tradition for subsequent generations of Ludworths to be named after characters from those legends. Arthur felt like he and his brother had gotten away lightly—considering his grandfather had gone full-bore ridiculous in naming his sons Uther and Lancelot—but their sister hadn't been so lucky. Refusing to be saddled with such a flowery name, she'd shorted it to Iggy, and woe betide anyone who forgot it.

'Arthur!' Lancelot's roar was closer this time. 'The hellbeast is on the phone for you.'

The last of Arthur's post-dinner good mood evaporated at the mention of his uncle's nickname for their mother. His soft groan was echoed by the other two. 'Perhaps she's called to wish us Happy New Year,' he said, more out of hope than expectation.

'Perhaps hell has frozen over,' Iggy muttered, as she played her fingers over the thick dark plait of hair curling over one shoulder and almost into her lap. The self-soothing gesture was a hangover from their childhood, and one of those unconscious habits she'd never quite managed to break.

Arthur wanted to reach out and stop her, to take her hand and offer the comfort she obviously needed, but he stopped himself. There was too much to say—nothing he hadn't already said a million times since he'd first become aware of the anachronistic inheritance rules attached to the Baronetcy of Ludworth that made him the rightful heir over her simply because he was their father's first-born legitimate *male* issue—but tonight, of all nights, was not the one. He'd try again, soon, before the gulf he could sense between them split any wider.

Using one hand to hold his beloved pup in place, Tristan sat up then drained the last of the cognac in his glass. 'If she asks after me, tell her I'm dead.'

'Tris...' Arthur hated himself for the soft admonishment the moment it left his lips.

Tristan shrugged, then checked his watch. 'It's nearly eleven, I'm going to sort Dad's stuff out.' Placing Pippin on the floor, he stood. The terrier cast him a baleful look at being so rudely disturbed then wandered over to jump up on the sofa Arthur had abandoned and wriggled his way into the centre of the dog pile still occupying most of it.

Iggy rose, all fluid grace and lean muscle from a lifetime spent more outdoors than in. 'I'll help you.' The two of them left the family room via the opposite door just as Lancelot's silvered head popped around the other one.

'Traitors,' Arthur muttered, before offering his uncle a weary smile. 'How is she?' He pointed at the cordless phone in Lancelot's hand.

'Poisonous, as ever.' His uncle made no attempt to lower his voice as he thrust the phone towards him, and Arthur winced at the indignant squawk coming from the handset. 'I'm off down The Castle for a pint.' The only pub in the small village that sprawled out from the edges of the Ludworth Estate wasn't the most imaginatively named establishment, but there was a guaranteed warm welcome for all who entered its front door.

Arthur wrapped his hand over the receiver. 'You're not coming out with us later?'

Lancelot shook his head, the fierce frown on his rugged features melting away, leaving behind lines of strain and grief. 'Can't do it, lad. Saying goodbye to him once was bad enough.'

Arthur swallowed. He didn't feel much like doing it himself, but his father had been very clear about his final wishes, so he would honour them together with Tristan and Iggy. 'We'll walk down afterwards and say hello to everyone.' And make sure Lancelot didn't fall down one of the grassy embankments, which were all that remained of the once-imposing moat that had protected the residents of Camland Castle from invaders for centuries, on his way home. With a brief nod, his uncle left the room.

Having no more excuses to avoid speaking to his mother, Arthur lifted the phone to his ear. 'Hello, Mother, how are you?'

'How am I? How can you ask me that? How could he have

3

been so cruel?' Helena Ludworth-Mills-Wexford-Jones broke down into noisy sobs which Arthur knew from long experience wouldn't produce enough tears to ruin her perfect make-up.

With a sigh, he rested his head back against the dark wood panelling lining the wall behind him and let the performance play out. His eyes strayed instinctively to the smiling portrait over the fireplace, and he wondered—not for the first time—how someone as jolly and lively as his dad had ended up married to someone like Helena.

Within less than a minute the sobs had quietened to a series of breathy gasps and he was able to make himself heard. 'Who's been cruel to you, Mother?' It was a pointless question. Deep down in his gut he knew what the call was about. He'd settled the last bits of his father's will with the solicitor the previous week. Not the best way to spend Christmas Eve, but the timing couldn't be helped and Arthur had just been glad to see the back of everything after several months trying to tie off the myriad strands of red tape tangled around his dad's sprawling portfolio. Once they'd untangled the mess of dodgy investments, short-term loans and several eye-watering overdrafts it had become clear to Arthur the estate he'd inherited was flat broke.

'Your father, of course. He waited until the last to drive a dagger into my heart. I bet he went to his grave laughing over it.'

'There wasn't much to laugh about at the end,' Arthur said, fighting to keep his voice steady as he pictured his father at the last. Uther's once hearty frame had been reduced to little more than skin stretched over bone by the cancer that had ravaged him in a few short months.

'But how am I supposed to survive on the pittance he's left me?' Helena wailed.

Arthur gripped the phone so hard his fingers turned white. God, she had a bloody nerve. 'Technically, he didn't owe you a penny.' Helena had walked out on the four of them before the triplets' second birthday, declaring her duty done, and had barely looked back. Even after she'd demanded a divorce to marry her second of four husbands—and counting—his dad had continued to support her financially over the next twenty-five years and had insisted on a final settlement for her in his will, one which the over-stretched estate could ill afford.

'How can you say that? He owed me! Giving birth to the three of you ruined my figure and destroyed my career.' Her voice wavered, and Arthur braced himself for another round of crocodile tears.

'One feature in a magazine thirty years ago doesn't exactly amount to a modelling career, Mother.'

'That's because I met your father shortly afterwards, and I had to give it up. I gave him everything he wanted—an heir, a spare and even a bloody brood mare to carry on the family line and look how he repays me!'

Anger shot through him. He hated the dismissive way she talked about them, especially Iggy. 'That's enough, Mother. The terms of Dad's will have been settled and there's nothing more to be said about it.' He'd cut out his own tongue before he'd admit to her the mess they were in. It was his business—well, his, Iggy's and Tristan's because they'd refused to let him shoulder it alone—and no one else's.

'But you're Baronet Ludworth now, Arthur.'

'Not officially.' In order to inherit his father's title, Arthur had been required to apply to the Department for Constitutional Affairs to be formally recognised and have his name entered onto the official Roll of the Baronets. As with most things of that nature, the wheels turned slowly, and he was still awaiting confirmation. He'd tried in vain to appeal to them for Iggy to be recognised as the rightful heir, but had been advised, not unsympathetically, that the restrictions laid down could not be overturned.

'Oh, you know what I mean.' His mother's formerly shrill tones turned soft and wheedling. 'You control the estate.'

Arthur laughed, a bitter snap of sound. 'You'll get nothing out of me, Mother. Not one more penny.' Even if the estate finances weren't teetering on the brink, he had nothing to give the woman who'd ruined his father's life.

'He's turned you against me! Listen, Arthur, you don't understand—'

*Bloody hell, the nerve of the woman!* His dad had never said a bad word against her, had done everything in his power to keep a relationship between his beloved children and the mother who'd never given two hoots for them. Arthur had shed his last tears for her after she'd failed to turn up to collect the three of them from school for a long-promised weekend. They'd been 13 at the time. Tristan and Iggy had given up after an hour and gone back to their rooms, but Arthur had stayed on the front steps convinced she'd come motoring up any second complaining about a holdup with the traffic. As each hour past he'd gone from excited, to hopeful, and eventually to worried she'd had some terrible accident. His housemaster had finally coaxed a tearful, frozen Arthur inside after putting in a call to his father who'd tracked Helena down at Ascot races. Having received an invitation to someone's box, she'd chosen to spend the day seeing and being seen by her society friends and couldn't understand what the fuss was all about.

With an echo of that sad boy in his heart, Arthur cut off her protestations. 'You abandoned us without a second thought, there's nothing left to understand. If you need money, I suggest you ask your *current* husband for it.' Arthur ended the call before any more of the bitterness welling up inside him could spill out. Shaking himself like one of their Labradors emerging from the pond after a dip, Arthur shed the cold shards of disappointment threatening to seep into his heart. She was never going to change. He'd known that at 13, and now, at 27, it was time to acknowledge it.

'What did she want?' Tristan entered the family room bundled

6

up in a navy padded jacket and a bright yellow scarf, a locked metal box balanced carefully across his arms.

'Money.'

'I hope you told her to get stuffed,' said Iggy who'd entered on Tristan's heels, equally well wrapped up and carrying Arthur's coat which she thrust at him.

'Close enough.' Accepting his coat, he tugged it on then moved to give Tristan a hand with the box. It wasn't heavy, but they didn't want to risk any accidents. 'Are we ready for this?'

'Nope, but let's do it anyway.' With a shrug, Iggy pulled a white knitted cap over her dark hair then tugged on a pair of matching gloves. God, she looked so sad. Arthur bet if he looked in a mirror right then, the same haunted look in her hazel eyes would be reflected in his. 'I've put your boots by the front door,' she said, pointing to the thick woollen socks on his otherwise bare feet.

'Cheers, Iggle-Piggle.' The hated nickname earned him a punch on the arm, but at least it eased some of the pain tightening her face.

It also sent him jostling into Tristan, who staggered a couple of steps, trying to keep the box steady. 'Careful! We don't want Dad going off by accident.'

Iggy patted the metal box with one gloved hand. 'Sorry, Dad.' The three of them laughed at the absurdity of it, further easing the stress of what was to come.

Steadying the box between them, Arthur and Tristan followed their sister through the echoing vaulted central chamber of the great hall. Once the beating heart of Camland Castle, it now belonged mostly to the dogs whose sprawling mass of beds and pillows occupied pride of place before the enormous fireplace which Arthur—at just a shade under six-feet tall—could still walk inside without ducking. Thick, evergreen boughs decorated with sprigs of blood-red holly berries and creamy-white clumps of mistletoe covered the high mantle, scenting the air with fresh pine. A matching display filled the middle of the enormous, age-scarred circular table positioned in the exact centre of the room.

As he did every time he passed through the space, Arthur paused to admire his sister's handiwork. Born with a green thumb, according to their great-aunt, Morgana, Iggy was never happier than when she could escape into the gardens and woodland stretching out around the castle.

Their progress halted by the front door for Arthur to stuff his feet into the dark-green wellingtons his sister had previously put out for him. Ever practical, she'd also left a large torch beside his boots, something he'd completely forgotten to think about when they'd been planning this evening. Arthur watched Iggy's face as she pulled opened the left-hand side of the imposing oak front door. The moment the chilly December air touched her skin, her whole body seemed to lift and lighten, as though she were some kind of sprite, only able to truly thrive out of doors.

Standing to one side, she ushered Arthur and Tristan out then shooed several disappointed dogs back into the warmth of the hall. 'No walkies for you tonight, darling, you won't like the noise,' she said, rubbing the silken ears of Nimrod, one of a pair of greyhounds they'd adopted from the local shelter.

Knowing they had the space to accommodate them, the shelter would often call if they were struggling to rehome any dogs. Large dogs; older ones; those at the less aesthetically pleasing end of the spectrum—Arthur and his siblings would take them in. The numbers in the pack had ebbed and flowed over the years, and those that passed on were buried together in a beautiful grove in the woods, so they could 'rest forever in the sunshine' as Iggy had declared when they'd first chosen it as children.

Nimrod snuffled her palm, then allowed Iggy to gently ease him back far enough to tug the heavy door closed once more. A few protesting barks followed them as they descended the steps, but Arthur knew they'd soon all be sprawled in front of the hearth in a tangle of heads and tails.

Iggy dug her own torch from her pocket and aimed it at the

8

gravel ahead of her, giving them a point of reference to follow. They followed the path as it wound around the western wall of the castle and beyond to the faded and overgrown formal gardens where it finally gave way to the gallops still used daily to exercise the horses from the successful Bluebell Castle stud their uncle ran from the stables.

The whimsical name was drawn from the incredible floral display the woods surrounding the castle put on every spring. The little flower had become so synonymous with the Ludworth family it had even found its way onto their family crest. Thoughts of what might become of his uncle's business haunted Arthur along with a million other worries. Lancelot's reputation was good enough the business could survive relocating elsewhere if the worst of their nightmares came true and Arthur was forced to sell up, but it'd be a devasting loss to the members of the local community who relied upon it for employment.

The circle of torchlight stopped as Iggy paused. 'Here?'

'Just a bit further, and then I reckon we'll be fine,' Tristan replied. 'What do you think, Arthur?'

It was hard to gauge distances in the dark, but he knew the land beneath his feet as well as the back of his own hand. They were almost to the edge of where the formal lands surrounding their home gave way to the wild escarpments of the Derbyshire hills. Their father had loved tromping over those hills and it was also a symbolic threshold. Free of all worldly responsibilities, Uther's spirit—or whatever—could escape back to the untamed wildness of nature. 'Here is probably as good a spot as any. We're well away from any trees.'

'I think it's perfect,' Iggy's voice held a slight tremor, but the beam of light cast by her torch onto the ground in front of them was steady as a rock.

'Are you sure you know what you're doing with these things?' Arthur asked Tristan as they bent to place the box gently on the ground.

'I'm sure. I've read the instructions at least half a dozen times, and I had a briefing from the manufacturers when I went and picked them up. Stop fussing.' The last was said with exasperated affection.

Taking up a position opposite his sister, Arthur pointed his own torch to increase the illuminated area and give Tristan enough room to work with. Trying to quell the nerves in his stomach, Arthur watched his brother unfasten the metal container and draw out the first of several massive rockets attached to long sticks. 'Trust Dad to come up with something as daft as this,' he muttered.

Tristan's broad grin flashed up briefly in the torch light. 'I think it's a fab idea, who wouldn't want to be turned into fireworks when they die?'

Just about everybody he could think of, but Arthur kept that to himself. Tristan had become enamoured with the idea from the moment they'd first read the request included in their father's will. Arthur had never heard of it before, but once they'd looked it up on the internet, it had proven to be more popular than he'd expected. After reading some of the touching testimonials on the manufacturer's site, he'd agreed to go along with it.

With their dad having passed away in early October, they could've done this on Bonfire night, but it had been Iggy's suggestion that they wait until New Year Eve's and mark the passing of the old year into the new with this final farewell and tribute. The symbolism of it had led Arthur to suggest this as the location, echoing as it did that transition from one thing to another: old to new; settled lands to wilderness; life to death.

Tristan paced out the placement of each of the eight rockets provided with the kit and set them firmly into the ground. He then removed the central piece of the display—a multi-firework barrage which could be lit by a single fuse. Straightening up, he checked his watch. 'Five minutes.'

They waited in silence until the first distant chime from the

10

village church, then Tristan stepped forward to fire the first rocket using the special ignitor kit provided by the manufacturer. A shiver travelled down Arthur's spine at the distinctive whoosh of the firework streaking high into the air, and then all his worries vanished as a huge boom echoed off the nearby rocky hills and a sparkle of silver and blue bloomed across the dark sky above their heads. Seconds later, the second rocket splashed golden rain, swiftly followed by the third, a bright silver starburst that ended in a series of crackles. Tristan lit two more, bright blue then bright green, five in total to mark each decade of their father's too-brief life.

Having lit the barrage, Tristan stepped back to join Arthur and Iggy who'd come to stand beside him and they watched in awed silence as the sky lit up with flash after flash of multi-coloured sparks sending their father on his way. Though the company had promised the barrage would last for two minutes it felt like much longer, and by the end of it Arthur found his face was aching from smiling so much at the sheer joy and exuberance. 'Well done, Dad.'

'That was fabulous, just perfect,' Iggy said as she squeezed his hand.

'Just the last three left.' Tristan offered the ignitor to Arthur. 'Age before beauty.' Arthur took it with a shake of his head. Apart from a pale scar bisecting Arthur's left eyebrow thanks to a fall from one of the mighty oak trees spread throughout their woods, they were alike enough to be mistaken for each other by anyone who didn't know the family well.

As he stepped up to one of the remaining rockets, all traces of humour fled and he found it hard to breathe around a sudden ache in his chest. The official memorial service they'd held back in the autumn had been the time for wordy tributes and eulogies. Now, he had only one thing left to say. 'Blaze bright, Dad, always.' With shaking fingers, he touched the ignitor to the fuse.

Bright silver sparks showered high above as Iggy placed a soft hand on his back before accepting the ignitor from him. 'Love you, Daddy, to the stars and back.' Her fiery tribute streaked into the sky, a perfect crackling match to Arthur's rocket.

'We'll always have Paris,' Tristan said as he lit the third and final fuse, and the three of them laughed. Stolen from *Casablanca*, it had been their dad's response to any awkward or emotional situation, and had become his traditional farewell phrase whenever he'd dropped them off at school.

As the final firework blazed above, they turned away towards the castle. Mixed amongst the smoke, the ashes of Uther Pendragon Ludworth, fourteenth Baronet Ludworth of Camland Castle drifted to settle over the lands he'd loved so much, and Arthur swore he'd do everything in his power to keep hold of them.

# CHAPTER TWO

'You've got this. You've done all the research, double-checked and triple-checked everything. Come on now.' Pep talk over, Lucie Kennington released her grip on the porcelain sink in the ladies' bathroom and turned on the cold tap. Running her wrists under the cool water, she practised a deep breathing technique she'd picked up at yoga class and squished down the last of the butterflies fluttering in her stomach.

A quick check in the mirror above the sink told her the carefully applied 'there, but not there' make-up she'd got up an hour earlier than normal to apply still looked flawless. One of the first things she'd learnt when starting at Witherby's Fine Art five years previously was the importance of presentation. Whether it was finding the perfect frame for a painting, a table from the right period to display an exquisite porcelain vase, or just ensuring you were immaculately turned out, presentation was an essential part of maintaining Witherby's reputation as one of the foremost auction houses in the country.

Having used a damp finger to tame a stray tendril threatening to escape from the sleek bun tied at her nape, Lucie dried her hands on one of the white hand towels stacked in neat rolled rows next to the sink then slid her arms into her navy jacket. Single button fastened at her waist, a quick half-turn and a smoothing hand over the matching pencil skirt and she was ready to face the music.

The low heels on her navy court shoes sank into the deep pile of the forest green carpet as she strode along the hallway then down the sweeping staircase which led from the upper floor staff offices to the ground floor housing the exhibition spaces. Witherby's occupied what had once been a grand Georgian mansion in the heart of London, and its high sculptured ceilings and painted half-panel walls added to the gravitas and atmosphere. Coming to work every day in the exquisitely beautiful building felt like a real privilege to Lucie—even if the ancient heating system and original sash windows left something to be desired in the cold depths of winter.

As she stepped down onto the creamy marble floor of the imposing entrance hall, a blast of cold from the open front door sent a shiver through her, and she was glad for the thermal vest hidden beneath her silk blouse. A strip of Wedgwood blue sky showed over the rooftops of the buildings across the street. It might be chilly, but at least the weather was fine which boded well for their first major sale day of spring. A quick, nervous smile to James, the doorman clad in a traditional set of tails, complete with top hat, earned her a wink in return. 'It's going to be a good one,' he said. 'They were queuing to get in.'

His declaration did nothing to quell her nerves, nor did the hubbub of conversation already spilling out of the open double-doors of the main auction room. The start of the auction was still three hours away. 'Better go and make sure everything's ready then!' Lucie kept her tone bright and breezy, like it was just another day and not the most important one to date in her career. With a quick wave, she headed down a short corridor to the left of the main entrance and into the private viewing area where select patrons were given time to peruse the best lots in relative peace.

One more deep breath as she paused on the threshold and then she swept into the room, head high, smile bright, eyes dancing over the people already gathered with a glass of Buck's Fizz. 'Something to drink, Ms Kennington?' Marnie, one of this year's new interns, offered her a silver tray topped with glasses.

'Thank you.' Lucie accepted a highball filled with sparkling water. The ice clinked, and she wrapped her left hand over the right to calm the slight shaking. She cast a glance around the room, trying to focus on individuals and not just the blur of chattering faces. Spying a famous newspaper art critic holding court in one corner, she took a too-large mouthful of water and almost choked as the bubbles fizzed up the back of her nose. *Smooth, Lucie.* Snorting out one's drink was most definitely not the 'Witherby's way' of doing things.

Hoping nobody had noticed her discomfort, she began to stroll around the edge of the room, catching snippets of conversations as she went. It came as no surprise how few of the discussions were about the painting they'd all gathered to see. Art was rarely appreciated solely for its ability to induce an emotional reaction, whether breath-taking joy, or shock and discomfort. It had become a commodity. A thing to own for the sake of owning it, or even as a way of reducing taxation liabilities. It was the ugly side of the art world, a necessary evil without which she wouldn't be able to do the job she loved. But it broke her heart to think of all the treasures secreted away in bank vaults and kept under lock and key. A shiver ran through her. Try as she might to escape it, the tendrils of materialism continued to thread themselves through her life.

'Ah, Lucinda, there you are.' The warm greeting from Carl Nelson, the head of her department, chased away the dark clouds gathering in her mind. He'd been nothing but supportive since she'd first joined the company as a shy girl fresh from university. Setting her shoulders, she lifted her face to meet the paternal smile he aimed her way and moved towards the small group gathered around him. 'I was just telling everyone about your remarkable discovery.'

A woman clad in a sleek black skirt and jacket that whispered of vintage Chanel from every stitch and thread gave Lucie an appraising glance before smiling. 'You really just found the piece hanging forgotten in the hallway?'

Lucie nodded. 'I was there to appraise another artwork entirely. I turned to take off my coat and caught sight of the Meileau from the corner of my eye.' She paused, lost for a moment in the memory of her first sight. Butterflies danced inside her, the same as they had in the dusty hallway of a suburban bungalow. The luminous blues and greens of the beautiful watercolour had glowed even in the half-light of a gloomy afternoon, stealing the breath from Lucie's lungs.

'And Impressionism isn't even her speciality.' The slightly hesitant voice behind her shoulder was another welcome balm to Lucie. Turning, she made room for a slightly rumpled-looking Piers Johnson to join them. 'So you can imagine,' he continued with a quick wink at Lucie, 'how green with envy we were when our Pre-Raphaelite-loving colleague stumbled across one of the discoveries of the decade.'

Fighting not to blush, Lucie found his hand and gave it a quick squeeze before dropping it again in case he got the wrong idea. With his kind blue eyes twinkling from behind the lenses of his wire-framed glasses, to the ruffled brown hair that always looked in need of a good comb, Piers had the kind of bookish charm that ticked every one of Lucie's boxes. Or should have.

They'd dated a handful of times the previous summer before Lucie had admitted reluctantly to herself that the only stimulation between them was on an intellectual level. When he'd finally kissed her in a quiet corner of the V&A where they'd been to visit an exhibition together, it had been…pleasant.

Though he'd been disappointed when she'd suggested they had too much to lose in terms of both friendship and their working relationship, he'd been nothing but gracious. Over the past twelve months he'd never intimated he wanted to resume their fledgling romance, but she caught the odd look from him now and then that made her wonder, so she was at pains not to act in a way he might take as encouragement. He was a decent man, and the last thing she wanted to do was hurt or embarrass him. Turning up to support her today was just the sort of thing he would do, and she wished, not for the first time, that she was attracted to him. He was perfect for her in every other way.

Swallowing a sigh of regret, she turned his compliment aside with one of her own. 'Oh, Piers, don't tease so. Everyone knows how much you've done to build Witherby's reputation to what it is today. I'm just a beginner in comparison.'

Casting her a grateful smile, he shoved his glasses back in place with his forefinger. 'You're too kind.' He turned back to the client. 'Since Lucie's find we've all been trawling the valuation enquiries inbox in the hopes of matching her success.'

Members of the public were welcome to submit requests directly to Witherby's via their website, and it usually fell to Lucy and the other junior valuation staff to comb through the emails and winnow out anything of interest. Her find had, temporarily at least, elevated the task from mundane chore to something of an in-house competition to find the next big thing.

'It was pure *luck*,' she stressed. 'Any one of my colleagues could've been assigned the visit. I was just in the right place at the right time.'

'Well, we're all on tenterhooks. When do we get to see this masterpiece?' The sleek woman asked.

Glancing past the woman's shoulder, Lucie spotted Carl making his way towards the cloth-swathed stand in the centre of the room. Immediately, the butterflies in her tummy were dancing once more. 'Any minute now.'

'Allow me.' With a smile, Piers offered the woman his arm, excusing himself from Lucie with a smile. No doubt he'd sensed her nerves and was giving her space to compose herself. Such a *good* man. As he strolled away, his words drifted back to Lucie.

'There were some questions over the provenance, but Lucie beavered away until she scraped together enough data to satisfy the committee.'

Lucie winced. It was true she'd faced an uphill battle to trace an unbroken line of ownership of the Meileau. Piers was no doubt just trying to make polite conversation, but she wished he would be a little more discreet. Someone might overhear him and assume there was some question mark over her research, which could be ruinous. Provenance was *everything* in the art community, and any doubt in its veracity might put off potential bidders. Trying not to let her nerves ratchet up to panic, she gave the pair a wide berth as she made her way towards the circular dais along with the rest of the converging crowd.

'Lucinda, where are…oh, there you are. Come on up.' Carl gestured to a spot beside him facing the gathered staff and guests.

Feeling heat prickle in her cheeks, Lucie edged towards the front to slip through a gap and join him. Never comfortable in the spotlight, she would've preferred to remain within the group. In the grand scheme of things, it didn't matter who had discovered the painting, only that someone had brought it back into the light for the world to enjoy once more. *Credit where credit is due.* The old adage drifted up from her memory, the words spoken by her grandfather when she demurred over him giving her a special present after she'd received an award at her school's speech night. When she'd pointed out her award had been for participating in a group project, he'd chucked her cheek with his finger. 'You're allowed to shine a little bit, sometimes. People will be quick enough to steal your glory, don't give it away so easily.'

With the spirit of her grandfather boosting her courage, Lucie forced her shoulders to relax and lifted her head to meet Carl's encouraging smile. He'd been instrumental in ensuring she received her due. He'd monitored her progress as she'd worked to pin together the bits and pieces of lost provenance caused in the main by the desperate flight from Paris a few steps ahead of the unrelenting press of the Third Reich sweeping over France's borders by the grandparents of Mrs Richardson, the now-owner, in the spring of 1940. Along with many other French Jews, their assets had been seized, the belongings they'd left behind ransacked by neighbours and former friends caught up in the anti-Semitic frenzy of those darkest of days.

It had taken many hours of delicate negotiation and correspondence with the great-granddaughter of a neighbour, before she'd allowed Lucie to search through the contents of their attic. In amongst boxes and suitcases stuffed with personal items and correspondence belonging not only to Mrs Richardson's grandparents but a host of other families who'd fled—or worse—Lucie had eventually found the original bill of sale for the Meileau. What other secrets might still be hidden in amongst the other boxes she'd left for others to uncover.

Lost in the memory of that dark, dusty attic filled with ghosts, Lucie didn't realise that Carl had launched into his speech until he mentioned her name again. With a little jump, she resolved to pay more attention, though it was hard to concentrate with so many eyes trained upon her. Mrs Richardson should've been there to celebrate the moment, but she and her husband had decided to avoid the limelight and inevitable press intrusion that would follow if the painting came close to achieving the sort of sales figure the valuation team were expecting, and had gone away on holiday. The auction house's legendary spring fine arts sale had been a calendar fixture for many years, and the Meileau was the star of the show. Lucie couldn't blame the Richardsons for wanting to stay anonymous.

Carl's tone increased in volume and enthusiasm as he built up to the finale of his speech. '...And without further ado...' Lucie took the agreed upon cue and moved to the other side of the painting to grip the velvet covering as Carl did the same on his side. 'Ladies and gentlemen, Witherby's is proud to share with you the first official unveiling of François Meileau's *Summer's Eve*.'

To a round of applause they lifted the cover, Lucie already turning eagerly to drink in the beauty of the painting. Secured safely in the vaults beneath the auction house, it had been several weeks since she'd last set eyes on it, and the myriad photographs she'd taken couldn't do it justice. Like a woman relearning the face of a long-lost lover, she let her greedy gaze rove over the entire surface of the work, waiting for the flutter of excitement she got every time she was up close to a masterpiece. And waited.

Whether it was too much excitement, or just plain nerves she wasn't sure, but the gut-punch of pure emotion she'd come to expect didn't come. The brushstrokes that had once seemed to dance across the canvas lay dull and flat, the delicacy of the colours she'd so admired missing somehow. Feeling strangely hollow, she edged back from the stand allowing the guests to crowd closer. Heat swept through her, churning her stomach and dampening the base of her spine until the silk of her blouse clung unpleasantly to her skin beneath her jacket. As she backed away from the stand, she watched Carl accept congratulations from one of the guests with a clink of their champagne flutes before they turned to face the painting. Arms waving like a windmill, he rabbited a mile a minute, oblivious to the dread creeping through Lucie. She waited for him to react, to notice what she had within seconds, but he continued to chatter to one person after another.

When a reporter clutching a notepad moved up beside him, Lucie found herself swallowing back a mouthful of bitter bile. Unable to watch anymore, she turned away and locked gazes with Piers. A deep furrow arrowing down between his brows, he worked his way across the room before her. Feeling hunted, Lucie backed up until her shoulders bumped against the dark wood panelling of the far wall.

Stopping barely inches from her, Piers cast a horrified glance towards the painting before fixing his confused stare back on Lucie. 'What,' he muttered low enough no one else could hear, 'the fuck is that?'

His unusual use of the expletive as much as the churning inside told her the worst of all possible truths. She hadn't been wrong, it hadn't been a case of first night nerves or over-anticipation. 'I don't know.'

Piers' eyebrows all but disappeared beneath the floppy strands of his fringe. 'You don't *know*?' There was a disbelieving edge to his tone, as though he was shouting at her even though his voice barely carried across the few inches separating them.

Feeling tears prickling behind her eyes, Lucie blinked hard. 'It's not the painting I found. It looks like it, but that's not the Meileau. I don't know how this has happened.' Her last words came out as a low wail and Lucie clamped her hand over her lips to stifle it.

Piers opened his mouth, and she flinched back against the wall expecting a tirade of abuse. Not that he was one to rage and shout, but the enormity of the disaster they were facing surely deserved it. It would be ruinous, not just for her career, but for the auction house as a whole. They'd made a huge song and dance about her discovery, had set the Meileau up as the star of the season and instead unveiled what to Lucie's eyes looked like a poor man's facsimile of the original. As though his knees were as weak as hers, Piers slumped against the wall beside her, stunned eyes fixed on hers.

'What are we going to do?' she whispered.

'I don't know,' he whispered back.

'We should tell someone.'

He shook his head. 'Not now. We can't. Not in front of this lot. It's not the *way*.'

The Witherby's way. God. Making a scene in public might almost be frowned upon more than the scandal of displaying what Lucie was almost entirely convinced was a fake painting.

21

*Almost.* She wanted to cry. No, she wanted the ground to open up and swallow her whole. She wanted her mum. But she wasn't a little girl anymore, and no one was coming to rescue her. 'Okay, okay. Here's what we're going to do. We're going to grit our teeth, smile and blag our way through the next hour that's what we're going to do.'

Piers stared at her for a long moment before throwing the remaining contents of his champagne glass down his throat. 'Okay, I'll get us another a drink.' With a wave, he summoned a server and swapped his empty glass for a new one. When he spotted the glass of water Lucie still clutched between numb fingers, he swiped it from her and thrust a second glass of champagne towards her. 'Here.'

'I wasn't going to drink tonight.'

He bit off the beginnings of a hysterical laugh. 'You're going to need it. And you might as well get something from the company whilst you can.'

Whilst she could? What on earth was that supposed to mean? *Oh.* 'They're going to sack me.'

Piers gave her a sad smile. 'Well, I don't think they're going to invite you to join the board of directors, that's for sure. Right, drink up and put a smile on your face. This is supposed to be your moment of triumph. If anyone catches you looking like a wet weekend, the game will be up. If one or other of us catches Carl alone, we'll have to try and warn him.' Following his own advice, Piers took a long swig from his glass then turned away from her. 'Ah, Charles, there you are! What do you think of our little masterpiece then?'

*

The hour that followed was one of the longest of Lucie's life. Fascinated by the backstory as much as the painting itself, one guest after another demanded her version of events from first discovery to finding the bill of sale. Jaw aching from the rictus grin she'd plastered on, Lucie drank and chatted like the life and soul of the party, her eyes never straying far from Piers as he worked the opposite side of the room. Carl maintained his position beside the painting, acting as master of ceremonies and still seemingly oblivious to the impending disaster.

When Piers moved towards him, Lucie feared the champagne churning in her belly would end up spewed all over the antique rug beneath her feet. Like witnessing a slow-motion car crash she watched the colour drain from Carl's face as Piers muttered into his ear. When Carl's disbelieving gaze met hers, there was nothing Lucie could do other than nod miserably to confirm the terrible news.

\*

'What the hell happened?' Carl asked for the dozenth time in the ten minutes since they'd entered his office after ushering out the last guest. Lucie had stopped trying to explain after the first five times he'd asked it. At least he'd stopped yelling. Her eyes strayed to the pile of shattered glass in one corner, the remnants of a Lalique paperweight he'd snatched from his desk and flung against the bookcase in his rage. She'd never seen him out of control and had Piers not stepped in front of her at the first signs of Carl's temper, she might have been more scared. As though he'd finally blown out the last of his fury, Carl dropped like a stone into the leather chair behind his desk and buried his face in his hands for a few seconds before lifting it to stare at them. 'We'll have to cancel the sale. Spin some story about the owner having second thoughts about parting with it. I'll speak to the publicity department first thing tomorrow.'

Feeling like it was safe to come out from behind Piers now Carl sounded so much calmer, Lucie edged to her right. 'I'll see if I can contact Mrs Richardson.'

'No.' Carl's sharp response ricocheted around the room like the bang of a gun. 'You will gather your things and leave this building immediately. Consider yourself on suspension until further notice. You won't speak a word to anyone about this other than the internal security team when they contact you.'

Feeling sick, Lucie swayed for a moment before forcing some steel into her spine. She hadn't done anything wrong. There had to be a logical explanation for this, if she could just stop the panicked swirl of her brain for two minutes, she knew she could fathom it out. 'I'm happy to cooperate, of course, but I'm sure it's just some kind of mistake.'

'Mistake? How can you stand there and tell me the most important artwork of the season has been replaced by a fake whilst it was under your care, and call it nothing more than a mistake? The word you are looking for is fraud.'

The word struck her like a blow, spinning her back almost fifteen years as she watched a team of policemen root through the contents of her bedroom as her mother sobbed in a heap on the landing. 'You...you can't...' Swallowing, she tried again. 'You can't possibly think I had anything to do with this?' She turned from Carl to Piers, hands held out in appeal. 'Why would I tell you it wasn't the right painting if I was trying to pull off some kind of scam?'

Piers glanced down at the carpet, clearly uncomfortable. 'But you didn't tell me, not until it was obvious I'd spotted there was something wrong with it.'

'What? No! That's not how it happened at all! As soon as Carl pulled off the cover I knew it wasn't right, I told you.' Frantic, she ran through the events in her head. As soon as she'd realised something was wrong, she'd...*oh*. She hadn't said anything, had she? She'd backed away instead of immediately making Carl aware of it. And it had been Piers who'd approached her, not the other way around. 'I swear to you both, I don't know anything about this. I *swear*.'

24

Piers flushed. 'I'm not accusing you of anything, not at all, but none of this makes sense.'

'I trusted you, Lucie.' The accusation in Carl's tone cut her to the quick. 'I should have listened to my instincts when I found out about your background, about the kind of family you come from. Instead, I gave you the benefit of the doubt, and this is how you repay me!'

A wave of nausea swept through her and she pressed a hand to her lips as though to hold it back. He couldn't be implying... 'You had my background investigated? Is that even *legal*?' Even as she said it, the fight left her. It didn't matter what she did, how diligently she worked to prove herself, she was never going to escape her name. Her past.

Drawing himself up to his full height, Carl shot her a look of such contempt she knew it was true. 'We are the premier auction house in the country for a reason, and protecting our reputation is tantamount!' There was no denial in any of that, he really had looked into her background.

'It was fifteen years ago! I was a child, I had nothing to do with anything my father did.' She could hear the pitch in her voice climbing and forced herself back into silence. *Like father, like daughter. The apple never falls far from the tree.* All those sayings existed for a reason—because people actually believed them.

Raising his hands to his face, Carl scrubbed at his eyes, tone quieter now, as though he was talking to himself. 'Employing the daughter of a convicted fraudster? What was I thinking! It won't be just you losing your bloody job over this.' He pointed towards the door. 'Get out of my sight!'

Only the neat crescents of her nails digging deep into the palms of her clenched fists stopped the tears of frustration from spilling over. Crying wouldn't do any good, it might even serve to demonstrate a guilty conscience. Lucie followed Piers with her eyes as he crossed the room to pull open the door. He muttered something to whoever was outside, then stepped back. To her horror, Mr Hazeltine, Witherby's head of security stood in the corridor. God, this was some kind of terrible joke. She looked from Carl to Piers and back again. Grim-faced, neither of them spoke.

'If you'll come with me, Miss Kennington, I'll take you to gather your belongings.' The security chief held out his hand indicating he wanted her to go with him.

With no fight left in her, Lucie did as he bade. To his credit, Mr Hazeltine took a slightly circuitous route to the restroom area which also contained staff lockers in an anteroom between the two sets of bathrooms and they only passed a couple of people she knew on the way. Neither spoke when it would be normal practice for both to say at least hello, and Lucie felt her insides cringe. The gossip mill was already churning, which was hardly surprising giving the volume of Carl's earlier yelling.

Mr Hazeltine checked the anteroom then nodded for her to enter. Lucie's low heels sunk into the plush carpet as she crossed to her locker, then paused key in hand. 'Did you want to search this?'

'I'll also require the keys to your office, and your access pass.' His voice was so bland, like they were discussing something as neutral as whether he took his tea with milk, rather than whether she'd got a load of stolen contraband stuffed under her spare pair of tights. 'Of course.' Lucie unhooked the lanyard dangling around her neck then sank onto the velvet banquette lining the wall before catching her slumped posture and forcing herself into an upright position. Body language and appearance were everything. It was the Witherby's way, after all.

It took about ten minutes to go through the meagre contents of her locker, and though he hadn't suggested it, Lucie took the opportunity to empty out the contents of the small rucksack she used to ferry her belongings back and forth to work. Laying out her trainers, a selection of old receipts, a spare pair of tights, two books—both of which were recent bestsellers—and a small cosmetic bag containing a few bits of make-up and a handful of tampons, she tried not to think about what it said about her life. It could be the contents of any woman's bag. There was nothing amongst the items that said anything about her, who she was, what she thought, what she felt. She'd tried so hard to present the perfect front, and yet it seemed there was no escaping the past.

'Right, I think I've got everything I need for the time being.' Mr Hazeltine closed the door to her locker with a decisive click then pocketed the keys. 'Now, before you go home, I should remind you about the non-disclosure clause in your employment contract.'

Bewildered, she could only blink at him. 'I'm sorry?'

If the smile he gave her next was supposed to be reassuring, it was anything but. 'When you signed your contract, you agreed not to discuss any matters which could harm or in any other way bring the reputation of Witherby's into disrepute.' The words tripped off his tongue in such a way she could tell it was a direct quotation. 'Until this matter is satisfactorily resolved, you cannot discuss it with anyone—legal counsel permitting, of course—outside these four walls.'

'L...legal counsel? Do you honestly think it might come to that?' And how the hell was she going to be able to afford it, if it did? 'I haven't done anything wrong. This is all a horrible mistake!'

There was that smile again, all teeth and no warmth. 'We'll be in touch in due course. Try to be patient, these things can take time.'

Lucie found herself thanking him, when she wanted to throw herself at him and beat her fists against his chest in frustration. *Not the Witherby's way.* Clenching the scraps of her pride together, she clamped her mouth tight against any further protests and gathered her belongings. As Mr Hazeltine escorted her out the rear entrance, Lucie knew she'd never be crossing the threshold of Witherby's again. Not now they'd found out who she really was.

# CHAPTER THREE

'Yes, yes, I understand.' Arthur spoke into the phone as he stared across the wide oak desk in what was now his office and met his brother's eyes. 'And there's no chance of recovering any of it?'

'I'm sorry, Sir Arthur, we tracked the funds as far as the Cayman Islands, but they're notorious for withholding cooperation.' Inspector Dillon sighed. 'Even if we could get them to let us inspect their records it's highly unlikely the funds are still in situ. It's taken us the best part of eighteen months to get Masterson's case to a verdict. We assume he's not acted alone, though he's not said as much. Hasn't said anything beyond "no comment" since his arrest, slippery sod.'

The very last of his hopes sinking, Arthur shook his head at Tristan's enquiring glance. 'Well, I want to thank you, Inspector, for all your hard work and diligence in bringing him to justice. Please pass on our gratitude to your team, also.'

'I will, Sir Arthur, I'm just sorry we couldn't get the justice you and all the other innocent victims deserve.' He sounded exhausted, poor man, which wasn't surprising considering Masterson's case had been splashed all over the tabloids. Ponzi schemes were nothing new, but it was the calibre of people who'd been caught up in Masterson's fraud that had the press pack slavering. Arthur's father hadn't been the only notable name to lose a fortune. From members of the peerage to pop stars and actors, the roll call of the duped and deluded had been a gossip columnist's dream.

'Not at all, and you have our profound thanks for keeping us up to date with developments in the case, I'm sure you have enough on your plate.'

'Well, the times I met your father, I was touched by what a decent man he was. I was very sorry to hear of his passing, and it seemed the least I could do under the circumstances.'

So, Arthur wasn't the only one who suspected the stress of the case had contributed to his father's demise. 'Thank you. I know he held you in very high esteem, Inspector, as do we all.' Having ended the call, Arthur dropped the handset into the cradle then let his head fall back. As he studied the brilliant crystal droplets of the chandelier hanging above the desk, he acknowledged how much hope he'd been clinging to—hope that Masterson would have a change of heart and enter some kind of plea bargain deal. The money was gone. And that was all there was to it.

'What are we going to do?'

Tristan's question made Arthur sit up straight once more. 'We're not going to do anything, little brother. You and Iggy are going to get the hell out of Dodge while you still can. No point in all three of us going down with the sinking ship, is there?'

Swiping the dark curls of his fringe out of his eyes, Tristan glared at him. 'Don't start that nonsense again, or you and I will have a serious falling out.'

'Stubborn fool.' Exasperation and affection filled the words in equal measures.

'Takes one to know one.'

He had a point. The two of them were similar in far more than looks, Arthur thought as he smoothed a hand through his shaggy hair, which was well overdue for a cut. He was looking more like Tristan every day, though Arthur was broader thanks to years spent rucking on a muddy rugby field. With his taller, more slender build, Tristan had been better suited to the cricket pitch. It had relieved them both to find their own sport to excel at, as people had tried to pit them against each other for as far back as he could remember. There'd never been any sense of competition between them, though. Their father and uncle had set an example which they'd been only too happy to follow— regardless of whose shoulders the family title rested upon, the Ludworths would succeed, or fail, together. Just lately though, Arthur had begun to regret this, desperate as he was to spare his siblings the pain of witnessing their family legacy collapsing before their eyes.

Frustrated, Arthur shoved his fringe from his eyes, an unconscious mirroring of his brother's earlier action. He'd never really bothered much with his own appearance, content with a short back and sides whenever he could be bothered to pop down to the little barbershop in the village, and a basic uniform of cords or chinos and a checked shirt. Tristan had always been the trendy one of the two of them, and he claimed the women loved his *Poldark*-esque mane.

Arthur was finding the tangle more hassle than it was worth and made a mental note to wander down to the village sooner rather than later. Besides, he'd never had any trouble attracting women even in his baggy old cords and rugby shirt. Being heir to a title was its own special pheromone, he thought with more than a shade of weariness. It had taken him a while—longer in fact that he was proud to admit—before he'd come to understand his popularity with women had more to do with his title than him as a person. He'd even got as far as considering asking one girl to marry him before the scales had fallen from his eyes when she'd been horrified by his attempts to promote Iggy into the position of official heir to the baronetcy. Now he was officially Baronet Ludworth—his name having entered the official roll the previous week—they'd be crawling out of the woodwork once

31

more. Well, if they were hunting for a fortune, they were going to be sorely disappointed.

A knock at the study door scattered the random musings his brain was using to avoid thinking about the enormous hole in their family finances. When the heavy wood remained resolutely closed, Arthur rolled his eyes at Tristan and hid a smile as he called out 'Come.'

The door opened to reveal Maxwell, their family butler, dressed in an immaculate charcoal trousers and waistcoat over a white shirt. The black tie at his throat was fastened in the same Windsor knot he'd taught both Arthur and Tristan to tie as young boys. 'Good afternoon, Sir Arthur, Master Tristan, your aunt has requested you join her in the yellow drawing room for afternoon tea.'

It was all Arthur could do not to let out a snort. Morgana Ludworth had never requested anything in all of her seventy-plus years. As delicate as a bird to look at, she had an implacable will and a tongue sharp enough to slice through steel. And a heart as big and fierce as a lion. She'd remained at home to nurse her ailing father whilst her peers had flown the coop, got married and had babies. 'I didn't just miss the boat, I missed the entire regatta,' she'd told them once with a laugh in her voice that hadn't reached her eyes. 'Then your father and Lancelot came along, and I stayed to help out your grandmother.'

Always a delicate woman, Arthur had few memories of his grandmother other than as someone they were always shushed into silence around. She'd died when they were still very young, and it had been Morgana who'd once again stepped into the void. Arthur adored his paternal great-aunt, as did his siblings, for as stern as she could be at times, she'd not blinked at taking on the three heartbroken, confused children Helena had left in her wake. 'Thank you, Maxwell, we'll be along shortly.'

'Very good, sir.' With the briefest incline of his head, Maxwell pulled the door closed behind him.

'He's got more starch in his pants than a virginal vicar. Can't you get him to relax a bit?'

Arthur shook his head. He'd tried to have a chat with Maxwell when he'd first inherited the title, but the butler had been so offended at the idea he might "move with the times and dispense with a few unnecessary traditions" that Arthur had abandoned the effort. Mrs W, their housekeeper, had been more on board and he'd given her free rein to discuss the issue with Betsy, the cook, and give him a proposal on improvements and updates they would like to make. Together, the three of them were in charge of the day-to-day running of the castle, with an ever-shrinking band of staff to assist them.

With March just around the corner, they were busy gearing up for the annual spring clean scheduled for next weekend. Mrs W and Betsy had been delighted when Arthur told them he, Tristan and Iggy would be rolling up their sleeves and getting down to it along with the team of paid volunteers gathered from the village. Maxwell had looked as though he were sucking a lemon at the very idea of members of the family dirtying their hands, but had refrained from commenting.

A building as old and extensive as the castle took a huge amount of physical effort to keep going, never mind the financial cost. They'd closed as many rooms as possible over the winter months, but with the latest utility bill lurking in Arthur's desk drawer like a malevolent toad, it had been a drop in the ocean. He dreaded to think what damage they were going to find now the weather was improving and they were beginning to pull back the dust covers.

Feeling suddenly queasy, Arthur swallowed hard then forced himself to stand. 'Come on, we'd better not keep Morgana waiting.'

Tristan gestured to the old fisherman's jumper Arthur had bundled himself into that morning, and then his own designer-branded sweatshirt. 'We'd better get changed, too, or we'll never hear the end of it.'

Hands and faces washed, jumpers and jeans exchanged for collared shirts and dark cords, the brothers entered the yellow drawing room. With a view to the woods behind the castle, it was their great-aunt's favourite room, and her unofficial domain. As usual, Morgana sat at the head of the small rosewood dining table, closest to the large stone fireplace. A cheery fire filled the room with the scent of pinecones, mingling with the ever-present fragrance of Penhaligon's Bluebell Eau de Toilette which was their aunt's signature perfume. Finding Iggy already seated to Morgana's left, Arthur bent to brush a kiss to the powdered cheek of his aunt before taking the empty chair to her right. Tristan repeated the greeting and slid into the seat beside Iggy.

Clad in her usual unrelieved black, Morgana cast an eye from Arthur to Tristan before nodding once. At the gesture, a maid stepped forward and began to pour tea into the bone china cups placed before each of them. As he waited for the maid to serve everyone, Arthur studied the silver stands laden with finger sandwiches, slices of Victoria sponge and fresh-baked sultana scones. Though it hadn't been that long since he'd wolfed down a bowl of soup for his lunch, Arthur felt the stirrings of appetite in his stomach at the fine spread before them.

Only once the maid had set the silver teapot down and left the room, did their aunt speak. Fixing Arthur with an expression that said she would brook no nonsense, she asked, 'What did the inspector have to say?'

That she knew who Arthur had been on the phone to surprised him not at all. Very little happened behind the stone walls of Camland Castle that didn't reach Morgana's ears sooner or later—usually sooner. 'We have to assume the money's gone for good.'

Iggy's sharp intake of breath told Arthur he wasn't the only one who'd been pinning his hopes on a different result. Morgana, however, showed no reaction. 'It's done then. The silly fool's scuppered your ship good and proper.'

'Morgana.' Iggy sounded pained, and Arthur saw Tristan reach beneath the table to give their sister's leg a comforting pat.

'Don't Morgana me, girl, when I'm only speaking the truth. Your father was as foolish with money as he was generous with his heart. Remember that race horse he bought for a fortune only for it to go lame the next week? Or that holiday resort in Dominica that got demolished by a hurricane and then it turned out the developers weren't insured? And what about—'

'Enough!' Arthur wasn't sure who was more shocked, Morgana at being cut off mid-flow or himself at having the balls to raise his voice to her. His great-aunt recovered first, raising her teacup to her lips and taking a sip as though nothing had happened.

Leaping in to fill the silence, Iggy reached for the stand of sandwiches and placed it next to her aunt's plate. 'Egg and cress, Morgana, your favourite.'

'I'm not a child to be mollified, Igraine,' Morgana said stiffly, but reached for a sandwich none the less.

Arthur and Tristan made themselves busy filling their own plates. Silence reigned over the table for a few minutes as they all tucked in. Only once Morgana had finished her first cup of tea and nodded to Iggy to refill her cup did she speak again. 'Regardless of *how* we got here, the dire situation can't be ignored any longer.'

'It's not your problem to worry about, Morgana, I can handle it.' Arthur said in his best 'head of the family' voice.

Morgana snorted. 'Don't try that tone with me, boy. You're not too old for a box on the ears.'

'You'd have to kneel by her chair so she can reach,' Tristan muttered causing Arthur to cough loudly to try and cover his sudden burst of laughter.

'Tristan Ludworth, I'll thank you to try and remember some of the manners I taught you,' Morgana snapped before turning away from the hot blush scalding Tristan's cheeks. Gaze fixed firmly on Arthur, she continued. 'The way I see it, you have very few choices, none of them particularly palatable.' She held up one slender hand, fingers gnarled with age. 'One, you can see if the National Trust will take this place off your hands. If we're lucky, they'll allow us to occupy a small part of it and open the rest up to the public.'

Arthur frowned at her rather unkind portrayal of the charity. 'They do a fantastic job, but I'm not quite ready to hand over the reins to someone else. I'm already seriously considering opening some parts of the castle to the public, but I want it to be on our terms and absolutely under my control.'

Morgana pursed her lips. 'Option two, you find some filthy rich foreigner to take the place lock, stock and—'

'No!' The triplets shouted her suggestion down in unison.

'There must be another way...' Iggy said.

'Can't we sell a few bits off?' Tristan asked.

Arthur raised a brow. 'Like what?'

His brother shrugged. 'I don't know, but the place is stuffed full of paintings, furniture and the like. Some of it must be worth something.'

Arthur shook his head. 'There's an old archive record somewhere, but I wouldn't know where to start with it.'

'If the three of you would let me finish,' Morgana said, her voice sharp, 'My third suggestion is to get an expert in to take a full survey of the contents of the castle. As well as being obsessed with all that Arthurian nonsense, the ninth baronet was friends with a very artistic set of friends. I believe several of them gifted him with works of art to thank him for his hospitality.'

Thomas Ludworth, Arthur's several times great-grandfather had become obsessed with a theory that rather than the traditional Cornish and Somerset connections, the legendary King Arthur had in fact been a Northern warlord and Camland Castle the seat of the court of Camelot. The majority of his peers had openly laughed at the idea, but there was a stack of research and papers Thomas had collated in the library which he'd sworn proved his theory. He'd even gone so far as to name his children after characters connected to the legend, a tradition the family had adopted to that day. As part of his obsession, he'd collected every bit of tat he could lay his hands on with even the most dubious connection to Arthur and Camelot. The walls were littered with rusting swords, battle axes and the like, and the family chapel held no fewer than three cups on the altar alleged to be the holy grail. He'd even gone so far as to commission the huge round table which dominated the centre of the great hall.

It kept the locals amused and gave the area a bit of a tourist boost, so Arthur didn't see any real harm in it, but he'd never given the theory any serious credence. 'I suppose it would be useful to get a survey done, for insurance purposes if nothing else.'

'And if you did decide to do some public open days, you could get this expert to curate the best of the Arthurian stuff into a proper exhibition. That'd be something to draw the crowds in,' Tristan said, sounding more excited than Arthur would've expected.

'It might work,' he mused. 'If we could get someone in quickly, we may even be able to put it together in time for the summer.' He would have to do some serious research, find out what some of the famous estates like Blenheim Palace and Highclere Castle charged for admission, and what sort of thing they offered the tourists who flocked there. The Arthurian connection gave Camland an eye-catching hook—regardless of how spurious it was.

'I could try and do something with the gardens,' Iggy said, eyes alight. 'A few themed walks to connect to the legend. There's that gorgeous glade in the woods we could suggest it was the meeting place for Lancelot and Guinevere; a more testing one out to the lake we could call the Excalibur trail.'

'With a great big rock somewhere along the way you'll claim is where King Arthur pulled the sword from the stone, no doubt,' Arthur said, half-joking.

'Yes! Exactly.' When she saw the doubt on his face, Iggy leaned forward. 'Come on, Arthur, in for a penny in for a pound. If we're going to go down, it might as well be in a blaze of tasteless glory!'

\*

'Are you sure we're not deluding ourselves with this?' Arthur asked Tristan as they surveyed a dusty collection of paintings in the long gallery. It was hard to imagine anyone looking twice at the gloomy-looking, mostly brown images lining the walls. Years of dirt and neglect made it almost impossible to make out the subject of most of them.

Tristan shrugged. 'We might be, but it's got to be worth a shot. If we can show the bank and the other creditors a viable business plan it might take a bit of the heat off you, at least for a little while. And as Iggy said, if we're going down let's go down fighting. We can call it Arthur's Last Stand,' he said with a wink.

'You and me on the drive wielding broadswords at the bailiffs? Lord, can you imagine it?'

'Morgana wouldn't need a weapon, she's already a battle-axe.' They both laughed, then glanced around guiltily. Their aunt had a habit of appearing at the most inconvenient of times, a bit like the witch some of the children from the village suspected her of being.

Only once they were sure the coast was clear did Tristan speak again. 'Look, worst-case scenario we're going to lose this place, so it won't do any harm to know what all this stuff is worth— separate the tat from the treasure, you know?'

Arthur nodded. He did know. He also had a sinking feeling in his stomach that there was more tat than treasure to be found hanging on the walls and littering the dusty surfaces of old bits of furniture. He took a breath. One thing he'd promised himself when he'd inherited the place was that he would face whatever came head on. No hiding behind dreams of a miracle, no banking on a deal that would never come off.

He'd loved his father, would always be fond of the fantastic memories his spirit of adventure had created for the three of them. But Arthur couldn't afford to be like him. Much as the responsibilities of his position might weigh on his shoulders and keep him tossing and turning in the middle of the night, he couldn't afford to show it. He was Baronet Ludworth and the people around him were depending on him. Not just his nearest and dearest, not even the direct employees who worked in the castle. If Arthur failed, it would cost the entire community.

He set his jaw. Failure just wasn't a bloody option, was it?

# CHAPTER FOUR

'Lucie, darling, time to wake up. I've made you a cup of tea.'

The coaxing tones of her mother's voice penetrated the foggy edges of sleep, and Lucie forced one eye open. 'I'm not thirsty,' she grumbled before rolling away to face the wall, but not before catching a glimpse of the worry lines etched into her mother's features. An unwelcome stab of guilt burrowed under the musty covers on her bed, making Lucie feel even more miserable. Why couldn't her mum just leave her alone as she'd asked?

Since walking out of the door at Witherby's two weeks earlier, a dull kind of fog had settled over Lucie leaving her unable to do anything. After attending a formal investigative interview where it had been clear nobody on the panel her employer had put together believed her protestations of innocence, she'd crawled under her covers three days ago and had barely shifted since. They hadn't gone to the police so far, hoping to keep the whole thing quiet to protect the company's name and reputation, but it was only a matter of time. Lucie had none of the answers they'd demanded, and a very valuable artwork was still missing.

'Well, I'll leave it here on your cabinet just in case, darling.' Silence hung long enough in the air for Lucie to believe her mother had left the room before Constance Kennington placed a gentle hand on her shoulder and said in a firmer tone than

Lucie had heard in years. 'It's a lovely day, you might feel better for a little bit of fresh air...?'

Shrugging off the touch, Lucie wormed her way deeper under the quilt, knowing she was being a brat but unable to help herself. It was about fifteen years too late for Constance to start worrying about her. If she'd only bothered to take an interest when it had mattered, they'd neither of them have been in the mess they were in now. As though on cue, the baby next door started wailing, the shrill sound penetrating the paper-thin walls of their twelfth floor flat in a rundown council block.

'I'll leave you to it then.' Constance's voice was back to its usual hesitant whisper, making Lucie feel lower than a slug. With Mr Hazeltine's warning over the non-disclosure agreement still rattling around in her head, Lucie had been afraid to go into detail over what was happening. Her refusal to say anything beyond that she'd been suspended pending an investigation was driving a wedge between them. She could tell her refusal to confide was hurting her mum—it was hurting Lucie, too—but aside from her worry over being found in breach of her contract on top of everything else, how on earth was she supposed to explain it without dragging her father's past crimes up?

Her mother had always been quiet and contained, the complete opposite of the brash, confident figure her father had cut through her childhood. Content to reside in the sheltered comfort of her husband's shadow, Constance had left everything to him. Like some Fifties' throwback to the image of the perfect housewife, she'd kept house and made sure she always looked nice. Any spare hours had been spent turning their back garden into a little slice of paradise.

Whenever she pictured her mum from those days, it wasn't in one of her neat Chanel suits as she clung to her husband's arm on the way to some function or another. It was in a simple day dress, a large straw sunhat shading her pale complexion as she tended the immaculate borders bursting with roses, foxgloves and lupins. She'd never seemed to care about the trappings, her world had been her husband and her daughter and the lovely haven she'd created for the three of them.

Lucie's gaze strayed to one of her favourite pictures in the frames that littered her bedside cabinet. Dressed in a mint-green pair of short dungarees over a white T-shirt, 6-year-old Lucie beamed with pride as she held up the first carrots she'd grown in the little vegetable patch her mum had created for her. One arm around Lucie's waist, the other held up to shade her eyes from the sun, Constance knelt beside her, smiling up at the taker of the photo. Such an innocent image of domestic perfection, would either of them ever feel that carefree again? A hot tear trickled down Lucie's cheek.

Lucie loved her mum, had never wanted for affection or attention from her, but at heart she'd been a daddy's girl. Oh, how she'd adored Paul Kennington with his bright smile and booming laugh, his generous nature and ever-flowing wallet. Nothing had been too good for Paul's girls as he'd referred to Lucie and her mum. Summer holidays in exotic resorts, winter skiing trips in exclusive mountain-top lodges, all the newest fashions—though Constance had never been one to put herself on show, sticking to timeless, elegant classics which suited her willowy frame. Though Lucie had been grateful for the wonderful presents and gifts, what she'd craved beyond anything was more of her father's time. Those holidays could've been in Bournemouth as easily as Disneyland as far as she had been concerned, as long as the three of them had been together. But it had always pleased her daddy to treat her like the princess he called her, so she'd gone along with things. Even when he'd sent her away to a private school, when all she'd ever wanted was to stay at home and be close to the two of them.

It had been a struggle at first to make new friends, but she'd just started to find her feet when it had all come crashing down around them. A few of the friends she'd made had tried to keep in touch afterwards, but Lucie had been too embarrassed and ashamed to return their calls or reply to the cards and letters they'd sent in the aftermath of her father's downfall. If the scandal of it all hadn't been devastating enough for her 13-year-old self to cope with, the seizure and sale of the Kennington's assets certainly had. The grand house where she'd enjoyed her own little suite of rooms—bedroom, bathroom and a huge playroom which had been converted into an entertainment and games room as she'd entered her teenage years—had been mortgaged up to the rafters and worth next to nothing when it was sold.

All the fancy clothes stuffing her wardrobes had gone too, declared to be profits from illegal activities and sold off, along with all the gadgets and devices as the police attempted to claw back at least some of the money her father had embezzled from his clients, friends and neighbours. Not that she'd cared about any of those things. It was the loss of security, of her little island of safety in the world being torn away much as her father had been torn from her sobbing arms when they'd come to arrest him that terrible night.

If she'd understood at the time it was the last time she'd see him, would she have fought harder to keep hold of him? She'd never know. Her parents had agreed she should be shielded from it all as much as possible and had refused to allow her to visit her father in prison. With an eight-year prison sentence, they'd hoped he would be out in half that time, but a heart attack eighteen months later had robbed Lucie of any chance to reconcile the confusing tangle of emotions that still threatened to overwhelm her whenever she risked thinking about him.

Once Lucie and her mum had been forced to take up residence in a tiny little flat miles from where anyone might know them, Lucie had become something of a hermit. Enrolled in the local comprehensive, she concentrated on keeping her head down as much as possible. Crippled by the desperate shame that people would find out what her father had done, Lucie had made no attempt to make new friends. Her only solace had been the quiet hours spent in the art department, where a sympathetic teacher had nurtured Lucie's small talents as a painter as well as her thirst for knowledge. A tough-love careers conversation halfway through her A levels had steered Lucie away from thoughts of a Fine Art degree to one in Art History.

Terrified of racking up any more debt than the basic student fees, she'd opted to attend UCL and stay living at home. When she wasn't in class, she would haunt London's myriad museums and art galleries, picking the brains of numerous volunteers and guides who were only too happy to spend wet Tuesday afternoons sharing their knowledge with an eager, interested girl. Weekends and evenings were spent pulling pints, waiting tables, and whatever other casual work she could pick up that would bring money in to supplement her mother's cleaning jobs, until one of her lecturers hooked her up with a contact at Witherby's and her apprenticeship—and what she'd hoped would be a new life—began.

Though she'd tried several times to persuade her mum to move, Constance had refused, saying she wouldn't be a burden on Lucie. She'd also encouraged Lucie to stay put and tuck away as much of her money into a savings account as she could rather than blow it on rent. Lucie had gone along with it, promising herself that as soon as she could afford it, she'd get them both out and into a nice little house somewhere in the suburbs. Somewhere with a garden so her mum could spend time on her knees tending her flowers rather than scrubbing kitchen floors. She had it all planned out in her mind's eye, down to the little shaded arbour she would build for Constance to sit and relax beneath.

And now those plans were withering before her eyes. Although no one had said as much, it had been made plain to Lucie that regardless of the final outcome there would be no place for her at Witherby's. Reputation was everything in the art world and word would slip out eventually—if the whispers hadn't already started, she'd be shocked. Innocent as she knew herself to be, it would matter naught if gossip tainted her name. She would have to find a new career, leave her beloved art behind and go back to waiting tables, the only other type of work she had any experience in. With the drop in income, she could kiss her little dream house in the suburbs goodbye, and with it her dreams of being able to give her mum a better life. The tears took hold in earnest, a keening wail escaping her lips before Lucie could bury her head in the pillows and muffle it.

A few moments later, her bedroom door flew open to bang against the flimsy wall, jolting Lucie upright at the noise. Bright light spilled in through the window as Constance flung open the curtains then turned to face her, fists on her hips. 'Lucinda Mary Kennington, you stop that now!' Though her voice quavered a little, there was no mistaking the determined gleam in her mother's eye. 'You've told me you've done nothing wrong, so stop acting like you're guilty. I want you up and in that shower, right this minute.' Her delicate nose wrinkled. 'It smells dreadful in here. You're 27, not 17, far too old to sulk.'

Shocked at this new assertive side her mother had never shown before, Lucie allowed herself to be herded into the little bathroom. When she emerged from behind the flimsy plastic curtain it was to find her grubby pyjamas had been replaced with clean jeans and a jumper, and her favourite pair of fuzzy socks.

Feeling better than she had for days, Lucie tugged a comb through her long hair as she wandered back into her bedroom to find the bed stripped bare and the window open to let in a chilly, but blessedly fresh breeze. The mugs, plates and other detritus she'd accumulated had all been swept away. Catching a hint of lemon polish in the air, Lucie shook her head in amazement. In the time she'd been in the shower, Constance had even managed to wipe a duster around the room.

Wondering which version of her mother awaited her, Lucie

slunk into the small open-plan living space they shared to find a fresh cup of tea and a plate of toast waiting on the little gateleg table squeezed beneath the window. A copy of *The Times* lay open beside her plate, with something circled in biro. Curious, Lucie picked up the paper as she sat down, eyes scanning the open page. It was the Register section, where people placed announcements of births, deaths, marriages and—she blinked at the circled entry—advertisements.

**Wanted: art historian, archivist, or other expert with relevant skills, to undertake a full assessment and survey of the Ludworth Collection at Camland Castle, Derbyshire. Full board and reasonable expenses covered for an initial two-month period, with room for extension on proof of need. No timewasters. Immediate start preferred. Apply to Sir Arthur Ludworth with full CV and covering letter to Ludworth@CamlandCastle.co.uk.**

'Well, what do you think, darling?' Constance asked as she slipped into the opposite chair with her own cup of tea.

'What do I think about what?' When her mother raised a sculpted eyebrow, Lucie prodded a finger at the advert. 'You can't be serious?'

'I think it would be prefect for you, just what you need to keep yourself occupied and a wonderful chance to get out of London for a bit. Some fresh air would do you the world of good and think how exciting it would be. The chance to live in a castle, for heaven's sake, even if it's only for a couple of months!' Constance gestured around the little room which even with her very best efforts to make homely was about as far from a castle as it was possible to get.

'But, I can't just up and leave you, and what if Witherby's want to interview me again?' Lucie still couldn't get her head around what her mum was suggesting.

'Of course you can leave me, darling, I'm not completely help-less.' Constance glanced down at her tea, a delicate blush heating her pale cheeks. 'Although I've given a fair impression otherwise for far too long. I can manage perfectly well here on my own, better in fact if I thought you were doing something with your life other than worrying about me.' She straightened up, the little flash of steel back in her eye. 'And as for whatever that nonsense is with Witherby's—' she held up a hand before Lucie could interject '—I know, you've told me you *can't* talk to me about it, darling, but it doesn't mean I can't be furious about the way they're treating you. What do they expect you to do? Sit here in suspended animation until they finally get their backsides in gear?'

'I can't leave town, Mum. I just can't.' Wouldn't running away just make her look guilty? Lucie sipped her tea, half-amazed she was even given credence to the idea. But then again, didn't it feel like Witherby's were already treating her like the guilty party? Damned if she did, damned if she didn't…

'You'll have your phone with you, so if they need to speak to you again, they can contact you,' Constance pointed out.

'I probably won't even get it. This Sir Arthur Ludworth, whoever he is, is probably looking for someone with a lot more experience…' Was she actually considering this crazy idea? Apparently so.

'That's as maybe, but there's no harm in applying, is there?'

'I suppose not.' And that was how Lucie found herself plonked on the sofa with her laptop on her knee as she worked and reworked her covering letter, trying to find the right combination of words to indicate she was immediately available without mentioning her current suspension. If she made it as far as the interview stage, she would speak to Sir Arthur face-to-face about what had happened, she reassured her pang of conscience.

*

A week later, Lucie was lugging her suitcase down the steps of the intercity train she'd boarded at St Pancras several hours previously. The crowds on the platform thinned out as her fellow travellers marched off in different directions, each apparently secure in their onward journey.

Unlike Lucie.

There'd been no interview stage, just a cursory reply accepting her application with instruction to report to the castle no later than the tenth of the month and a vague instruction that catching the train would be her best option. Her Google searches hadn't revealed a great deal about the Ludworths or Camland Castle other than a dubious link to Arthurian legend she'd quickly dismissed. No pictures of the family beyond the odd image on the *Hello!* website of a middle-aged, slightly portly man. In one he was dressed in full top hat and tails at Ascot, the caption beneath it stating simply 'Baronet Ludworth'. Another showed the same man in amongst a group of similarly aged men clad in dinner jackets and women in flowing evening dresses, snapped at some grand party held to celebrate the birthday of somebody she'd never heard of.

There were plenty of images of the castle walls, a few that showed a glimpse of grey stone in the distance taken through thick, high iron gates and tree cover, so clearly the castle wasn't open to the public. Most of the tourist photos online were of the village that shared a name with the castle, and showed a mix of stone cottages, a handful of shops and a pub. The surrounding dales looked wild and untamed, and her heart had fluttered in both excitement and a little trepidation at living in the shadow of those mysterious hills. The family holidays she'd enjoyed as a child hadn't involved a lot of trekking or hiking and she could imagine how easy it would be to get lost in that beautiful, if bleak, Derbyshire wilderness. The pictures which had really captured her imagination, though, were those accompanying a feature article listing some of Britain's hidden natural treasures. Beneath the tangled limbs of what was clearly an ancient wood, a sea of dancing bluebells spread out to a faded blur in the distance. The ground looked untouched, as though no one had walked beneath those ancient boughs for years. A magical place, like the photographer had strayed through the barrier between reality and fantasy and if the observer just looked hard enough, they might spot a fairy, or sprite peeking out between the roots of one of the ancient oaks. Would she get a chance to see it with her own eyes? Gosh, she hoped so.

Of the Arthur Ludworths listed on social media, none looked to be likely candidates, although she couldn't be sure as several of the accounts had their security settings locked so she could do no more than view their most basic information. A reference she'd found in the *Gazette* to Sir Arthur's recent listing on the Roll of Baronets had led her down a rabbit warren of searches into the weird and wonderful world of the Honours and Peerage system, fascinating but ultimately worthless to the job she'd been hired to do.

As she wrestled with the stubborn handle on her suitcase which was refusing to be pulled out, Lucie spotted a man dressed in the navy and red uniform of the local rail network and gave him a wave. 'Excuse me, I'm looking for the next train to Camland?'

Tucking the signal paddle he was holding into one voluminous trouser pocket, the guard retrieved a timetable from the other. 'You'll be wanting Platform 7B, my love.' He pointed to the farthest platform from where they were standing, and then to a concrete and corrugated panel construction behind him. 'Up and over the bridge, there.'

'Okay, thank you!' Lucie staggered a little as her final tug released the locking mechanism and the handle of her case flew up.

'Need a hand with that, my love?'

Though she knew he meant nothing by it, and likely referred

to every female he encountered from 8 to 80 in the same manner, the man's colloquial endearment rankled her feminist sensibilities almost as much as his assumption she couldn't manage her own luggage. 'I'll be fine, thanks. Platform 7B, right?'

'Up and over.' The guard nodded, then turned away towards what looked like the main ticket office. The moment he stepped inside, a vicious whip of cold wind blew down the platform, followed by an ominous rumble from the dark clouds overhead. Lucie glanced from the ticket office to the far platform that appeared to offer no form of shelter with a sigh. Up and over it was.

By the time she'd panted her way to the top of the concrete incline and onto the bridge itself, Lucie was regretting not accepting the guard's offer of assistance. In a panic over what might be deemed suitable clothing for residing in a castle, she'd stuffed pretty much the entire contents of her wardrobe into her suitcase—including a bottle-green velvet formal dress she'd found in a charity shop for the university leavers' ball that no one had invited her to. In addition to the weight of her case, the rucksack on her back was stuffed to bursting with every reference book and cataloguing guide in her considerable collection. Rubbing her red and aching palm against her leg, Lucie hitched the rucksack a little higher on her back, ignoring the dull ache spreading across her shoulders. Switching hands, she towed the case over the bridge, thankful that at least the walk down the opposite slope would be easier.

When the case banged into her ankle for the third time, its weight and the momentum of the slope causing it to career a little unsteadily, she realised she'd been too quick in giving those thanks. With a huff and an angry shove that sent the unwitting cause of her misery spinning into the chain link fence lining the rear of the station platform, Lucie sank down onto the cold metal bench nearby. She scanned up and down the platform for an electronic sign, or a timetable noticeboard at least, but there was nothing as far as she could see. There was nothing she could do, it seemed, but wait.

Wanting to make a good impression, she'd chosen to wear a skirt suit and a pair of low heels, teamed with her best wool coat. A decision she now regretted as the cold wind whistled past her once more, sending a run of goose bumps over legs clad only in thin nylon tights. To add insult to injury, a fine drizzle began to fall from the clouds overhead, soaking through the wool of her coat in a matter of minutes. Unable to face the return journey back over the bridge, and with no idea how much longer she would have to wait, Lucie tugged a beret from her pocket to cover her hair, hunched her shoulders and willed the train to hurry up.

Ten long minutes later, a single carriage train pulled up at the platform disgorging several passengers who scurried past Lucie with barely a glance. With no sign of any member of staff around, Lucie approached the open door of the train and peered inside just as the internal door to the driver's area slid back. 'Eee, you startled me, love!' A grey-haired man with the kind of creases on his cheeks that said he smiled a lot clutched at his chest and staggered back in an exaggerated movement, the twinkle in his eyes telling her there was no harm done. 'Are you all right, there?' he added, taking in her bedraggled state with a quick once-over.

'I'm looking for the train to Camland.'

'Then you're in the right place. Hop on, love, and I'll get you there in two shakes of a lamb's tail, or forty-seven minutes if you go by what the timetable says.'

Grateful at the chance of shelter, Lucie hurried to retrieve her suitcase, and didn't demur when the driver reached down to help her lift it into the train. 'Blimey, love, you running away to join the circus?'

His kind, familiar manner was so unlike the brisk efficiency of London, she smiled. She would have to get used to being called 'love' or spend the next couple of months in permanent offence if he and the guard she'd spoken to previously were anything to

51

go by. It could be worse, she mused, unbuttoning her wet coat and hooking it over the back of the seat in front of her. She'd take chatty over being ignored any day of the week. The door shushed closed behind her, and Lucie settled back in her seat, grateful for the warmth of the carriage. Well, for the first few minutes until she could feel dampness beneath her armpits and her wet coat started to steam. The central heating on the train had clearly been set to tropical.

Standing up, she tugged open the nearest window with a sigh of relief as a blast of cold air hit her glowing face, followed swiftly by a much less wanted shower of raindrops. Another gust drove more rain through the open window and she shoved it closed with a gasp. She could either boil or drown. Great.

Over the next ten minutes, the train door opened and closed as a handful of other passengers climbed aboard. As was human nature, they scattered around the carriage with as much space between each other as possible, and were soon plugged into headphones, or had their noses buried in e-readers, tablets or paperback books. Not everyone was social in this part of the world, apparently, and Lucie was grateful for that as it gave her time to gather her wits and think about what lay ahead.

From almost the moment she'd opened the email offering her the position at Camland, she'd been thinking about what she should say if Sir Arthur asked any awkward questions about why she'd left her position at Witherby's. On her application, she'd said she wanted the chance to explore a collection in depth, and highlighted the six months she'd spent in the cataloguing and records section at the auction house as part of her training. Not a lie, but also not the truth, and it was beginning to sit uncomfortably with her. That bloody non-disclosure agreement had tied her hands. Then again, who in their right mind would let someone suspected of what she'd been accused of doing cross their threshold? Talk about a Catch-22 situation. She'd just have to hope the topic didn't come up. As the train pulled out of the station, she leant her head back, closed her eyes and began to run over the introductory speech she'd been working on.

*

In what seemed like a matter of moments, Lucie woke to a hand shaking her shoulder lightly. 'Wake up, love, this is the end of the line.'

Panic and adrenaline shot through her. 'Have I missed my stop?'

The driver shook his head with an amused smile. 'No, love, Camland *is* the end of the line. The end of the world some folks might say.'

Fuzzy from the heat and her impromptu nap, Lucie tried to concentrate as she collected her belongings, shrugging on her now only slightly damp coat and shouldering the cursed backpack once more. When she reached the luggage area, it was to find the driver had already lifted her suitcase down onto the platform and popped up the handle with apparently no problems. 'That's very kind of you, thanks.'

'My pleasure, love. Now you know where you're headed?'

'The castle. I'm hoping it shouldn't be too hard to find,' she said with a grin.

The driver laughed. 'Not hard at all, love. Just keep heading up until you can't go any further.'

Oh. Great. Trying not to let her smile slip, Lucie gave him a wave and trundled down the little platform towards the open gap at the end which led onto a tiny car park big enough for no more than a dozen cars. 'The end of the world, indeed,' she murmured to herself at the idea of any place small enough to manage with so little parking.

The stone cottages she'd seen on her computer screen looked a little grimmer in real life, set as they were against a heavily leaden sky. Without the pretty hanging baskets and blooming

53

window boxes of summer it was easy to see the peeling paint, the cracked and weathered pathways, the moss on the roof tiles. The front of more than one was marred with the ugly wheelie bins that pervaded housing estates throughout the country, even remote areas such as this, it seemed.

Glancing left, then right, it wasn't immediately obvious to Lucie which way she should go, and the tiny car park didn't bear something as metropolitan as a taxi rank. Did they do Uber in Derbyshire? Lucie retrieved her phone from her pocket, stared at the single bar on her screen and tucked it away with a sigh. They might do Uber, but they didn't do 3G.

The path to her right was the more appealing of the two, with its gentle downward slope, but that's not what the driver's instruction had been. Taking a deep breath, Lucie grasped the handle of her suitcase and turned left. Up, the driver had said, and boy, he wasn't kidding.

# CHAPTER FIVE

The yammering and barking of what sounded like every dog in the castle echoed around the great hall, the wild cacophony enough to draw Arthur out of his bedroom where he'd been changing his shirt ready for dinner. With only the cuffs on his navy-blue dress shirt buttoned, he strode along the landing then leaned over the thick oak bannister that edged the top of the stairs. Like a churning maelstrom of black, gold and brindle fur, the dogs circled a small black-clad figure who was edging away towards the side of the room. 'Sit!' Arthur bellowed, gratified as the noise cut off in an instant as he bounded down the stairs.

'What the hell is all the fuss about...?' He glowered at the now quivering pack of dogs who lay flat on their bellies, all eyes fixed on him.

'I...I did knock several times, but nobody answered.'

The soft response drew his eyes away from the unruly mongrels he was unfortunate enough to call his pets towards the small woman perched awkwardly on the edge of one of the sofas which lined the room, a large backpack making it impossible for her to sit properly. Beneath a sorry looking beret, he could make out a straggle of dark red hair and a smudge of pale skin. Weaving through the dogs, Arthur moved closer and realised her coat

55

wasn't black as he'd first imagined, but a paler grey turned dark by the rain pummelling the windows outside.

'I didn't mean for you to sit,' he said, unable to help a grin as he realised it wasn't only the dogs who'd responded automatically to his harsh command. Offering his hand, he nudged Nimrod, who'd planted himself at the woman's feet, gently aside. 'And I'm sorry for the unholy greeting you received from this rabble.' A whine came from beside his hip, and Arthur dropped his free hand to caress the silken ears of Bella, the other of the pair of greyhounds who'd come over seeking forgiveness.

When the woman continued to gawk up at him, Arthur shook his extended fingers impatiently in her direction. 'Let me give you a hand up and out of that wet coat, you'll catch a chill.'

'I'm not the only one,' she replied, cheeks flaming with colour.

Following her gaze downwards, Arthur noted the expanse of bare chest showing through the open sides of his shirt and drop his hand to hurriedly button it. 'Sorry, I was dressing for dinner when these hell hounds started up.' Once he looked halfway decent, he extended his hand once more. 'Arthur Ludworth, at your service, Miss…?'

Fingers freezing a couple of inches from his, the woman's head jerked up, giving him a first full glimpse of her face. And what a face, it was. Like one of the carved marble statues in the long gallery, her alabaster skin was smooth and flawless. Those deep-set green eyes were nothing like the dead stares of those goddesses and nymphs though. Nor the mane of glorious russet red hair, a shade or two deeper than a fox's pelt, that spilled down her back now she'd tugged off that ugly hat. 'A…Arthur Ludworth? As in Sir Arthur Ludworth?'

'That's right.' From the startled expression on her face she'd clearly been expecting someone else. 'I'm sorry, you have me at an advantage.'

'Oh, yes, I'm Lucinda Kennington, you're expecting me…'

Ah. The art expert. Bloody Tristan and his stupid idea to post an ad in the paper. Of the dozens of responses to his advert, she'd been one of the few who hadn't been either a crank or a blatant charlatan. By the time he'd reached Miss Kennington's email, he'd been about ready to throw his laptop out the window in disgust over so much of his morning wasted.

Her ability to use the correct grammar had been cause enough for celebration even before he'd glanced over the CV she'd attached. Arthur had fired back an immediate response and consigned the remainder of the unread applications to his electronic trash bin. She'd acknowledged his job offer and promised to confirm her arrival date and then he'd heard nothing further. 'I didn't know you were arriving today, Miss Kennington, forgive my confusion.' Mind racing, Arthur wondered how long it would take Mrs W to get a room ready. From the looks of her, their unexpected arrival looked in dire need of a hot shower and a change of clothes.

Russet lashes flickered in surprise. 'I sent you an email confirming I would be travelling today.' A warm blush brought colour to her creamy skin, highlighting the delicate arc of her cheekbones, the deep hollows around her vivid eyes. God, she really was quite lovely. The punch of attraction which followed that thought took him by surprise. Delicate porcelain beauties weren't normally his type. He liked robust girls with laughs as big as their...personalities. He watched, fascinated, as Miss Kennington raised a hand to sweep a stray lock of hair from her forehead. Her wrist was so tiny he found himself wondering if he could span it with his thumb and forefinger. A man his size would have to be gentle around a woman like this. He found the idea oddly appealing.

Giving himself a shake, Arthur pulled his phone from his pocket and stared at the blank space in the top left corner where the signal icon should have been and then rubbed his forehead in frustration. 'We've been having problems with our internet the past couple of days, I didn't think...' Problems was putting it mildly. After months of double-billing them because they'd refused to close the old account in his father's name without a copy of the certificate of probate, their provider had closed off both accounts without warning and was refusing to reinstate the new one Arthur had set up. Unable to get a decent mobile signal for more than a few minutes at a time had resulted in endless dropped calls leaving Arthur ready to scream as he was forced to renegotiate the endless 'press one for new accounts, press four if you have lost the will to live' automated menus that served no purpose he could see other than to thwart attempts to speak to an actual human being. Tristan had headed down to the village pub a couple of hours ago to try and use their pay phone in a last-ditch attempt to get the problem resolved.

Miss Kennington visibly shivered, dragging Arthur away from his reverie. Really, he was being the most terrible host, what must she think of him? 'Here, let me help you with your coat.' He tugged her to her feet, an action that took almost no effort as she barely seemed to weigh anything, then tried to help her separate the wet wool from the suit jacket beneath it. The material didn't yield easily resulting in a somewhat undignified tug of war as he pulled her coat one way whilst Miss Kennington wriggled in the other. Thinking it was some kind of game, Nimrod, Bella and a few of the other dogs who'd stayed at his side rather than wander over to bask before the fireplace tried to join in. 'Get down, Nimrod! You too, Bertie. Bloody hounds, I'll stick you all out in the stables if you don't behave.'

'I'm fine, it's fine, I can manage,' Miss Kennington was muttering, her attempts to avoid the dogs and escape her coat more hindrance than help.

'Just hold still,' Arthur found himself snapping with more force than he'd intended. Her cheeks flushed red, but at least she stopped faffing around long enough for him to get the soggy coat free. Holding the dripping coat away from himself, Arthur cast a mock-glare over the panting, prancing dogs who seemed delighted he'd won the game and were waiting to see what excitement lay in store for them next. 'On your beds, go on!'

With expressions that might have broken a softer heart, the mini pack retreated, all apart from Bella who'd taken up station in front of Miss Kennington, seemingly determined to protect her from the others. 'You've won a friend there,' Arthur said with a grin. When Miss Kennington didn't return his smile, a terrible thought occurred to him. 'Unless you don't like dogs?'

She shook her head. 'I'm not really used to them, that's all, and you do have rather a lot…'

Arthur let his eyes roam over the motley furballs splayed out before the fire. 'I'm not sure how we ended up with quite so many, to be honest.' *Other than the fact everyone around knows we're a bloody soft touch when it came to anything on four paws.* 'They can be a bit overwhelming en masse, but I promise you they'd never cause you any harm.'

To his relief, Miss Kennington dropped her fingers to caress the top of Bella's head, and the brindle greyhound responded by pressing closer, her entire body vibrating with delight at the attention. 'She's beautiful.'

'That's Bella,' Arthur said, unable to keep the note of affection out of his voice. He adored all their dogs, but as Pippin the little terrier was Tristan's particular pet, Nimrod and Bella held a special place in Arthur's heart.

Miss Kennington sank into the chair behind her once more as she lavished more attention on the ecstatic greyhound. 'Hello, Bella, you're a gorgeous girl, aren't you?' Her long fingers stroking over the dog's head held him mesmerised. Musician's fingers, he thought, eyes fixated by the neat little nails unadorned with polish, and he wondered if she played an instrument. To everyone's surprise—not least Arthur's own—the compulsory music lessons at school had sparked a brief passion for playing the violin. Though the music master had despaired over his chunky fingers, it hadn't stopped Arthur from learning, just made it a bit harder to find his way around the strings until he'd got the hang on it. As with his rugby, he'd never pursued it seriously, despite the urging of his tutor. What had been the point when his future had been mapped out for him thanks to a bunch of archaic inheritance laws?

Arthur reached for the length of blue rope hanging beside the door. Within moments Maxwell appeared, summoned from the depths of the castle via the bell pull. 'You rang, Sir Arthur?'

Trying not to roll his eyes at his butler's studied formality, Arthur gestured towards Miss Kennington. 'We have a guest, Maxwell. Can you track down Mrs W and make sure a room is made available for Miss Kennington?'

Maxwell inclined his head. 'I believe Mrs Walters has already prepared the rose room in anticipation of Miss Kennington's arrival. It shouldn't need more than the covers turning down.'

Of course she had. Arthur might have known as much, as their housekeeper was the very model of efficiency.

The butler extended one white gloved hand towards the stairs. 'If you will allow me to escort you, Miss? Arrangements will be made for your luggage to be brought up shortly.' He shouldered the backpack when Miss Kennington would've reached for it.

Her eyes flickered uncertainly between him and Maxwell, so Arthur gave her a reassuring nod. 'Go on and get settled. I'll speak to Betsy and ask her to hold dinner for an hour, so you'll have plenty of time to have a shower and get yourself warmed up.'

'Oh, you don't have to go to any trouble on my account.' That rosy blush highlighted her cheeks once more.

'It's no trouble. I'm sure whatever Betsy has prepared can be held for a bit.' Arthur raised an eyebrow towards Maxwell.

'Beef and barley stew, sir,' the butler provided helpfully.

Arthur clapped his hands together. 'That's settled then. I'll speak to Betsy and track down Mrs W. She'll pop up and see you shortly, just in case there's anything you need.'

Miss Kennington hesitated before nodding. 'Thank you.'

With a shrug of one shoulder, Arthur tucked his hands in his pockets and backed up a few steps to watch her follow Maxwell towards the upper floor. 'It's no trouble,' he repeated, wanting to make it clear. 'This will be your home for the next couple of months, so I want you to be as comfortable as possible.'

He watched her slender figure trailing up the stairs after the butler, a strange sensation tugging at his chest as though he should be the one going with her. Would she like it here? Would she find her room to her satisfaction? Would she want to stay after she got a chance to look around the castle, or would both the castle and its owner fail to pass muster? As the dogs swarmed around his ankles once more, he found himself willing her to glance back over her shoulder. She reached the top of the staircase, hesitated with her hand on the rail, and *yes!* The instant their gazes met, Arthur felt something, a little zing like he'd touched a charged particle.

Suddenly Tristan's idea to put that advert in the paper was looking to Arthur like a very good one indeed.

# CHAPTER SIX

From the moment the butler—*the butler, for goodness' sake!*—pushed open the heavy oak-panelled door to what he'd referred to as the rose room, the reality of where she was hammered home to Lucie. Opulent velvet drapes hung in thick swathes around an honest-to-goodness four-poster bed so high she thought she might need a ladder to climb onto it. The pale cream wallpaper covered in roses of every shade and hue from palest pink to deep red it was almost black were clearly what had given the room its name. So realistically drawn were they, she might have been tempted to trace a finger over one of the buds had the butler not been standing stiff at attention beside the open door. Not sure what he was expecting, she told him the room was beautiful and he withdrew with a bow, closing the door behind him.

Alone at last, she took a few moments to explore the rest of the room, from the heavy wardrobe carved in the same dark wood as the bedframe complete with a neat row of padded coat hangers waiting for her clothes—no nasty tangle of wire ones here!—to a matching dresser which held an old fashioned china washbasin and matching ewer. Everything looked authentic and her fingers itched to explore the delicate finials and carving. Even the thick rug covering the cream carpet next to the bed whispered of quality and age. She might still have been evaluating the age and origin of the furniture an hour later had she not poked her head around the door inset in one wall and discovered the delights of the bathroom. After that, her only thought was to strip out of her ruined suit and laddered tights, and to wash the cold from her bones.

*As comfortable as possible...* Sir Arthur's parting words slipped back into Lucie's mind as she closed her eyes and leaned her head back under the stream of blessedly hot water cascading from the shower head. His voice had rolled through her, rich and velvety like quality dark chocolate, and the glimpses of his body she'd caught through the open front of his shirt! It was simply criminal for any man to be as good-looking as that. Lucie banged her head gently against the tiles behind her. She could not possibly fancy Sir Arthur Ludworth. She. *Thump*. Could. *Thump*. Not. *Thump*. Turning beneath the stream, she tilted her face up into it determined to wash any ridiculous thoughts right out of her head.

When she'd seen the bathroom with its ancient-looking fixtures and fittings, including a vast roll-top bath offset on a pedestal in one corner, she'd worried there was an equally ancient boiler lurking somewhere in the vast expanse of the castle. To her relief, the water had blasted out of the taps in a reassuring stream when she turned them on and it was only her desire not to keep anyone waiting any longer than necessary that had made her opt for a shower rather than the luxury of a bath. She couldn't remember the last time she'd had one. The bathroom in the flat she shared with her mum held only a poky square shower stall, a sink and the toilet, and there was still barely room to swing a cat. Once she'd found her feet, so to speak, she would make time for herself and the row of luxury bath products she'd spotted sitting beside the tub, the same brand as the gorgeous shampoo that was filling the air with the zingy scents of ginger and lemongrass and putting some energy back into her tired body.

After using the matching bodywash, Lucie rinsed the bubbles somewhat regretfully from her skin and turned off the water.

Wrapping herself in a cloud-soft white bath sheet that covered her from breastbone to ankle, she was just securing a second, smaller towel around her sopping-wet hair when a knock on the bathroom door startled her. An image of Sir Arthur flashing an expanse of muscled bare chest sprang into her mind once more, her good intentions no match for the hints of a six-pack she'd seen. He hadn't been at all what she'd expected after the research she'd done. Instead of the slightly overweight middle-aged man she'd seen in that Ascot picture, she'd been faced with some Adonis, all high cheekbones, patrician nose and with a smile that could knock a girl into next Tuesday. No, no, no! She could not, *would not* have a crush on her new boss. It was beyond humiliating.

The knock came once more. 'Hello?' she called out in a tentative voice, hoping like hell his rich drawl wouldn't be the one she heard back.

'Miss Kennington?'

A woman, thank God! Lucie tugged open the door and found herself facing an elegant woman somewhere around her mum's age. With her pale blonde hair swept up into an elegant twist and a blouse and skirt straight out of a Boden catalogue, she looked the epitome of a country lady. Was this the housekeeper Sir Arthur had mentioned? Lucie cringed at the thought of the high-street and value-store brands that made up the majority of the items stuffed in her suitcase.

'I'm sorry to disturb you, I did knock on the main door but then I heard the water running. I'm Mrs Walters—Mrs W to everyone but Maxwell.' A hint of humour twinkled in her brown eyes, softening her expression into something much warmer and Lucie relaxed in response to it. 'I just wanted to make sure you had everything you need.'

'I…I think so. Mr Maxwell said he'd arrange for my case to be brought up?'

Mrs W tsked. 'Don't let him catch you calling him *Mr* Maxwell, dear, or we'll never hear the end of it. And in answer to your question, yes, your case is here. Would you like me to help you with your unpacking?' She was already stepping away from the bathroom door and back into the bedroom where Lucie's case rested on the bed on top of a blanket which hadn't been there earlier.

'Oh no, it's fine really.' Lucie hurried in her wake, stepping on the edge of the bath sheet in her hurry which began to unravel. By the time she'd rewrapped herself and tucked the ends firmly in at the front, Mrs W had already unzipped her case and was lifting out that silly green evening dress Lucie was regretting having packed.

Holding it up to the light, Mrs W gave a nod, apparently seeing nothing untoward about another member of staff—because rose room, or no rose room, that's exactly what Lucie was—packing a formal gown. 'I'll hang this for now, and if the creases haven't dropped in a couple of days then let me know and I'll give it a steam.'

'There's no need,' Lucie said, feeling a little desperate as the housekeeper, having hung the dress, was now lifting out handfuls of underwear and stacking them in neat piles on top of the bed.

'Nonsense, Miss Kennington, it's what I'm here for.' Mrs W ploughed on like a perfectly-coiffured bulldozer, apparently heedless to Lucie's growing sense of embarrassment.

'Lucie, I'd much prefer it if everyone would call me Lucie.' She scrabbled in the piles looking for a half-decent bra and a matching pair of knickers, rather than the days of the week pants her mum had bought her for Christmas one year as a joke and which she'd packed because they were hardly worn.

'As you wish, Lucie. Now we don't stand too much on formality here, so I think these slacks and this top will be perfectly fine for dinner, don't you?'

Lucie could've kissed her for that kindness as she'd been panicking a bit about what would be acceptable since Sir Arthur had mentioned he'd been dressing for dinner when her arrival disturbed her. Embarrassment flashed through her at the way she'd dropped into the chair in instinctive response at the tone

65

of command he'd used to order the dogs to sit. What a terrible first impression she must've made, cowering like a fool and dripping water all over the flag-stoned floor. She'd have to do much better at dinner. Speaking of which, there would be no time to dry her hair beforehand. Lucie sat on the velvet-covered stool in front of the dressing table and unwrapped the towel from her head. She'd just have to plait it and pin it up out of the way.

'Oh, what a gorgeous colour.' Lucie turned on the stool, wondering what could possibly have caught Mrs W's eye as apart from the green dress, her wardrobe was a mass of neutral shades, and black. She found the housekeeper's eyes locked on her, a hand clasped to her cheek. 'I always wanted red hair when I was little girl and first read the *Anne of Green Gables* stories,' Mrs W sighed. 'Such a romantic colour, and with your lovely, creamy skin, I bet you were the envy of all of your friends.'

Hardly, but Lucie kept her snort of derision to herself. 'Thank you.' Turning back to hide her blush at the unexpected compliment, Lucie focused on twisting and securing her hair up into a neat plaited bun at the nape of her neck whilst Mrs W busied herself with the few remaining bits in Lucie's case.

Only once everything had been hung up or laid with care into the dresser drawers did the housekeeper step back. 'That's you all sorted, Lucie. I shall leave you in peace to get dressed. Come down when you are ready, everyone will gather in the family room.'

'The family room?' Lucie wondered who exactly *everyone* was, but didn't dare ask.

'It's the second door on the right leading from the great hall.' Mrs W smiled, obviously thinking that helped. 'Where you entered the castle,' she added once Lucie continued to stare blankly.

'Oh, yes, of course.' The vast, vaulted space had been more than large enough to be considered great, what with that fireplace taller than her head and the enormous table in the centre of it. 'And, I'd get back there how?' She should've paid better attention to the route Maxwell had taken, but it had been hard to concentrate when her brain had been overwhelmed by the fact she was going to be staying in a real, stand-against-all-invaders castle complete with battlements and a round tower.

Mrs W's smile turned sympathetic. 'It's a bit of a maze until you get used it. Once you've met with Arthur in the morning and gone over your duties, I'll show you around the place and help you get your bearings.' It didn't escape Lucie's attention that the housekeeper attached no honorific to her employer's name, unlike the butler. 'Turn right as you come out of your room and follow the corridor to the half-stair down to the next floor where you'll turn left and find the main staircase at the far end.'

'Thank you. *Again.*' Lucie emphasised the final word with a grateful smile.

'My pleasure, Lucie. I can't wait to see what you unearth during your investigations. It's all rather exciting.' With a whisper of stockings definitely more silk than nylon, Mrs W swept out of the room.

*

A few minutes later, dressed and with just a hint of make-up to darken her lashes and put a bit of colour in her cheeks, Lucie followed Mrs W's instructions and found herself at the top of the enormous double-sided staircase that overlooked the great hall. She hadn't had much of an opportunity to take in the grandeur of the space during her arrival, focused as she had been on getting out of the rain, not getting knocked over by the dogs' enthusiastic greeting and then rather more on Sir Arthur's naked chest than she should've been. Pausing now at the top, she let her eyes drink in the beautifully carved vaulted ceiling beams, the grimly imposing stone walls softened here and there by thick tapestries in muted shades of green and blue. Impressive as they were now, she could only imagine how incredible they must've been when newly woven—not to mention the hours of pains-taking work stitched into them. Between the tapestries large sconces held modern electric lights. The grey stone behind them looked to have been left stained by decades of soot as though to remind the observer of the burning torches they would've once held.

Dominating it all was the enormous circular table set in the very centre of the room. She hadn't noticed more than its sheer size earlier, but from her bird's eye vantage point on the balcony she could see now that it was elaborately painted to resemble an enormous shield, or target, in alternating segments of green and white. A huge stylised red rose filled the centre of the table, tickling something in the back of Lucie's memory. As she slowly made her way down the stairs, the decorations around the edge of the table morphed into medieval script and her stomach began to churn. *She'd seen this before.* As she finished her descent and crossed to examine it, her worst fears were realised. She was staring at a replica of an artefact which hung on the wall of the great hall at Winchester Castle.

Fingers tracing the outline of *Pelleas*, the name inscribed closest to her, Lucie recalled what she'd read—and dismissed—during her research into the Ludworths about a family obsession with all things Arthurian. *Pelleas, Kay, Ector de Maris,* the names stretched the circumference of the table. Sir Pellinor, Sir Kay, Sir Ector, all fabled Knights of the Round Table. A bubble of laughter escaped her lips, and she clapped her hand over her mouth before it could rise into hysteria. The joke was on her, that much was for sure.

Bloody knights of the bloody round table! She'd thought taking this job at Camland Castle would be a chance to expand her skills and perhaps even salvage her reputation a little, instead she was on some wild goose chase for the scion of a family of lunatics. No wonder she'd got the job, she was probably the only person naïve enough to apply for it!

Furious, she marched around the table, heels clicking on the tiles in a staccato beat to match the drumming of her heart. The door to what the housekeeper had referred to as the family room stood slightly ajar and she stomped straight through it to confront the man lazing on one of a pair of matching sofas set either side of the fireplace. The brindle greyhound who'd been resting before the fire leapt up to press herself against Lucie's thigh, but she was too angry and too focused on the object of her ire. 'Is this some kind of bloody joke?' she snapped.

A dark eyebrow angled itself into a position that could only be described as haughty as Sir Arthur somehow managed to stare down his nose at her, even from his semi-reclined position. The pink shirt he was wearing tucked into a pair of indigo-blue jeans did nothing to soften the masculine hard planes of his face. 'Are you lost?'

'Lost?' she sputtered. 'Lost! Yes, of course I'm bloody lost! Lost in the back-end of nowhere with an arrogant idiot with wild delusions of grandeur! No timewasters, you said, and yet here you are wasting *my* time on some kind of fantastical wild goose chase!'

A grin played about Sir Arthur's lips, and, though never previously inclined towards violence, Lucie had to clench her fists against the sudden urge to punch him right on the end of his nose. 'It's not funny,' she ground out between clenched teeth.

'Oh, I rather think it is.' Sitting up straighter, Sir Arthur dislodged a wheat-coloured terrier who'd been curled across his lap and folded his arms across his chest, the movement tugging the pink shirt tight across his broad shoulders.

Pink? But hadn't he been wearing navy when they'd met not an hour earlier? It took very little effort to recall the image of him standing before her almost half-naked. In fact, it sprang forth so readily she feared it might be permanently imprinted on her brain. 'You changed your shirt.' God! Why had she even said that, and what did it matter if he had? She needed to stop gawking at him and get back to the point. 'I may be young, but I'm not to be trifled with, *Sir* Arthur, and I won't be dragged into whatever nonsense you've got in mind. I'll be on the first train home tomorrow.'

As the object of her ire continued to smile that irritating smile, the first clouds of her anger lifted and she took a proper look at him. Though he certainly resembled the man she'd met in the great hall earlier, it was clear—to her absolute horror—that whoever he was, he wasn't Sir Arthur. 'Oh. But you're not...I just assumed...Oh my goodness, I'm so terribly sorry,' she gasped, hands flapping ineffectually towards him.

Grin slipping not one inch, he scratched the terrier behind one ear as he continued to stare up at her. 'No, I'm not, and more's the pity. I'm sure my brother will be most disappointed to hear you won't be trifled with. If I were him, I'd have all kinds of glorious *nonsense* planned for you.'

The way he said the word nonsense made it sound positively filthy and Lucie could no more stop the blush heating her cheeks than she could the sun from rising in the east. Her tendency to flush over the smallest thing had been the bane of her existence. As the initial embarrassment faded, her brain caught up with the rest of what he'd said. 'Your brother?'

The man on the sofa was all but laughing now, enjoying her discomfort. 'Yes, Red, there's two of us—well, three if you count Iggy, but she's not a man no matter how hard she might try to outdo us. I'm Tristan Ludworth, youngest by a handful of minutes and therefore title-less and of no significance whatsoever.' He rose to his feet, towering over her even with her heeled pumps lending a small advantage. 'And you must be Miss Kennington.' Reaching for one of her hands that now hung limp at her side, Tristan raised it to his lips for a kiss. 'Charmed, I'm sure.'

Cheeks aflame once more, Lucie tugged her hand free and spun away only to almost run into a towering figure who'd been standing almost at her back. Strong hands cupped her shoulders.

70

'Hey, steady on there, where's the fire?' Sir Arthur steadied her for a moment before releasing his hold. 'Miss Kennington? Is everything all right?'

Head swivelling between Arthur's hazel eyes shining with concern, to Tristan's identical pair glittering with amusement, Lucie felt a flutter of panic. They were both so big, and so close, and so *gorgeous*, it was overwhelming. Arthur…Tristan…the round table…In a flash her initial anger reignited, and she poked Sir Arthur in the chest. 'You got me here under false pretences. I took your advertisement in good faith and thought this was going to be a serious project!'

Sir Arthur stared down at the finger planted against his breastbone, then back up to meet her gaze. 'Believe me, I take the prospect of potentially losing my home very seriously indeed, Miss Kennington. What's upset you?' His eyes flicked over her head to stare at this brother. 'Is this your fault? Have you been messing with her? You promised me you would be on your best behaviour.'

'Hey, don't blame me!' Lucie glanced behind her to see Tristan backing up with his palms raised in protestation. 'Pippin and I were minding our own business when this flaming Valkyrie burst into the room and started yelling. I thought you must've done something to piss her off, given your dodgy track record with the ladies.'

'Dodgy track record?' Seemingly to have forgotten about her, Arthur stepped around Lucie to confront his brother. 'Says the man with a string of conquests that'd line the road from here to Chesterfield and back again!'

Tristan scoffed. 'Not every woman wants to snag the heir. I'll leave the fortune hunters to you, thanks, bro.' Laughing, he ducked as Arthur took a swing at him that Lucie could tell from her position had never any intention of landing.

'Excuse me?' She waved when they both glanced around. 'As entertaining as this brotherly banter is, can we get back to the point, please?'

71

Sir Arthur folded his arms across his chest, his brother—his triplet, she supposed, for hadn't Tristan mentioned a sister?—mirrored the action. Side-by-side and as close to her as they were, Lucie could see that apart from their colouring and general build, they were actually quite dissimilar. Tristan's face was a little thinner in the cheeks, his build more slender than his brother's stockier frame. There was a slice through one of Arthur's eyebrows, a remnant of some old scar or just a tiny natural defect, she couldn't be sure, that gave him something of a rakish air. He quirked that brow at her now. 'And what exactly *is* the point, Miss Kennington?'

Rolling her eyes at his persistence at pretence, Lucie gestured to them both before waving her hand towards the open door leading back to the great hall. 'Arthur, Tristan, the round bloody table. That crazy ancestor of yours who believed this is Camelot.'

Sir Arthur shrugged. 'What of it?'

So, at least he wasn't going to deny it! She supposed she should be grateful for small mercies. 'I thought this was a serious position, that you wanted someone to assess and catalogue works of art, not replicas and rubbish.' Lucie clamped her lips shut. The paintings and pieces she'd seen on the landing hadn't been rubbish, though, had they?

There was no hint of that smooth rich chocolate in his tone now, only an ice that told her she'd overstepped the mark. 'I'll admit part of your role will be to go through some of the more interesting items my ancestor, Thomas Ludworth, accumulated, but as I said before, I'm deadly serious about the financial threat looming over Camland which is why I need someone to urgently update and review our archives and collection records. If I can't rustle up some serious cash in the very near future, then over four hundred years of my family's history could be broken up and sold for scrap.' It was his turn to glower. 'If you're not up to the job, Miss Kennington, then tell me now and I'll find somebody who is!'

Oh.

Lucie opened and closed her mouth a couple of times as

responses flew through her mind. His claim about the risk of losing everything struck far too close to home, and she was once more the bewildered teenager watching her possessions being loaded onto the back of a bailiff's truck. Did she honestly think she had the knowledge and experience to do a good job for Sir Arthur and the rest of his family? If he was serious, then maybe she should get out whilst the going was good. What she'd thought would be an interesting project, a way to escape from her current work nightmare and lose herself deep in the castle archives had taken a deadly serious turn. Confidence already close to rock bottom, it took a further nosedive. Was she *really* up to it? What if she blew it and missed some fantastic treasure worth a fortune, and they lost everything?

Or worse, what if that treasure was just waiting here for her to discover it and she missed the opportunity? A decent find would surely help to redeem her reputation...Chances like this didn't come along very often, and slinking back to her tiny bedroom to hide once more under her duvet would be the end of her. Pushing her shoulders back, Lucie straightened up to her full and entirely unimpressive five-foot-three height, and thrust out her hand. 'It's Lucie, Sir Arthur, not Miss Kennington, and I'm your woman.'

Arthur enveloped her hand in his much-larger tanned grip and shook it firmly. 'Just call me Arthur. If your other skills match your temper, Lucie, then I think you're definitely my woman.' His hazel gaze locked with hers and Lucie found herself thinking about all the different ways she'd like to be his woman.

Face burning, she tried to tug her hand free, but Arthur held her fingers tighter for a long moment, making it clear the clasp would end only when he was ready for it to. God, that arrogant possession really shouldn't be attractive, but her bones were in danger of melting from the heat generated from just their palms pressing together. What would happen to her if he should press other parts of himself against other parts of her? *Never going to happen, Lucie!* Giving herself a firm mental shake, she reclaimed her hand from his and tucked it safely beneath her arm before it could get her into any more trouble.

'In your dreams.' Tristan nudged his brother's arm then clapped his hands together. 'Right, now we've all called a truce, how about a drink to celebrate?'

As though on cue, a panelled door at the end of the room swung open and Maxwell appeared, a silver tray laden with tall glass flutes balanced on his right arm. 'Champagne, Sir Arthur?'

'You're a bloody mind-reader, Maxy, old boy!' Tristan crowed as he swooped down on the tray and gathered three of the glasses between his hands. The butler's lips twitched at the irreverent nickname, but Lucie didn't miss the sparkle in his eyes as he watched the two brothers laughing over something together. He might be a stickler for protocol, but there was real affection in his manner for them—perhaps not the same relaxed fondness with which Mrs W had spoken of Arthur, but it was clearly more than a run-of-the-mill job working for this family.

Before she could consider the strange employer-employee dynamics at the castle, a stunning brunette dressed in a sapphire-blue smoking jacket over skin-tight black jeans swept into the room and claimed a glass of champagne from the tray. Though the line of her jaw was softer, the cheekbones finer and higher, she had the same strong nose and wide brow as the brothers. No sooner had she arrived than two more people entered the room. The middle-aged man's brown hair carried more than a dusting of grey, but he still cut as imposing a figure as the younger Ludworth men. The woman on his arm looked at least a generation older, though there was no lack of vigour in the piercing gaze she fixed on Lucie as she accepted a drink.

If two had been intimidating, five were positively terrifying. Feeling an utter fish of water, Lucie wondered if it was too late to retreat to the staff quarters and eat her supper with Mrs W and Maxwell.

# CHAPTER SEVEN

'How did you get on with the internet company?' Arthur asked his brother as he watched the rest of the family descend on Lucie. The fire and fury of her earlier outburst had been replaced by a wariness he didn't like to see in her green eyes. He could still feel the imprint of the outraged finger she'd jabbed into his chest and he raised an absent hand to rub the spot as he wondered if he should've done more to prepare her for the task ahead. Her reaction to his family's eccentric past had been exactly the type of thing he'd been dreading, which was the only reason he could account for blurting out his dire financial situation to a practical stranger. She was a lot younger than he'd expected—a lot prettier too. In his mind's eye, Ms Lucinda Kennington had been a lady in her middle years, fond of tweed skirts and sensible walking shoes with thick glasses she wore around her neck on a string of beads. Mind you, from the shocked look she'd given him when he'd introduced himself earlier, he hadn't been what she'd expected either.

'...So I told him that no, he couldn't speak to the bloody account holder as what was left of Uther had been shot into the sky stuffed in a firework.'

Tristan's exasperated voice cut into his musings, making Arthur realise he'd not been paying attention. Dragging his eyes from Lucie, he turned to face his brother. 'You didn't?'

'I bloody well did, stupid jobsworth.' Tristan took a mouthful of champagne. 'I eventually got through to a grown-up who was most apologetic once I started bandying the title around a bit, told her it *was* most inconvenient when I couldn't contact my good friend, *Harry*—' Tristan lowered his voice to a theatrical whisper '—about a planned visit to the castle.'

Arthur groaned. 'Please tell me you didn't tell some poor call-centre supervisor that we have connections to the royal family.'

Unrepentant, Tristan shrugged. 'I didn't tell her that, but I didn't disabuse her when she jumped to that conclusion. Besides, Harry and I are good friends, and he is visiting The Castle this weekend, so it wasn't a lie.' Harry Wilks, the son of Bill and Morag Wilks who ran the namesake pub in the village, was around the same age as them. 'Cut a long story short, a new account has been set up and the connection should be restored before 10 a.m. tomorrow.' Tristan clicked their glasses together. 'Now, let's talk about something far more interesting like your delectable Miss Kennington.'

Even before Tristan had finished saying her name, Arthur was already searching the room for her. She seemed to have recovered from her earlier uncertainty at meeting the family and was cosily ensconced on one of the sofas with Iggy and Morgana book-ending her. The three women were listening to Lancelot tell what Arthur assumed was one of his wild anecdotes from the way he was waving his arms around. 'She's off limits,' he growled at his brother. Tristan would never press his attentions on any woman who wasn't interested any more than Arthur would, but that didn't stop him flirting outrageously at the drop of a hat. There would be no dropping of hats by his brother, or any other items of clothing for that matter, in Lucie's vicinity. Not if Arthur had anything to do with it.

Tristan held up his hands. 'All right, I won't rain on your parade.' He heaved a sigh of false regret. 'Shame really, as she's a stunner.'

'There's no parade. Lucie is here to do a job and we are going to let her do it in peace. She's a professional, and we should respect her right to work without harassment like any other employee.' He'd reached that rather disappointing conclusion during the past hour when he'd been holed up once more studying the dreadful state of their current overdraft. As he watched, Lucie laughed at something Lancelot had said to her, her whole face lighting up with joy. Arthur let his warning to Tristan settle on his own shoulders. Pretty she might be, but Lucie was off limits. Capital O. Capital L. Full stop, underlined. Do not pass go, do not collect two hundred pounds. Do not think about kissing the pretty new member of staff.

Draining his glass, Arthur checked his watch. 'Right, shall we make a move? Dinner must be ready by now.'

They made their way to the sofa where Tristan offered his arm to their great-aunt with a flourish. 'Silly boy,' she said, patting his cheek with her free hand.

'Come on, dearest girl, help your old, arthritic uncle, won't you?' Lancelot crooked his elbow towards Iggy.

Hooking her hand around his arm, Iggy rolled her eyes. 'Old and arthritic, my ars…my eye,' she said, catching herself just in time from swearing within earshot of Morgana who had very definite views about the kind of language suitable for ladies. 'I saw you out on the gallops earlier putting that new mare through her paces.'

Lancelot laughed. 'She's a goer, all right, and so responsive. About the only female in my life who I can say that about, more's the pity!'

After wincing at his uncle's departing back, Arthur relieved Lucie of her empty glass then popped it onto the mantelpiece together with his own. When he turned back, she'd risen from the sofa and was standing slightly off to one side of him with her hands clasped in front of her. Not quite sure what to read from her body language, and not wishing to make her feel uncom-

77

fortable, though his instinct was to offer his arm, Arthur settled for gesturing towards the door. When she moved forward, he kept his arm slightly behind her, not touching but ready to offer support if required.

Their pace across the great hall and down the corridor leading to the dining room was set by Morgana's slow gait leaving plenty of time for polite conversation. 'How's your room? Do you have everything you need?'

Casting him a quick sideways glance, Lucie nodded. 'It's fine.' She gave a little laugh. 'More than fine, it's beautiful, much grander than what I'm used to.'

'And what's that?' He'd only meant it as a general question, something neutral to carry them through the rest of their walk to the table, but from the hitch in her step, he wondered if he'd blundered somehow. 'Sorry, I don't mean to pry,' he added.

She shot him that little flash of side-eye again. 'It's fine.' She paused. 'Sorry, I keep saying that.'

He laughed. 'It's been a bit of an awkward start for us, hasn't it? I can only apologise for the mess with the internet and not getting your email. Tristan seems to have worked a miracle, though, and they've promised to get us back up and running tomorrow morning. Around 10 a.m., something like that.'

When she met his eyes this time, she didn't glance away. 'That'll be good. I'm so used to my phone being permanently connected, it's a bit odd. However did people manage before?'

'Well, it's often a bit hit and miss around here so we've kept the landline. I hadn't realised how many people don't have them these days until I started seeing those stories on the news when one of the networks crashes.'

They were almost at the door to the dining room. Arthur stepped to one side to allow Lucie to proceed ahead of him. 'Did you need to use the phone, to call home, I mean, and let them know you're okay?' Her refusal to answer earlier had him more than a little intrigued. Hopefully she'd have a boyfriend waiting

78

for her, and Arthur could forget about the annoying tug of attraction he felt towards her.

'It's fi…' Lucie burst out laughing, then raised her hand to cover the red flush on her cheek. 'Gosh, I need to work on my stock responses, don't I? I managed to get a bar on my phone earlier and sent Mum a quick text. I'll message her properly once we're back online tomorrow.'

Pondering the connotations of Lucie mentioning her mum, Arthur showed her to a free chair next to his sister before taking his own place at the head of the table. It still felt a bit awkward to be sitting there, even though it had been almost six months since his father's passing, but he was slowly coming to terms with it. Protocol worked because it made people comfortable, helped them to understand the rules. His own discomfort was secondary to ensuring those who lived and worked at the castle were happy and at ease.

With Mrs W's help, he was breaking down a few of the most constraining barriers, though. Gone were the terrible, stuffy dinners they'd endured as small children when their grandfather had still been alive, and which their father had perpetuated, although with a more relaxed air. With the ready agreement of the rest of the family, they now sat at one end of the dining room table, and dinner had been reduced to one course plus a bit of cheese or some fruit for those that wanted anything else.

If Arthur could really choose, he'd be happy with a tray on his knee in the family room, but as Mrs W had pointed out, that would put the ladies who came up from the village to assist with service at breakfast and dinner out of a job. Which might have made sense given the economising they needed to do, but it was such a drop in the ocean he had sworn they would be facing the bailiffs before he would cut anyone's hours or wages. It was like walking a tightrope sometimes. He thought once more about the hideous blackhole in the family finances and added juggling and breathing fire to his veritable circus act.

Maxwell appeared at his elbow. 'Will you want wine with dinner, Sir Arthur?'

He was fine, but he raised a quick eyebrow at his aunt on his left and Tristan on his right. When both shook their heads, he said. 'Not tonight, thank you. I think we'll be fine with water.'

'Very good, sir. Perhaps some elderflower cordial for you, Ms Ludworth?' The butler asked Morgana. When she inclined her head with a smile, Maxwell gave her the slightest of bows and left the table to return moments later bearing two large jugs, one clear, the other cloudy which he placed on the table before Arthur. 'Dinner will be served momentarily.'

They were soon all sat with bowls of steaming beef and barley stew and hunks of Betsy's fresh baked bread in front of them. Arthur let the conversation flow around him, thoughts focused on the food before him and his plan for the coming day. With Maxwell's help, he'd located the old archives, purchase ledgers and other records they thought might assist Lucie. For all his love of tradition, the butler had certainly moved with the times and had produced a memory stick containing the electronic database he used to keep track of the family collection of silver and other small valuables such as the vases, snuff boxes and other things accumulated over the years and displayed in various rooms around the castle. He'd told Arthur it made doing regular inventory checks much easier as he could print off a list for each room and do a quick inspection for damage or see if anything had been misplaced. Arthur wasn't aware of any instances of theft happening within his lifetime, but things inevitably got moved around, knocked down the back of cupboards, or whatever.

Even with the documents they'd been able to pull together, it was still clear to Arthur there was a lot of missing information and Lucie would have her work cut out for her. Well, that was what he was paying her for after all. The stew started to churn uncomfortably in his gut. He really hoped he wasn't throwing good money after bad, and that there would be something worth enough money to help them out of the hole. He'd better start working on a plan B, just in case. Maybe a plan C, D and E whilst he was at it.

Though he'd been hesitant about the prospect of opening the house to the public, it was starting to look like their most viable option. The bluebell display the woods put on each year was renowned in the local area—and beyond. Perhaps he could test the waters with some sort of event around Easter. He filed the idea away for later; there were still hosting duties to be discharged. Pushing away his plate, Arthur refused the offer of anything else as it was cleared away. He watched Lucie do the same then stifle a huge yawn. She looked up just at that moment and gave him an embarrassed smile. 'I'm sorry, it's been a long day.'

Arthur stood. 'Not at all. Would you like to take a cup of tea or coffee up to your room?' He gestured to the side table where Maxwell was just setting out a couple of large thermos jugs.

Lucie came to stand beside him. 'You won't think I'm rude if I do?'

'Oh, absolutely, but I'll get over it in a couple of days,' Arthur deadpanned as he stared down at her.

Her eyes widened for a moment before she giggled. 'I suppose it's a bit late to worry about being rude after I yelled at you earlier and called your family lunatics.' She ducked her head, making herself busy as she studied the selection of tea bags laid out in a china bowl. Aunt Morgana was the only tea drinker amongst them and she insisted on lapsang souchong loose tea made in a silver pot, so heaven knew where Maxwell had rustled up such a mixed selection. Knowing him, he had a box of every assortment stored in the pantry 'just in case'.

Reaching for the thermos containing the hot water, Arthur poured it over the peppermint teabag Lucie had placed in her cup. 'I probably should've warned you about the King Arthur stuff. I know it seems a bit weird, but the ninth baronet was convinced there was a connection. He dedicated more than half his life, and a great deal of his fortune pursuing it.' He gave her a rueful smile. 'That's the first time the family nearly went bankrupt.'

'Are things really that bad?'

'I can cover what we've agreed to pay you, if that's what you're worried about.' There was an edge of hurt in the look she gave him, and Arthur could've kicked himself for being so clumsy. 'That came out wrong.' An awkward silence settled over them as he quickly fixed himself a black coffee in a travel mug. It had become a nightly ritual of his to take his last drink of the evening when he gave the dogs their walk.

Lucie tapped her spoon on the edge of her cup, breaking the silence. 'We've been doing a lot of that today—saying the wrong thing and jumping to conclusions. Perhaps we should have a fresh start tomorrow?'

Relieved he hadn't offended her too badly, Arthur relaxed. 'That sounds like a great idea.' She finished making her tea and reached for the cup. 'Well, good night, then.'

'Good night. Breakfast will be in here tomorrow morning whenever you're ready, and then I thought we could meet in the library and we can through the documents I've managed to put together so far.'

'Sounds good. Mrs W's offered to give me a bit of tour as well, to help me find my feet.' She picked up her mug. 'Good night.'

'I'll see you back to the great hall, I need to let the dogs out for a bit anyway.' With a brief exchange of farewells to the rest of the family, they left the dining room.

Their arrival back in the hall was greeted by the dogs as though they'd been gone for weeks rather than just over an hour. Arthur stood in front of Lucie to block the worst of the wagging tails and enthusiastic tongues. 'Yes, yes, we're going out in a minute,' he assured them and pointed towards the door. Recognising the signal, all bar one surged towards the entrance before turning to stare expectantly at him. Only delicate Bella remained, nuzzling at Lucie's hand for a stroke. 'You've definitely made a friend,' he said as she petted the greyhound. 'If you let her, she'll follow you upstairs.'

'Oh, are they allowed upstairs?' Lucie raised her eyes to meet his, surprise arching her brows.

'It's their home too, so they can go where they like, though they choose to stay down here for the most part. And no one, not even the dogs, enters the yellow drawing room without strict invitation from Morgana.'

'I'll bear that in mind,' Lucie bit her lip as though trying to hide a smile against the dire warning he'd put into the words.

'No doubt you'll be summoned for afternoon tea, and a full inspection.' He wasn't quite joking. Having been under Morgana's stern eye more times than he cared to remember, he knew what an intimidating experience it could be—even at his age.

'Should I be worried?' There was no sign of that smile now.

'No, not really. She has a heart of gold, but she'll steamroller you given half a chance, so stand your ground.'

'That sounds faintly terrifying.'

Arthur shook his head. 'I'm sure you'll be fine, and if you can get her talking, she knows a great deal about the history of this place.'

Lucie perked up at that idea and there was a real sense of keenness when she spoke next. 'Has she lived here all her life?'

'Yes. She never married—I think there's a story there, but Iggy knows more about it than I do. Added to that, she ended up taking care of one member of the family or the other—first her father, then my grandmother suffered what today would be called post-natal depression, so Morgana had a big hand in raising my father and my uncle. Finally, she took on the three of us.' It was funny how history had repeated itself. One of the unspoken truths of the family was that Ludworth brides never seemed to stick around for long, whether through tragedy, illness or other more selfish reasons.

Not funny, awful. To the point some idiots in the village, who had nothing better to do than gossip, whispered about a curse on the family.

Not wanting to let his thoughts dwell on such dark things, Arthur shifted the conversation back to their previous topic. 'As for the dogs, well, Pippin shadows Tristan everywhere and Bella and Nimrod have a blanket in my room where they sleep more often than not. If you keep your door shut, they won't bother you.' They'd found their way into his bedroom not long after the family had taken them in and he'd discovered the pair curled up on a tweed blanket they'd stolen from the end of his bed. Once claimed, it had never been returned to his possession, although he did rescue it for a run through the washing machine now and then. From the way Bella was glued to Lucie's side, it looked like Arthur wasn't the only one who'd be sleeping alone that night.

He regretted the thought the moment it entered his head as it was followed immediately by visions of russet hair spilling over the pale-grey cotton of his sheets. No! Arthur wrenched his thoughts back under control before his mental vision could dip lower to the more interesting things the rest of his bedding would cover.

Sleeping on his own wasn't a bad thing, it was a good thing. More space to stretch out and sprawl his long limbs without encountering a feminine ankle that didn't appreciate being kicked as had accidentally happened with one girlfriend. No snoring, other than his own, to disturb him. No scattering of make-up and underwear in his neat, tidy en-suite bathroom. No stealing of his shirts and jumpers, no random knick-knacks that seemed to breed in any private space a woman occupied. There was a lot to be said for protecting one's personal space.

Not that Lucie looked in any danger of laying siege at his bedroom door. Her attention was all fixed on Bella. *Lucky dog.*

A sharp bark of demand from by the door snapped him back to attention. 'Better get this lot out, or there'll be mayhem,' he said. 'Bella, are you coming out, sweetheart?' He offered a coaxing hand to the greyhound who responded by huddling closer to Lucie's side. 'Rejected!' Arthur clutched at his chest as though suffering a mortal blow and staggered back a few paces. 'Looks like it's just us boys,' he said to the waiting furry melee as he waded through them to retrieve his waxed jacket from one of the hooks hanging in the arched alcove of the doorway.

Having shrugged it on and turned the collar up against the impending cold outside, he glanced back to see Lucie was more than halfway up the stairs, Bella at her heels. When she reached the landing, she paused to give him a little wave, which he returned in kind. Still not quite sure what to make of their new arrival, he ushered the dogs out into the chilly evening air his footsteps and his mind already turning towards the woods and the forthcoming bluebell display. There was a hell of a lot to do before they'd be ready to let members of the public start wandering around the estate.

# CHAPTER EIGHT

Lucie woke to the sound of rain rattling against the thick glass of the leaded window set deep into the stone wall of her bedroom. As she surfaced to full consciousness, she became aware of a jabbing pain in her neck, caused no doubt by the unfamiliar pillows. Moving with care, she eased herself up on her elbows until she had room to rotate her head. With a crack like a twig snapping, the stiffness in her neck released and the wash of sweet relief as the pain vanished made her sag back down onto the bed with a sigh. In the dim light peeping through a gap in the curtains, she noticed the fleur-de-lis pattern embroidered into the canopy overhead, a detail she'd missed when lying down the night before. That little sumptuous detail was enough to bring the reality of her circumstances crashing back. She'd really spent the night in a castle!

Eager to explore, Lucie tossed back the sheets, blanket and thick eiderdown enveloping her bed in strange layers so unlike the modern hollow-fibre duvet she was used to. It had taken a bit of adjustment to get them tucked around herself, but their added weight had sent her off to sleep well enough. So well, in fact, she realised as an urgent need overtook her, that she hadn't got up once in the night, which was very unlike her. Scrambling down from the high bed, she almost tripped over Bella, who'd sprawled herself out on the rug beside the bed. With a quick pat of apology, Lucie skipped past the dog and into the bathroom.

Twenty minutes later, she was showered, had secured her hair in a messy bun on the top of her head and dressed in a pair of her most comfortable jeans and a long-sleeved navy-blue T-shirt beneath a three-quarter sleeved cream knitted jumper with a big, slouchy polo-neck over the top. Given the amount of walking she'd likely be doing, she slipped her feet into a pair of lightweight trainers. She'd noted the mix of smart and casual wear the family had worn to dinner and had abandoned her original idea of wearing one of her skirt suits. It just didn't make sense to truss herself up in her usual work outfits if she was going to be traipsing around a building the size of the castle.

By the time she was ready, Bella had taken up position by the closed bedroom door. Hurrying over, Lucie let her out and followed the greyhound as she trotted along the corridors and down the stairs into the hall. A few lazy woofs greeted them from the furry pile before the fireplace, but none of the other dogs did more than raise a head to watch their descent. Bella made a beeline for the enormous front doors, clearly needing to go out. The ease with which she was able to open one of them surprised Lucie the same as it had on her arrival.

She'd barely made a gap before Bella was wriggling through and shooting down the steps and across the driveway in a scattering of wet gravel. The brindle dog was soon a dark smudge in the distance, sending Lucie into a bit of a panic. Should she have just let her out like that? What if she didn't come back? Worried, she glanced around the deep alcove, but there was no sign of any dog leads in amongst the jumble of coats, wellington boots, hats and walking sticks. Recalling that Arthur had taken the other dogs out the previous evening without using a lead on any of them, she crossed her fingers that Bella would find her way back.

A little anxious when there was no sign of the greyhound a few minutes later, Lucie hugged her arms around herself and stepped outside. The alcove of the door stretched as far on the outside as it did on the inside, so she was able to take a couple of paces and still remain under cover. What she saw, even in the gloomy overcast morning light stole her breath.

Low lines of box and yew hedges marched out before her in the geometrical shapes and rows of a formal garden set in the middle of a wide green lawn. Away to the left stood a wild expanse of trees, making it seem like the garden had been reclaimed from the forest and at any moment the woodland might swoop in and take it back. Beneath the lowering clouds, she could just make out the dark grey and brown escarpment of the Derbyshire dales.

Even in these earliest days of spring everything was so lush and green, a million miles away from the car-packed streets she was familiar with. Her father's delusions of grandeur seemed very small in comparison to the generations of power and privilege it took to command a private view such as this, and she wondered once again why he'd bothered. It was one of many questions that would ever go unanswered, though it haunted her still. What had he been hoping to achieve? What deficit had he grown up with that was so great it could have driven him to steal from others to give her and her mother a lifestyle they'd never needed nor desired? A shiver ran through her, though the jumper she'd put on was thick and cosy. She couldn't let him intrude today, not when she needed to make the very best impression with her new employer.

Drawing in deep calming breaths, she let her avid gaze roam free over the landscape. The gate through which she'd entered the previous evening was the only point of entry she could see in the towering curtain wall she recognised from the pictures she'd seen online. The pale grey stone stretched as far as her eyes could see and she wondered if it reached as far as the natural stone hills in the distance. She could find out for herself, but on another day, when the elements were more conducive to exploring. And, she reminded herself, sternly, when she didn't have so much work waiting for her. After yesterday's debacle, it really wouldn't do to turn up late for her meeting with Arthur.

Lucie checked her watch. It was still only 8.15 a.m., so there was no immediate cause for panic. Never one for a big breakfast, she could grab some toast and a cup of tea and still be ready for the half-eight start time she'd set for herself. As long as Bella showed up soon. Straining her eyes, Lucie peered through the rain at a dark shape. Was it moving, or was that just an optical illusion caused by the bad weather? The indistinct blob soon resolved itself into the sleek graceful outlines of a greyhound in full flight.

Heaving a sigh of relief, Lucie stepped back inside, grateful to be out of the morning chill. Moments later, Bella barrelled through the big oak door, almost losing her back legs from under her as she screeched to a stop at Lucie's feet. Tongue lolling, she raised two muddy paws ready to place them on the front of Lucie's clean jeans. Stepping back, Lucie grabbed an old towel she'd noticed earlier in the muddle of items in the alcove and managed to wrap Bella's paws in it before she could do any damage to her clothes.

The poor thing was shivering from head to toe, although she seemed happy enough as Lucie knelt and scrubbed at her short fur until the greyhound was warm and mostly dry. Bella shoved her cold nose into the warm spot of Lucie's neck then scampered across the stone flags to join the rest of her pack before the leaping flames of the fire. 'Gee, thanks,' Lucie muttered as she straightened up and closed the front door once more.

'Good morning!' Turning at the greeting, Lucie watched Igraine bounce down the last couple of steps.

'Oh, hi there!' She waved the soggy towel in her hand. 'I just let Bella out and now I'm not sure what to do with this.'

Smiling, Igraine pointed to a doorway to the right. 'Leave the towel on one of the hooks to dry out, we'll no doubt need it later if this awful rain keeps up. You can wash your hands in there whilst you're at it.' Heading in the direction indicated, Lucie found a small washroom and did just that.

They made their way towards the dining room together, with Igraine chatting about her plans for the day. 'I need to get out and check the fences. We lease out a couple of farms, well, small-holdings, really, and there was a nasty storm last week. I was hoping to ride out, but at this rate I'll have to take the Land Rover instead.' She turned to Lucie as they entered the dining room. 'Do you ride?'

'I had a few lessons, but that was a long time ago.' There'd been a stables associated with the boarding school she'd attended, and although her father had been willing to listen to her pleas for a pony, her mum had insisted Lucie try it out first. She'd been a little upset at the time but was grateful now looking back because it had been barely six months later that he'd been arrested, and it had all gone to pot. Losing her personal possessions had been a terrible enough shock, how much worse to have had to give up something she'd have formed an emotional attachment to, like a pony.

'Well, let me know if you want to go out sometime,' Igraine said as she headed for the sideboard to make a cup of coffee. 'We've got a couple of sturdy hacks, I'm sure one of them would suit you.' She offered the large thermos to Lucie. 'Do you want a drink?'

'I'll have a cup of tea, please, but I can make it myself.' It felt a little awkward having a member of the family wait on her, but then Arthur had done the same the previous evening so perhaps they were just well-mannered, and Lucie was being a dolt by reading more into every situation than there was to see.

'It's no trouble. You can pour us some juice if you like?'

Within a few minutes they were at the table in the same seats they'd occupied the previous evening. Though they'd only spoken a little, Lucie had found the other woman to be genuinely warm and friendly, and she felt like given a bit of time there was the potential for a friendship there. It felt like so long since she'd had a proper friend, though there was nobody to blame for that other than Lucie herself.

There'd been plenty of invitations out with co-workers at the auction house, but central London prices were always through the roof and she never fancied the long trek back to the end of the tube line late in the evening. All pathetic excuses, really, but ones she'd used as a shield against letting anyone get too close. Perhaps it was time to let a few of those barriers down. After all, her time here at the castle was finite, and, once the spring was over, she'd be on the train back home again. Getting to know Igraine, and the rest of the family, didn't seem like it would be a hardship. They'd all been very pleasant to her, even after the utter fool she'd made of herself to Tristan and Arthur. She raised a hand to her cheek as embarrassment struck once more.

'What's up?' Sharp-eyed Igraine hadn't missed her blush.

Lucie pulled a face, then confessed to a wide-eyed—and then hysterically laughing—Igraine. 'Oh, it was awful,' Lucie said, burying her face in her hands as she tried to stifle her own laugh.

'I wish I'd been a fly on the wall! Poor Arthur, he's never very good when it comes to confrontation. I bet Tristan loved it, though!'

Arthur did well enough when it came to confrontation, but Lucie kept that thought to herself as she recalled the annoyance flashing in his eyes, the way he'd drawn himself up to his full height and towered over her. Other than those few moments of ire, he'd been much more softly spoken, even a little defensive, so perhaps his sister was right. As someone with a first-class honours degree in defensiveness, Lucie knew the signs.

Perhaps that was why they rubbed each other up the wrong way a bit? Only time would tell. Lucie had suggested a fresh start that morning, so she would have to play her part and not be quick to jump to conclusions. Easier said than done, but she could treat it as part of her experiment. No one at the castle knew anything about her, other than what she chose to tell them. She didn't have to be worried about them judging her for what had happened in the past: not the terrible mess with her dad, or the awful misunderstanding at Witherby's. She could be anyone she wanted to be—within reason of course. What would it be like to be as self-assured as Igraine appeared to be? How refreshing to not be in a blind panic all the time, not to feel the weight of opinion pressing down her. As long as she was diligent in the job they were paying her to do, that was all that mattered.

She didn't have to be poor Lucinda, the conman's daughter, or shy Lucie who didn't fit in with the other people at school. Dutiful Lucie, trying to protect her mum and not rock their already waterlogged boat, or her latest, and worst, re-creation— timid, pathetic Miss Kennington desperate to do a good job and impress everybody at work. She could be…Lucie stared down into her rapidly cooling tea, stunned to realise that she had no idea who or what she really was. It was like she'd spent her life stuffed into pigeonholes of other people's design.

Maybe she shouldn't be looking to play another role whilst she was here at the castle, maybe she should use the time to try and figure out who she really was, and more importantly, who she *wanted* to be.

Feeling almost giddy, she helped herself to a couple of slices of brown toast from the silver rack in the centre of the table. Her hand was halfway towards the low-fat spread when she hesitated. When was the last time she'd allowed herself the luxury of butter? With a little grin, she tugged the golden rectangle sitting in a silver tray that matched the toast rack closer. Perhaps it should've bothered her, the overt displays of wealth everywhere, but it didn't. The Ludworths weren't showing off, this was normal to them. It wasn't flash to have silver on the dining room table, it was just… their stuff. And it was one thing to be rich in possessions, but quite another to be financially secure. Hadn't Arthur intimated as much?

The reality of her situation dawned. If she did find something valuable, some rare and refined treasure, it wouldn't be going on display somewhere in this magnificent building, it'd be heading straight for the auction block and no doubt into the private vault of some millionaire. It was quite depressing. Maybe being surrounded by such fabulous things all the time took some of their power to impress away, maybe that was why he'd sounded so blasé about the prospect of selling the family's treasures. Lucie couldn't imagine feeling the same way, but not everyone had the same appreciation for art as she did. *Their loss.*

Turning her attention back to her breakfast, she took a bite of toast. As the rich butter melted across her tongue, she allowed her lashes to flutter closed. 'Wow, I think I'm having an out of body experience.'

Igraine laughed. 'Betsy makes it herself, it's rather magnificent, isn't it?'

'Betsy?' The two ladies who'd served them at dinner had been introduced to her, but she didn't remember either of them being a Betsy.

'She's our cook.'

Cook, housekeeper, butler, ladies to serve dinner…goodness, how many more members of staff did they have in this place? There must've been some of her shock on her face because Igraine rolled her eyes. 'God, we must seem horribly spoilt to you.'

Given where and how they lived, she was finding them all surprisingly down to earth. 'No, not at all. You can't run a place like this yourself. It's just taking a bit of getting used to.' She took a deep breath. Wasn't she in danger of shoving Igraine and her brothers in the kind of pigeonhole she hated? Any insecurities she was suffering from in comparing her home and background were her problem, not theirs. Reaching over, she placed a hand on Igraine's arm. 'Please, don't feel like I'm judging you. I think this place is incredible. It must've been an amazing experience growing up here.'

Igraine smiled, the tension around her eyes softening. 'We're world class hide-and-seek champions, that's for sure.'

They were laughing over that when Arthur walked in. 'Morning, Lucie, morning, Iggy.'

Lord, if he looked appealing in the shadowy light of evening, he was devastating in the daylight. Curling the hand she held in her lap into a ball, Lucie dug her nails into her skin and willed herself to stop staring at him. 'Morning.' She managed a quick smile, then dragged her eyes away.

Apparently oblivious to Lucie's discomfort, Igraine waved her half-eaten piece of toast towards her brother in greeting. 'Hey, did you sleep well?'

'Not bad, thanks.' He moved to the sideboard to make himself a coffee. The thick muscles packed across his shoulders rolled beneath the cotton of his rugby shirt as he went through the motions of making the drink. Unable to stop herself, Lucie followed the line of his spine to where his waist tapered in slightly, then further down to the impressive thighs cased in faded denim. Everything about him was solid, physical. *Vital.* She recalled walking beside him the previous evening, the way he'd curled his big frame slightly as though trying not to over-power her, or as if his natural instinct was to protect her. What would it feel like to curl up against all the warm strength? To rest her head upon his shoulder and let him shield her from the outside world for just a few moments? Like being behind the thick walls of this castle, she supposed. Secure; sheltered.

*Dangerous ground, Lucie, you're treading upon such dangerous ground.* Clearly being in the fantasy environment of the castle was doing funny things to her head. She needed to put an end to these ridiculous daydreams once and for all. Arthur wasn't a hero. He was just a man. A very handsome man who lived in a freaking, bloody castle, but a man just the same. And for all the fabulous things surrounding him, he was still obsessed with money, just like her father had been. Yes, they had very different reasons for it, but he could only see beautiful things in terms of what they were worth to him. He'd never walk the halls of this place and be able to see it the way she did—not like Piers would. Yes. Piers. She needed to think about him, concentrate on a man who understood her, who appreciated the aesthetic over the monetary value of art. Coffee in hand, Arthur strolled towards the window to cast a frown outside. 'This rain is never going to end, is it?' He sighed, then raised the mug to his lips and Lucie found herself watching the way they pursed around the edge.

*Think of Piers!* The admonishment fell on deaf ears. She'd never found his mouth fascinating, not even when it'd been pressed against her own. It was all she could do to sit still and not thunk her head against the rich mahogany of the table.

'That's March in Derbyshire, for you,' Igraine answered, briskly. 'I'm taking the Land Rover over to Tumbledown Farm, check those fences.'

Arthur nodded but didn't say anything, his back still to them. Lucie snuck a quick glance at her watch. It was almost eight-thirty, her self-imposed start time. Arthur had said something about holding their initial meeting in the library, so she could make her way there and begin reviewing the documents until he was ready. It would give her time to get her head straight her and shake off this ridiculous infatuation.

If only she had the first clue which of the maze of rooms on the ground floor was the library. She could excuse herself and go exploring, she supposed, but wouldn't he find it weird if she upped and left? As she wrestled on the horns of her dilemma, the discreet door tucked in the far wall swung open and one of the women who'd served them at dinner appeared with a fresh rack of toast.

'Lord, you half scared the life out of me!' she exclaimed, clutching at her chest with her free hand. 'I didn't know anyone was down yet. Nobody rang.' The last was said with a faint air of accusation.

'Apologies, Vera, I've only just come down and hadn't quite decided what I wanted for breakfast.' Arthur turned to face inwards as he spoke but made no move to approach the table.

Vera placed the fresh toast on the table, swapping it for the couple of cold slices left in the other rack then straightened up. 'No rush, sir. You take your time and give us a tinkle when you're ready.' Her kind blue eyes scanned over Lucie. 'And what about you, Miss?'

Still not entirely comfortable with the idea of someone fetching and carrying for her, Lucie shook her head. 'I'm happy with some toast, thank you.'

Vera didn't seem convinced. 'That won't keep the wolf from the door. You sure I can't get you a poached egg, maybe a slice or two of bacon? It's proper local stuff, prepared and cured by the village butcher. Not like that supermarket rubbish, all preservatives and added water.' She shuddered in horror.

Though tempted, Lucie wasn't sure her stomach was up to it. In addition to her dilemma over Arthur, nerves over the task she faced ahead had been building since she'd opened her eyes. She cast a quick glance at her watch again, then up to see Vera was still waiting for a reply. 'Another morning, when I have a bit more time…'

'Speaking of which,' Igraine said, pushing her chair back, 'I need to get on the move. Vera, can you ask Betsy to rustle me up a packed lunch? I'll be out and about for most of the day. Tell her I'll come and collect it in a few minutes as I want to talk to her about the menu for Aunt Morgana's birthday next month.'

'Crikey, I'd forgotten all about that.' Arthur finally stirred himself from the window. 'I'll have some scrambled eggs, Vera.'

'Right you are, sir.' With a nod, Vera left the room.

Strolling towards the table, Arthur assumed the seat at its head. Now was the time to excuse herself, to let him know she was going for a look around and that he could find her once he'd finished his breakfast. She hesitated a moment too long for it to feel natural and ended up blurting his name. 'Arthur!'

Pausing in the act of shaking out a napkin to lay across his lap, Arthur glanced up. 'Yes?'

Lucie cringed inwardly. If she didn't get a grip, he'd know something was up. And if he found out she'd been mooning over him…God, it didn't bear thinking about! He was still looking at her, that imperfect brow quirked in a quizzical arch, and she realised she'd been silent for too long. 'Oh. I, err, I just wanted to say how much I was looking forward to getting started this morning.'

Arthur glanced at the napkin still in his hand. 'Right. Did you want to start now? Sorry, if I'd known you were champing at the bit, I wouldn't have ordered anything.' He placed the crumpled linen beside his plate and looked ready to rise from his chair.

'No!' Lucie all but shouted, then bit her lip. 'What I meant was there's no rush. I'm keen to get started, of course I am, but not to the point where I'm expecting you to skip your breakfast. Take your time, really, it's fine.' *It's fine.* God, they were going to chisel those bloody words upon her headstone.

Bemused, Arthur smoothed the napkin across his lap. 'As long as you're sure.'

'Of course, you're the boss, after all!' Lucie's laugh sounded so horribly forced to her own ears that a little bit of her curled up inside and died to hear it. Grabbing for her cup, she took a large mouthful of tea, then had to choke it down as she realised it had gone cold. With a grimace, she stood up. 'I'll make a fresh one,' she muttered before scurrying to the relative safety of the sideboard.

To her relief, Arthur and Igraine chatted for a few moments about the arrangements for their aunt's birthday celebration. Either they hadn't noticed her off behaviour, or they were both too polite to mention it. Reaching for a fresh cup, Lucie decided against any more caffeine and rummaged instead in the bowl for one of the camomile teabags she'd spotted the previous evening. Something to soothe her nerves would be just the ticket. So much for all her grand plans for a fresh start. 'You can be anyone you want to be, Lucie Kennington,' she mocked herself silently. Unless Arthur was in the room it seemed, and then all she was capable of being was an absolute ninny.

A light hand touched her shoulder, making her jump and sending the teaspoon skittering across the sideboard. 'I'll catch up with you at dinner,' Igraine said. 'You can tell me how you get on with everything, and maybe we can fix up a day for that ride we talked about.'

Lucie nodded, pleased that Igraine seemed as keen to be friends as she was. 'That would be nice. Have a good day, and I hope the rain lets up soon.'

Igraine grinned, her cheek dimpling in the exact same spot her brother's did. 'Me too.' And with a flick of the thick plait hanging over her shoulder, she was gone. With no other choice, Lucie resumed her seat at the dining table, resolving to keep her mouth shut and leave Arthur in peace to enjoy his breakfast. Once they were in the library and she could get on with what she was supposed to be doing, things would be easier.

Arthur it seemed, had other ideas.

# CHAPTER NINE

Arthur watched Lucie closely as she resumed her place at the table. She seemed different this morning, a little bit skittish like she had been when she'd first arrived. She'd been much more relaxed before bed last night, and he'd been relieved at her suggestion for a fresh start, had resolved on his walk around the castle that he would lay all his cards on the table that morning and ensure she was fully apprised of the position the family was facing. He felt sure that once she understood the urgency and importance of what he hoped to achieve through appointing her, she would be more receptive to helping to curate the Arthurian collection alongside everything else. Arthur sighed. At least she and Iggy had been getting on well. 'I heard my sister mention something about the two of you going out. Do you get much opportunity to ride in London?'

Lucie jerked, spilling a drop of tea on the back of her hand. Arthur grabbed his napkin, ready to blot it, but she'd already dropped her cup back into the saucer and hidden her hand beneath the table. Really, what was the matter with her this morning? 'I…I don't want you to think I'm taking advantage of the situation here. Going for a ride was Igraine's idea, not mine. I know I'm here to work.'

Ah, so that was it. 'It wasn't a trick question,' he said, keeping his voice soft. 'Part of your job will be to get to know not just the castle, but the entire estate. I think the more you understand about the family, and our position here, the better it will be. Going out with Iggy will really help you with that.' Arthur steepled his fingers beneath his chin as he considered his next words. 'I know you said earlier that I'm the boss, but that's not how I see things. Yes, I'll want a regular update on your progress, and I'll always be available if there's something you want to consult me about, but from my point of view, you're the expert here and I want to give you as much autonomy as possible.'

She was quiet for a long moment. When she finally met his gaze, there was a sense of resolve in her eyes. 'I appreciate that, thank you. Once I understand the scope fully, I should be able to put together a bit of a timetable. I think that will be useful for both of us.'

'Sounds good to me.' The door creaked behind him, signalling Vera's return. In addition to the scrambled eggs he'd requested, Betsy had added a couple of rashers of lean, crispy bacon. 'Thanks, Vera. I think that'll be everything for now.' He glanced at Lucie, who nodded her agreement.

'I'll be back in a bit to clear up, then.' The ever-cheerful Vera bustled back out, the swing door swooshing a couple of times in her wake.

Arthur cut a mouthful of food. 'Anyway, we were talking about riding. I suppose it must be more difficult to arrange in town?'

'I wouldn't know.'

Arthur paused mid-chew to look at her, noting the telltale red spots on her cheek that he was recognising as a sign of discomfiture.

Lucie sipped her tea before continuing. 'As I was telling Igraine, I used to ride a bit at school, but I haven't been on a horse for many years. She promised me you have a couple of docile mounts.'

Riding at school? Arthur mulled that interesting titbit. The private school he and Tristan had attended had offered a huge range of extra-curricular activities, but even it hadn't had a stables. She must've gone somewhere pretty decent for that kind of set-up. Intrigued at the chance to learn a bit more about her background, he couldn't help but ask, 'Which school did you go to?'

'Wessingdean.'

'Nice.' Arthur gave a low whistle of appreciation when she mentioned one of the most prestigious girls' schools in the country. 'I was best man at a friend's wedding in the summer. His dad and mine were best friends at school so Joss and I have known each other all our lives. He married a Wessingdean girl, Henrietta Warner-Mills. Perhaps you know her?' He laughed at himself almost immediately. 'Sorry, that's like meeting an American and them assuming we Brits all know each other.'

'I don't recall the name. I only went there for a couple of years and then my father underwent a career change and I moved schools as a result.' Lucie's responding smile was somewhat thin-lipped, and he cursed himself for prying.

He didn't know exactly how old she was; it wasn't something one asked, and information like that had been expunged from CVs years ago. He'd guessed her to be somewhere around the same age as him, and Wessingdean wasn't a huge school, but if she'd only been there a couple of years… Not sure quite how but feeling like he'd committed some kind of faux pas, Arthur moved back onto safer ground. 'Well, I'm sure we can find you something suitable if you do decide to go out riding. How tall are you, five-four?'

'Five-three, and that's only if I stand up really straight,' she said with a genuine grin which made him feel better.

'Tristan swears he's taller than me, claims to be six foot one. I told him, yeah, but only if the one is a centimetre rather than an inch.' He forked up another mouthful of food and contemplated which member of their small stables would be best suited to her. 'Lancelot's the real expert, so you might want to consult with him, but I think Lightning would probably suit you best.'

He winked when she looked askance at him. 'It's an ironic name, I promise.' He finished the last couple of bites of his breakfast, wiped his mouth then drained his coffee. 'Right, shall we get started?'

*

The library was in the west wing of the castle and he knew Mrs W had planned a full tour with Lucie later. Still, he couldn't resist showing off one of his favourite spots, so he took her via the orangery which ran along two-thirds of the rear of the castle. Modern in comparison to most parts of the castle, the enormous conservatory had been added towards the end of the nineteenth century. An elaborate under-floor system of heated pipes kept the space warm even on cold, blustery days like today. He'd considered closing it as one of many options he, Maxwell and Mrs W had reviewed when trying to save on household running costs, but it provided the family with a source of fresh fruit throughout the year, and there were a number of rare tropical species in amongst the dense greenery. It would also have broken Iggy's heart, and he'd cut out his own before he did that.

As he watched Lucie explore the room, touching a finger to the shiny leaves of a rubber plant here, bending to inhale the scent of an orchid there, Arthur admonished himself. There was always an excuse when it came to making the hard decisions. Crossing his fingers and praying for a miracle wasn't going to cut it. His father had tried that and look at where it had got them all.

Once he got Lucie settled, it was time to sit down and review everything again. Making more savings was imperative. Yes, he was hopeful for some of the plans he was coming up with for the future, but even if they managed to pull some of them off, there would be no immediate income forthcoming, and—like the fee he was paying Lucie to investigate their artworks and other valuables—they would all require a financial outlay up front.

'It's so amazing in here, I had no idea there'd be something like this hiding away.'

Arthur let Lucie's obvious pleasure push away his darkening mood. 'It's one of my favourite places in the castle. This, and the secret room at the top of the tower.'

'Secret room?' Lucie's eyes were round as saucers.

'Well, that's what we called it, anyway. It's got a huge lock and these enormous bolts that slide deep into the stone floor. The key was lost for years, so nobody knew what was inside. Iggy became obsessed with idea that one of our ancestors had used it to lock up a mad wife, or something.'

'Like *Jane Eyre*.' Lucie sighed. 'One of my favourite books. Can we see it?'

Arthur shook his head. 'Not today. The tower isn't accessible from the main part of the castle, so we'd have to go outside to get to the entrance. There's rumours of a secret passageway that can be used to enter the tower from inside the castle, but I can promise you we've turned the place upside down trying to find it.' He and Tristan had even gone so far as to clamber up inside one of the huge fireplace chimneys looking for it, getting filthy into the bargain.

'Another day then.' Lucie sounded a bit regretful before straightening her shoulders. 'You'll have to fit me with a set of blinkers to stop me getting distracted by all the wonderful sights the castle has to offer.'

'If that's the case, perhaps we should rethink your work area.' With a smile, Arthur ushered her along the rest of the orangery and through the double doors which led to the library. As he listened to Lucie's gasp of delight, Arthur revised his list of favourite places in the castle. With its double-height lit by an enormous teardrop chandelier and the two side walls covered in shelves from floor to ceiling, it was a beautiful space. Thick

Turkish rugs littered the polished wooden floor and a huge mezzanine balcony space spanned over the oak door opposite them.

'Oh, *Arthur.*' The way she said it, sent his blood rushing. Had a woman spoken his name with such passion before? Glancing sideways, he gave a rueful shake of his head. Lucie's transfixed gaze was all for the leather-bound tomes lining the walls. *Probably just as well.*

Not the slightest bit consoled by that thought, Arthur pointed to the spiral staircase which led to the balcony area. 'We've set you up on the mezzanine. The family archives, papers and other records are filed up there, and it's also a bit out of the way so you're less likely to be disturbed.'

Nodding in a distracted manner that said she was only half-listening to him, Lucie crossed the room to run a hand down the side of one of the rolling ladders hanging from the left-hand bookcase. 'I've never seen one of these outside of a film.' There was a sense of wonder in her voice that had him viewing the space as though a newcomer to it. Leaving Lucie to examine the bookcases he made his way to the freestanding globe suspended from a cherrywood frame. With wondering hands, he spun the faded ball as he once had done as a boy marvelling at all the countries and continents. His fingers paused over the dent in the middle of Africa caused by an ill-thought game of indoor cricket he and Tristan had played one rainy afternoon. Familiarity might not have bred contempt as such, but they had certainly taken the wonderful things around them for granted. To them the library had been an ideal space to play in with its easily rolled-back rugs and wide expanse of empty floor between the two walls of shelves. He covered his face with his hands. God, they were lucky the ball had never gone through one of the windows in the patio doors and damaged the orangery in the process!

'Are you all right?' Lucie touched his shoulder.

'What? Oh, yes, I'm fine, just recalling what a pair of idiots

Tristan and I were.' He turned the globe to show her the dent. 'Indoor cricket.'

'In here?' Her sense of horror was palpable. Best not confess to the football match they'd played in the village church which had resulted in the loss of a marble angel's wing. Though it had been a mis-kick from Iggy that had knocked the statue from its plinth, they'd each accepted the punishment meted out. Every piece of brass, every pane in the stained-glass windows had shone for months after their father had seconded them to the team of volunteers who cleaned the church for the rest of the school holidays.

Arthur found himself grinning at the memory. 'We were absolute heathens, tearing around the place without a thought to the value of anything.' The ladies had attempted to co-opt Iggy into their flower arranging group, much to his sister's horror. To distract them, Tristan had volunteered in her stead, and, to everyone's surprise had developed a real knack for it. He still lent a hand for big events like Easter and Christmas, and it was his stylish touch that lifted many of the living spaces in the castle.

'I suppose growing up with this around you lessens the impact of it somewhat,' Lucie said, her tone thoughtful. 'Although I can't imagine ever walking into this room and not feeling a little over-whelmed.'

'But you must be used to being surrounded by beautiful things, and a lot rarer than most of what we've got here,' Arthur replied, thinking about her experience working at one of the foremost auction houses in the country.

'At Witherby's, you mean?' She seemed to hesitate, the way a person did when they were going to say one thing before changing their mind and saying something else, and it made him wonder for the first time why she wasn't working there anymore. She seemed a bit young to be taking a sabbatical.

She started speaking again, and he let the thought slip away.

'Yes, I was, but we worked in such a controlled environment it was sometimes like being in a laboratory. The auction house itself is a fabulous structure, but not on the same scale as this.' She waved her arm towards the shelves.

'I'm sure you'll get used to it soon enough.' Arthur led her over to a roll-top desk near the globe. 'There's a catalogue system of sorts.' He pushed up the front of the desk to show her two long thin boxes filled with handwritten cards. 'Though I'm not sure it follows any conventional library system, it works once you get the hang of it.'

'Is it alphabetical?'

'Sort of. Things have been grouped into categories and then alphabetised from there.' He pulled up a faded divider; once blue, it had bleached over the years to a dull grey, though there were traces of the original colouring towards the bottom end of the card. 'Blue is flora and fauna.' Leading the way across to a section of the shelving, he showed her the corresponding strip glued to the shelf marking where the section started. It was a somewhat eclectic mix of everything from gardening books and seed catalogues to a copy of Darwin's *On the Origin of Species*.

'Interesting system.' Lucie said with more than a touch of wryness.

Arthur shrugged. 'My great-grandfather started it and we've just followed along.'

Lucie's gaze travelled upwards to the mezzanine gallery. 'And what about up there in the family archive?'

'Perhaps you'd better take a look for yourself.' He headed for the spiral staircase and climbed upwards. Having reached the top, he turned to offer Lucie his hand as she appeared below him. 'It's a bit disconcerting when you first come up here,' he warned as he pointed to the low wooden railing which lined the central edge of the mezzanine. It came to about hip-height on him. 'I'm pretty sure it would fail all modern health and safety rules, but it's not something I can afford to replace right now.'

106

She eyed the railing. 'I'm a bit shorter than you, so it's not quite so bad, but I see what you mean. I'll be sure to keep a safe distance.'

Arthur nodded. 'I've set you up over here,' He led her to a corner desk that was securely walled in by three sides of shelves. 'But if you'd rather work down below, I can help you move whatever files and records you might need.'

Lucie slid into the chair then placed her hands on the green leather blotter in the centre of the desk. 'Oh, no, this is lovely.' Her eyes traced the shelves around her which were filled with a jumble of old ledgers, leather and cloth bound books and even some rolled up documents and maps of the castle, before she turned her attention to the items he'd laid out on the desk.

'If you need a laptop, I can lend you mine.' There was an ancient desktop computer in his study that his father had used, but Arthur preferred his more portable device.

'I have my own. I left it in my room, I suppose I should've brought it down with me.'

'You'll want to get your bearings first, no doubt.' He slid a stack of hardbacked record books towards her. 'This is the last attempt at an archive from what I've been able to find. It seems to have been started in the 1930s.' He pointed to a pile of ledgers next. 'These are some of the old purchase ledgers for the castle. My father implemented an electronic record when he took over, but there's not much of interest on the database and the old stuff has never been transferred. As you can see, they've all got red covers so at least they're easy to pick out from the shelves.'

'Okay, well that's something to be grateful for, at least.' Her attention returned once more to the shelves. 'And what's the filing system used up here?'

'Haphazard, I'm afraid. Once Maxwell and I started looking for things we thought might be of use to you, we realised it's a bit random. Things are generally grouped in the same era, but beyond that...' He cast her a helpless look. 'In the end we decided

107

to leave it up to whoever we appointed to organise things as they wanted, and that'll be you.'

'That'll be me.' Lucie heaved a huge sigh, but there was at least a smile on her face.

'Sorry.'

She laughed. 'No need to be, it's actually quite exciting. I can't wait to get stuck in.'

Tucking his hands in his pockets, Arthur backed a few steps away from the desk. 'Well, I'll leave you to it, then, unless there's anything you need that you can think of, off the top of your head?'

'I've got more than enough here to keep me occupied.' She checked the cheap plastic watch on her wrist. 'Perhaps I should try and find Mrs W first, before I bury myself in a mountain of files and ledgers.'

He'd forgotten about the tour his housekeeper had arranged with Lucie. 'She's probably in the kitchen. I can show you the way, or send her to meet you here?'

'I'll come with you, if that's all right? Otherwise I'll be too tempted to start digging through these records.' With a smile, Lucie shut the ledger she'd already opened before her and stood.

The route he took back to the kitchens was a bit more convoluted, thanks to the very necessary installation of what was then a modern plumbing system early in the twentieth century. The works had required extensive internal alterations whilst preserving the integrity of the most important rooms within the castle. As a result, a number of the old passageways had been utilised to run the pipework so getting from A to B was no longer always straightforward.

When they entered the great hall, Lucie was looking thoroughly confused as she turned in a slow circle. 'I have absolutely no idea how we ended up here. I always thought I had a good sense of direction, but obviously not as I could've sworn we were heading towards the other end of the castle.'

'We'll have to get you a ball of string, so you can use it to trace your way back,' he joked, referring to the legend of Theseus and the labyrinth.

'As long as there aren't any monsters lurking, I'll be all right.'

Pleased she'd recognised and entered into the joke with him, Arthur smiled back at her over his shoulder. 'We haven't finished the spring cleaning yet, so there might be a surprise or two lurking in a dusty corner.'

'*We?*' From the sceptical expression on her face, it was clear she thought him incapable of wielding so much as a feather duster.

'We,' he repeated, voice firm. 'Keeping this place up and running is a team effort and I'm very much a part of that team.' Okay, that might have come out a little bit too defensive, but he hated the assumption he sat around on his arse all day with a team of lackeys ready to do his bidding.

Lucie held up her hands. 'I surrender!' she said with a grin. 'I was just struggling a bit with a mental image of you in an apron and a pair of rubber gloves.' Her expression sobered. 'No offence, Arthur, honestly. It's easy to see how much the castle and your heritage means to you from the way your face lights up every time you talk about it. I just hope I can play my part in helping you keep it.'

He hoped so too.

# CHAPTER TEN

The next week flew past. In order to try and get to grips with the magnitude of the task facing her, Lucie had decided to split her days up into three parts. Her mornings were spent verifying the information in the original archive ledgers and updating and transferring the records for each room onto a spreadsheet. With the help of her smartphone, and thanks to the castle's internet service getting back up and running, she created a corresponding image album. Though it was hard to do, she forced herself to mark up anything that caught her eye for a later, more in-depth study.

If she let herself get side-tracked, she'd never get the basics finished and she was keen to demonstrate tangible proof to Arthur that hiring her would be worth his while. He'd given her access to the family's online cloud account so her work could be automatically backed-up and available, and she'd noticed a couple of times that the timestamps on some of the files were different. She hoped that was just him showing an interest rather than him checking up on what she was doing.

Her afternoons were dedicated to sorting out the jumble of records in the family archive. They really were a mishmash of everything and after a couple of hours getting nowhere fast on her second afternoon, she'd taken the bold step of stripping everything off the shelves and starting from scratch. The floor of the mezzanine looked like a disaster zone, but she was slowly making order from the chaos.

As Arthur had already started to do, she'd pulled out all the purchase ledgers and filed them in date order. There were still some gaps, but an enterprising steward had taken to numbering the ledgers in the late eighteen century, and his successors had continued the practice. She had a list of missing records and had left spaces on the shelf in the hope she would come across them as she continued to sort through the mass of papers.

Maps and sketches of the castle had been stacked together in one corner. It would be an interesting intellectual exercise to trace the building and alteration from start to present day, but it wasn't a priority for Lucie, nor strictly within her remit. Once she'd got to grips with everything else, she might suggest it to Arthur as an extension of her work, depending on how well the rest of it went.

To her delight, quite a few members of the Ludworth family had been avid diarists and she had several stacks of books filled with their personal observations to trawl through. She was restricting herself to browsing them only in the evenings, and though the often spidery handwriting took some effort to decipher, she'd been up until the early hours paging through the diary of one Isabella Ludworth who, from what Lucie could work out, was Arthur's three-times great grandmother.

The one thing she hadn't found and desperately needed was a proper family tree. She'd come across an old family bible with the start of one, but it only covered four generations and hadn't been kept up to date. It was one of many items on her list of things to ask Arthur when she found time. They'd hardly seen each other, apart from meal times, and she invariably had her nose buried in a book or was busy flicking through her tablet to review her progress of the day. She still didn't feel entirely comfortable joining the family to eat, especially in the evenings, so tried

111

to keep herself to herself and not pay too much attention to their discussions. For their part, the Ludworths took her presence as entirely natural, and it was only her own reluctance that kept her on the periphery of the conversation. That, and fear over making a goose of herself in front of Arthur. She'd managed to get a hold on her attraction to him for the most part, but every now and then he would do something like throw back his head and let loose a glorious bellow of laughter, or catch her eye as though to share some private secret with her, and she was lost once more in a flight of inappropriate daydreams.

As she poked her head around the dining room door, she was relieved to find the long table empty of occupants. Stacking her tablet, notebook and phone next to what had become 'her' seat, she helped herself to a cup of tea and a bowl of muesli from the sideboard. With only half an eye on her bowl, she spooned the delicious homemade mix of oats, dried fruit and almonds into her mouth as she flicked through the photos she'd taken the previous day.

The blue room, as Mrs W had referred to it on her tour, had been pretty enough, but nothing in there had sparked Lucie's interest. The furnishings were of quality—if a touch worn on closer inspection—but nothing had screamed 'look at me'. It had been the same story in the other rooms she'd documented so far, and although it had only been a week, a nervous ball of tension was already starting to grow in her stomach that she wouldn't find anything exciting.

'Stop running before you can walk, Luce,' she muttered as she shoved the tablet to one side and reached for her tea.

'Did you say something?' The familiar drawl from the breakfast buffet made her jump, and she only just managed to steady her tea before it spilled into the remains of her cereal.

'You startled me,' she said as Arthur approached the table clutching his usual black coffee. *Well, duh, Lucie. Talk about stating the bloody obvious.*

'Sorry.' He didn't look the slightest bit repentant. In his usual checked shirt rolled to the elbows to reveal tanned forearms and a pair of black cords several washes past threadbare, he shouldn't have looked quite so devastating to her as he did. Try as she might to ignore it, she still got a funny little flutter every time he was in the vicinity. And it wasn't just his good looks, as she'd discovered to her chagrin that Tristan had nothing like the same effect upon her—only Arthur.

It was another reason she tried not to get involved in dinnertime discussions. He made her so tongue-tied, she worried her ridiculous little crush on him would be obvious to everyone. This morning, a lock of dark hair had broken loose from his neat, practical cut to hang over his right eye. It gave him an air of vulnerability, a tiny crack in his aura of control. He brushed it back with an impatient gesture revealing a dark stain along the underside of his arm.

'You've got something on…'Lucie trailed off with a gesture, embarrassed to give away the fact she'd been studying him.

Appearing oblivious to her mooning over him, Arthur twisted his arm to glare at the offending mark. 'Damn, I thought I'd cleaned it all off. I had a disagreement with a printer cartridge this morning.' He licked his thumb then rubbed at the spot. Not something she'd ever have listed as one of the top ten sexy things a man could do before that moment, but apparently just the sight of his tongue was enough to send a shiver running through her.

*Lord, stop it, you dozy moo!* Lucie admonished herself and forced her eyes down towards the congealing remains of her breakfast. The last of the milk had been absorbed into the muesli, turning it to a cloggy mush.

She'd just shoved a spoonful into her mouth when Arthur abandoned his attempts to clean the ink from his arm and spoke to her. 'What are your plans for the morning?'

The oaty mixture swelled almost to choking point, and it felt like the more she chewed, the more it expanded until she wasn't sure she'd ever be able to swallow it. Throughout her interminable battle with the offending mouthful, she could feel his eyes upon her, could sense his growing amusement as struggled to rid herself of it.

Why wouldn't it go down? She'd had twenty-seven years to learn how to eat, and managed most of those without humiliating herself like this. Her eyes began to water, and she feared if it carried on much longer, she'd have to resort to spitting the whole claggy lump into her napkin. It was that or choke to death on it. Given she'd likely expire from shame if she had to cough it up in front of Arthur, it appeared she'd reached the point of her demise either way.

Finally—*finally!*—when she was almost at the point of imagining the inscription on her tombstone, a tiny chunk of the cereal worked its way down her resisting throat and hope bloomed that she might make it alive from the table, yet. Grabbing at her tea, she forced a tiny sip between her lips and the additional moisture was enough to aid the rest of the muesli in the right direction. Only once she was sure it had all gone did she risk another drink to ease her poor abused throat.

Unwilling to meet the eyes she could feel burning into her from the end of the table, she kept her gaze resolutely down. Her nemesis stared back up at her, and a heated blush scalded her cheeks. There was no rescuing the situation, she'd made an absolute fool of herself and she couldn't bear to look at Arthur and read amusement, or worse, sympathy at her plight. Time to make a break for it.

'Well, lots to do!' she said in a shouty-hearty tone she'd never before used in her life. God, she sounded like her old P.E. teacher who'd believed yelling encouragement would make the horror of a freezing, muddy cross country run somehow fun for her miserable pupils. *Just get out!* Grabbing up her things, Lucie fled the room without a backward glance.

Running like the devil himself was after her, Lucie dashed

along the corridor from the dining room and straight across the great hall, disturbing the dogs who were lounging in front of the fire place as usual. Thinking it was a great game of some sort, they joined Lucie in her headlong flight, barking excitedly as she turned first left, then right before they entered the long gallery.

With a fleeting glance of apology to the rows of stern-faced portraits peering down their aquiline noses at her from the damasked walls, Lucie kept running until she reached her destination for that morning—the west drawing room. Paws scrabbled at the backs of her jean-clad legs and more than one chilly nose poked her hand seeking a treat as she balanced her tablet, book and phone in one hand and reached for the brass handle of the door with the other.

Before she opened the door, she turned to glower at the rambunctious pack milling around her. 'All right, all right, you lot, calm down!' She might not be able to say much to Arthur without blushing fit to burst into flames, but she'd learnt to talk to the dogs in a tone that brooked no nonsense, thanks to Mrs. W.

'They're as soppy as anything,' the housekeeper had told her. 'Just show them who's the boss and they'll give you no trouble at all.' Surveying the wagging, panting bunch now sprawled at her feet, Lucie had to admit the housekeeper had been right.

Inching open the door, she placed her work things on a table conveniently positioned just inside then settled on her haunches to pet the dogs. Apart from one Jack Russell who bullied his way to the front and shoved his head under her hand until she stroked his ears, now they had her attention the dogs were patient enough to wait their turn. Keeping one hand on the wriggling white and tan terrier, she made sure to pat and fuss each one of the dogs in turn, muttering nonsense and praise as though they could understand every word.

A shrill whistle pierced the air just as she was pushing back to her feet, and the dogs leapt up as one, ears pricked. The whistle sounded again, and they were off and running back the way they'd come, answering their master's summons. Not even Bella could resist the lure of Arthur, picking up her dainty feet as she tumbled along the corridor with the others.

Not that Lucie could blame the pretty greyhound; if Arthur whistled at her, Lucie might find herself running after him, too. Although after the breakfast debacle she wasn't sure how she would face him again. With a sigh over her own retched foolishness, she entered the drawing room and closed the door firmly behind her. Time to stop worrying about that morning's awkward encounter and get to work.

With the door shut, there was barely enough light in the room for Lucie to locate the wall switch. Flipping it on did little to improve the atmosphere as most of the bulbs in the matching pair of ceiling light fixtures were either dead or missing. Judging from the dust covers and the general staleness of the air, the west drawing room was one of those still to receive a spring clean. Tucked away as it was in the far corner of this wing, it felt to her like a forgotten space.

The heavy drapes had been drawn, to protect the paintings and carpets from sun damage, she assumed, but it only added to the gloomy, depressing atmosphere. Not prone to superstition, she still had a sense that something terrible had happened in the room, something heartbreaking, or tragic, which had left a layer of sadness hanging in the air. She suppressed a quick shiver. If she started thinking about ghosts and spirits, she'd end up hiding under the bed. A building as old as the castle was bound to hold some terrible secrets.

Lucie fiddled around beside one set of curtains until her fingers located the heavy, woven pull cord. Not wishing to disturb too much of the dust which had likely settled into the folds of the material, she pulled gently to open the drapes, letting the warm spring sunshine spill in through the grubby window panes. The bands of light lifted the atmosphere in an instant and she hurried to the opposite window to repeat the action. Now she looked again, it was simply a neglected, dusty room, one of many around the castle, no doubt.

Peeling back the covers from the furniture without sending clouds of dust into the air was a painstaking process, and she was soon lost in the rhythm of checking the original archive record for the room, updating it to the electronic record on her tablet and adding pictures to the cloud. She made her way methodically around the room in an anticlockwise direction, and was almost back to where she'd started when her stomach rumbled. Checking her watch, she was surprised to find over three hours had passed in what felt like a blink of an eye. She raised her arms to stretch out the kinks in her back from either bending over to examine the furniture, or tilting her head to study pictures and prints on the walls.

There was a nice collection of four watercolours she'd marked up on her records for further study. They weren't attributed in the original archive, other than with a generic 'four seasons' title. The landscapes had each been painted from the same spot, a clearing surrounded by trees with a small circle of broken stones dotted around the centre of it. Whether an ancient pagan ring or a more modern Victorian folly version, it was impossible to tell from the paintings themselves, but the image was striking. In the first, the stones popped out from a sea of nodding bluebells, in the second a shaft of sunlight pierced the lush green canopy of the trees to shine on one of the stones. The third showed those branches stripped bare, a carpet of fallen leaves covering the clearing, and the last showed the stones half-buried in a blanket of thick snow.

Whatever their material value, they were too beautiful to be tucked away in a forgotten corner room, she thought sadly. Her stomach rumbled again, and she checked the copy of the archive list to see if she'd missed anything. One entry remained unticked, *sketch of a woman's head, circa 1862.* Turning in a slow circle, she studied each of the walls in turn, wondering if she'd somehow missed it. No, everything hanging had been photographed and added to her spreadsheet. Puzzled, she retraced her path around the room, ducking down to check nothing had fallen under one of the tables, or was propped against the wall behind the larger pieces of furniture. Nothing.

About to give up and mark the item as missing, a flash of inspiration hit, and she twitched off the dust sheet covering a Queen Anne style desk. Even dull from a lack of polish, the burnished walnut wood sang of its quality, and she couldn't help but trail her fingers along the intricate carving at one corner. The delicate, slightly bowed legs didn't look strong enough to hold it up, but there was no sign of wobbliness in the piece, even balanced as it was on the thick carpet. She tugged open the first drawer and was disappointed to find it empty. The one below it was also bare, as was the larger central drawer and the upper right one. Ready to dismiss her own folly, Lucie slid open the final drawer and was stunned to see a small frame facing downwards in the bottom.

With shaking fingers, she lifted the frame and turned it over. What she saw knocked the air from her lungs and sent her bottom crashing into the dust-cover draped chair behind her. When she'd seen the date entered into the ledger, her stomach had given a little flip because it was at the height of the Pre-Raphaelite era, her personal favourite and specialty. It had come and gone in an instant, of course, because there was nothing she'd seen so far to indicate anyone in the Ludworth family had a penchant for the once-controversial group of rebellious young artists she adored.

*Until now, that is.*

Tracing the outline of a stubborn, almost masculine jaw, a nose too broad to be considered fashionably dainty, the thick waves of hair captured in a few swirling strokes of charcoal, Lucie felt her heart thudding against her ribs. Though it was barely finished—a five-minute scribble rather than a serious study—

118

there was no mistaking the face she'd seen staring out of many a masterpiece. Eudora Baines, muse and mistress of Jacob James Viggliorento. And she'd bet her right arm, JJ, as he'd been known to his friends, was the artist behind the pencil.

Fascinated, Lucie carried the picture over to the window to study it in full light. As she tilted the frame. she noticed the left-hand edge of the paper was ragged, as though it had been ripped casually from a notebook or sketchpad. Her fingers itched to pry open the back of the frame and remove the image, but she resisted the urge. Best to wait until she had her tools with her; if she accidentally smudged the charcoal, she'd never forgive herself.

'What are you doing here, Eudora?' she murmured as she hugged the little frame close to her chest. It was a mystery, and one she was determined to solve.

119

# CHAPTER ELEVEN

It was with some trepidation that Arthur stuck his around the dining room door that lunchtime. After Lucie's performance at breakfast he didn't want to be the cause of any more choking fits, or have her fleeing the room at the sight of him. Thankfully, it was empty, so he helped himself to a bowl of soup from the warmer and a couple of bread rolls from the large Tupperware box they used to keep them fresh. With everyone busy doing their own thing it was the easiest way to keep lunch as flexible as possible without giving the staff any more to do.

Helping himself to a glass of water, Arthur propped his tablet up on its stand and opened his newspaper app. He liked to keep abreast of things, and lunch was normally quieter than breakfast so the perfect time to catch up on the day's news. Today's soup was chicken noodle, a particular favourite of his, and he was two-thirds down his second bowl when the door swung open and Lucie bounced in.

There was no other way to describe it. The high ponytail she'd tied her gorgeous red hair in swung from side to side with the excited movement of her body. Her face lit up when she caught sight of him, and he swallowed a sigh of relief that she'd apparently decided to forget any awkwardness from earlier.

'Oh, Arthur, there you are!' Eschewing her normal seat further along the table, Lucie dropped into the chair at his left elbow. Propping her chin in her hands, she beamed up at him. The full force of that lovely smile did inexplicable things to his insides. She looked so full of joy, he wanted to reach out and touch her cheek as though some of it might rub off on him.

'Here I am, what do you need?' *A kiss, perhaps?* Though he'd sworn to himself he would keep things strictly professional, he was only a man after all, and she was so pretty and sparky in that moment he wanted to snatch her up and forget about anything other than the most basic demands of his nature.

'I need a copy of your family tree; do you have one?'

No snatching, then. Whatever had her lit up like a beacon, it wasn't the current baronet, but one of his ancestors. Arthur swallowed his disappointment with a mouthful of water then settled back in his chair. A little distance between them would help banish the last of those snatching thoughts. 'There's one in my study. When you have a hereditary title like ours which requires presenting proof to an appointed council before you can assume it, it pays to keep very good family records.'

Lucie frowned. 'Doesn't it just pass down from father to son, like other peerages?'

'It's not a peerage, it's something different.' Arthur waved a hand. 'It's all a bit complicated, but in order to use the title I had to present proof of my birth and lineage to get my name entered onto the Roll of Baronets. There's an old Debrett's guide somewhere in the library, that explains it all.' He paused. 'They've probably got a website, everyone and everything does these days.'

'I'll have to look it up, it sounds intriguing.'

'Then I've oversold it to you,' Arthur replied, with a grin. He'd been schooled on the why's and wherefore's of his family history and could list them all back to before the Civil War, but he wouldn't wish the knowledge on anyone else. The weight of all that history, the intimate knowledge of those past baronets—both successes and failures—had hung around his neck like a millstone since his earliest days in the school room. He would have to find a better way to do it when he had children of his own, assuming there was anything left for them to inherit by the time he got around to continuing the family line.

'Well, if I can get a look at this family tree, I can get on with my research.' A long, low growl of sound echoed around the room and a red-faced Lucie clapped a hand over her stomach. 'Oh, my goodness, how embarrassing. I can't seem to sit at this table without humiliating myself one way or another.'

She made to stand, but Arthur was too quick for her. With a firm hand on her shoulder, he pressed her back into her seat. 'You dashed off this morning with your breakfast half-eaten, and you've clearly not had anything since. I'll get you some soup.'

'I…I'm fine, really.'

'I'm going to ban that bloody word from your vocabulary! You can take five minutes.' Arthur stomped over to the sideboard, ladled out a bowl of soup then returned to place it in front of her. 'Eat.' He went back to retrieve a couple of rolls for her, not giving her the chance to argue with him. A glass of water was next. When he saw the spoon lying untouched next to her bowl, he scowled. 'As I seem to be the source of your discomfort, I'll be in my study when you're finished, but I don't want to see you there until you eat something.'

He was halfway to the door, when she stopped him. 'Arthur, please, this is silly. You don't need to go.'

Needing her to eat was more important than his pride. She was clearly uncomfortable around him so better to make himself scarce. Glancing back at her, he shrugged. 'I want you to feel at home here, but I don't seem to be making a very good job of it.'

'It's not you. Please, come and sit back down.'

Having resumed his seat, Arthur reached for a bit of roll he'd left on his side plate and began to butter it. Perhaps if he was eating, too, she'd feel less self-conscious. A bit of distracting conversation might help. 'You were excited about something when you came in a few minutes ago, is it to do with my family tree?'

Lucie nodded. 'I found a little sketch dating back to the 1860s.'

A sketch. Well that didn't sound too promising as far as the family coffers went, but it had clearly got her engine revving. Mulling over the dates, he chewed the mouthful of bread, pleased to note from a corner of his eye that Lucie had picked up her spoon and was making headway with her soup. '1860s would've been Thomas, the ninth baronet. He inherited the title in 1857 after his father came a cropper whilst out riding. Thomas was quite young, had to give up his studies in London if I remember, rightly. He's the one who got obsessed with all the Arthurian stuff.'

He finished the last bite of his roll. 'Aunt Morgana said he hung out with a bit of an arty set, now I come to think of it.'

'Did she mention any names?' Lucie was practically on the edge of her seat, that eager light shining once more in her eyes.

'Not that I can recall, but then again, I wasn't paying that much attention. You should ask her...' He checked his watch. 'Although not just now.' Aunt Morgana retired to her room for a lie-down after lunch. At 75, she could do whatever the heck she liked that kept her happy, as far as Arthur and the others were concerned, so they made sure to never disturb her.

'That's okay, I can ask her over dinner. I'd still like to make a copy of the family tree, though. I've been trying to sort out the archive into a better order. I've already put things like estate ledgers, staffing records, personal correspondence and so on into their own sections, and I think it would make life easier if I could further break those groups down by each generation.'

Given the way everything was jumbled together now, anything sounded like a vast improvement to Arthur. 'I'm happy to go along with whatever system works for you.' Folding his arms, he rested them on the edge of the dining table and leaned forward. 'Are you going to keep me in suspense about this sketch?'

123

She glanced down, and then back up again. 'I'm trying not to let myself get too carried away until I can find some verification, but I think it might be of Eudora Baines.'

Which left him none the wiser. 'And she is…?'

'Oh, sorry!' Lucie laughed. 'I forget not everyone is obsessed with the same things I am. She was, amongst other things, the muse of a famous Pre-Raphaelite artist.'

Pre-Raphaelite? Now that was something he *had* heard of. 'And you think this sketch is by someone famous?' *Don't get ahead of yourself, Arthur…*

'I think it might be.' Arthur's heart began to pound at her words. 'But it's unsigned and really not more than a scribble.' And there went his hopes again, dashed against the rocks of reality. Of course there wasn't some hidden masterpiece lurking in some forgotten corner of the castle, real life didn't work that way.

'So, your interest is more of an academic thing?'

'What? Oh, yes.' Lucie bit her lip, realisation dawning across her pretty features. 'You didn't think…? Oh, of course you did, how stupid of me!' She reached back to tug on her ponytail, stroking it through her fingers. 'I'm sorry, Arthur.'

She sounded so upset, he couldn't bear it. 'Don't be. I just got a bit carried away with myself, that's all. If you're excited about this sketch, then so am I.' Well, he could be if he put a bit more effort into it. Not wanting to snuff out the bright fire of her enthusiasm, he gestured for her to continue.

'It's like finding a new piece to a puzzle. Another little clue into their lives.' She raised one shoulder. 'I'm not sure I can explain it, but I spent so much time researching into these people, they almost feel like friends.' High colour splashed across her cheeks. 'That sounds a bit pathetic, doesn't it?'

'Not at all,' Arthur assured her. 'I think it's great that you have something you feel so passionate about. Where did you find the sketch?'

'I was working in the west drawing room today. After my tour with Mrs W, I decided the only way to tackle such a big project was to be logical about it. The temptation was to focus on the most impressive spaces, but then I worried about getting side-tracked and missing something. I found a set of plans in amongst the archive which look like they were drawn up early in the twentieth century. The rooms are all named, which is very helpful, so I decided to start at one end of the ground floor and work my way from west to east.' She was babbling a bit, like she expected him to interrupt her, or criticise the working method she'd chosen, and he wondered who'd been responsible for putting such a dent in her confidence. Whoever it was needed a swift kick.

'That sounds a lot more sensible than any suggestion I might have come up with. Can I have a look at the plans you're using, just to make sure they are the most up to date?' In not wanting to interfere, he could see he'd been a bit too hands-off with the project, leaving Lucie to flounder around and make the best of things. 'I should've thought to provide you with a proper layout of the place—*and* the family tree.'

She gave him an abashed smile. 'I've quite enjoyed poking around, but it would be more efficient to check with you I was working off the right information.'

At this rate they'd be apologising to each other for the next half an hour. Arthur stood and held out his hand. 'Well, then let's agree that we were both a little bit at fault and remedy that from now on.'

'It's a deal,' she agreed, shaking his proffered hand. As their fingers slipped apart, he noticed a callus on the side of her middle finger. Capturing her hand once more, he soothed the hard lump with the ball of his thumb. 'I...I always hold my pen too hard,' she murmured, staring down at their joined hands. 'Always have.'

Arthur released his hold and set his hand next to hers, comparing his smooth straight fingers to hers. 'I never did enough work at school to notice if I held the pen too tight.'

125

Shy green eyes peeked up at him through her thick russet fringe. 'I find that hard to believe.'

He shook his head. 'Believe it or not, it doesn't change the truth of it. Tristan was the brains of the outfit. I've always been the brawn. I was too busy running around the rugby pitch. I did enough to get by, but I didn't really see the point as my future was mapped out from the day we were born.' A bitter laugh escaped his throat. 'A stupid quirk of fate and some archaic bollocks meant running this place was my only career option, so I didn't much see the point in studying a bunch of stuff I'd never get to use.'

'But you went to university? I'm sure I heard Tristan mention a reunion invitation the other night.'

'Rugby scholarship. I let Tristan have his pick of courses and tagged along.'

'And Iggy?'

Arthur smiled, shaking off some of his unexpected melancholy. It wasn't like him to be all moody and introspective. Life was as it was and there was no use bemoaning a fate many people would consider blessed. 'She couldn't wait to see the back of us! Went to Cirencester, to the agricultural college, which is what I should've done if I'd had any sense.'

'I can see it would've had its benefits running an estate as large as this. What did you study instead?'

'Business studies, a couple of elective units on book-keeping. It was all right, actually, which was just as well as I blew out my knee during the first winter there and couldn't play rugby after that.' When he caught her looking down at his legs, he tugged up the left leg of his cords to show her the white scar stretching from just above his knee to a couple of inches below it. 'It's fine now, as long as I don't do anything stupid. And it comes in handy for predicting the bad weather.' He released his trouser leg and shook it back into place.

'Makes my callus a bit pathetic by comparison.' Lucie rubbed her thumb over the bump, echoing his action from a few moments before. Apart from the little ridge, the rest of her skin had been incredibly soft and smooth to the touch.

Surprised at how much he wanted to take her hand again, he tucked his hands behind his back. 'That's it? No other flaws?'

Her musical laughter filled the air. 'Oh, plenty of those!' She waved a hand towards her face as though pointing some of them out.

'What am I supposed to be looking at?' Arthur tilted his head from one side to the other before shaking it. 'Nope, can't see anything wrong with you.'

She tugged a lock of her fringe. 'Apart from this carroty mess, and enough freckles for a dozen people, you mean?'

Stepping close, he grasped her ponytail gently then let the waterfall of silken strands run through his fingers. 'I think it's very pretty.' It came out gruff; a roughened caress as the intimacy of his action struck. He should let her go, before he did something unforgivable like wrap it around his fist and tug her close for a kiss...

'We should get back to work.' She turned away, pulling her hair free from his lax grasp, the movement almost natural enough for him to miss the sudden warmth glowing in her cheeks. Perhaps he wasn't the only one thinking inappropriate thoughts.

She was right; damn it, he knew she was right, but for an instant he wanted to ignore all the very sensible reasons why taking her into his arms would be a terrible idea and just go with it. They were both young, and from what he'd worked out so far, both free and single. Would it be so bad to give in to this attraction and see where it took them?

Before he'd finished the thought, he knew the truth of it. It would be bad; more than bad, quite possibly ruinous. Because after she'd slapped his face for behaving inappropriately and stormed out, what would he do then? Maybe, just maybe, she was onto something with this Pre-Raphaelite connection. If he let his stupid libido get in the way of saving the family fortunes, wouldn't he be just as bad as those ancestors of his who'd got them in this mess in the first place?

He'd thought himself free? What a bloody joke that was. With a quick wipe of his hand against his leg to try and dispel the lingering feel of her silky hair, he gestured towards the door. 'Right, let's go and find that family tree, I promised you, and then perhaps you can show me this sketch of yours?'

# CHAPTER TWELVE

For the rest of the afternoon, Arthur was the absolute soul of propriety. Having made a copy of the family tree on his printer-cum-scanner, he followed Lucie to the library mezzanine and showed a great deal of interest in the beginnings of the new filing system she'd set up. At no point did he give any hint of mention of that super-charged moment in the dining room when he'd stroked her hair and for one blissful, foolish moment she'd thought he might want to kiss her. He made sure to not lean in too close as they sat side-by-side to review the items she'd flagged as warranting further study once the initial full survey had been completed, and all in all acted exactly as he had during all of their other encounters—scrupulously polite.

When their knuckles made accidental contact as she handed him the frame holding the sketch of Eudora, it was Lucie who leapt back as though burnt whilst Arthur gave no sign of noticing either the brief contact or her stupid over-reaction to it. By the time the daylight was fading outside, she was beginning to wonder if she'd imagined the whole thing.

*I think it's very pretty.* A shiver rippled down her spine. No. She hadn't imagined that, nor the way he'd stared down at her as though he wanted to devour her.

'Here.'

Lucie blinked at the cardigan Arthur had unhooked from the back of her chair. 'What's that for?'

Arthur draped the garment over the arm of her seat. 'My mistake. I thought you were getting chilly.'

Was he teasing her? She stared at him, trying and failing to read anything other than a mild concern in his warm hazel eyes. 'I...umm, it was nothing,' she stuttered, for what else was she going to say? *I was thinking about that moment when you almost kissed me?* Hell would freeze over before she told him the truth. And melt again before she would utter the question burning her tongue. *'Why didn't you?'* If it was because she'd been stupid enough to open her mouth and say they should get back to work, she'd kick herself from here to next Tuesday. It had been a reflex action, a fleeting attempt by her conscience to remind herself of her position at the castle, rather than any kind of serious protestation.

She pinched the underside of her arm to banish the foolish notion. If he'd wanted to kiss her, he would've kissed her. Arthur didn't strike her as the kind of man who was backward about coming forward. He was always in motion. Even when he'd given her his full attention as she'd shown him the photos on her tablet, he'd been moving. Tapping a pen he'd picked up against his thigh one minute, running a hand through his thick hair the next. He was never still. It made sense that he'd been a sportsman at school, he had that kind of solid physique and confidence in his movements she remembered for her own classmates.

She risked a glance at him from under her lashes, but his attention was once more on the tablet. 'I like these,' he said, tapping the screen. 'Where did you find them?' He tilted the screen to show her the grouping she'd made of the four seasons paintings.

'They're in the west drawing room, where I found the sketch. They're unattributed, but beautifully rendered.'

Arthur turned the tablet back for another look. 'Whoever

painted them, they were connected to the castle in some way.'
When she raised an eyebrow, he pointed to the stone circle in
the centre of the first image. 'This is out in the woods behind
the castle, we used to play there all the time. It'll look just like
this in a few more weeks.'

'The bluebells?' She remembered the photos she'd seen when
she'd been Googling the family and the castle.

He nodded. 'A huge carpet of them as far as the eye can see,
that's how this place got its nickname, Bluebell Castle.'

*Bluebell Castle.* A fanciful, romantic name for such an imposing
fortress. 'How old is the circle?'

'A hundred and fifty years or so.'

Lucie rolled her eyes. 'Don't tell me, it was built by my favourite
baronet.'

'The one and only.' They exchanged a grin. 'It's actually a copy
of an ancient circle out on the moors about five miles from the
boundary of our lands. At least he had the good sense to leave
the original undisturbed, and just have a replica made to enter-
tain himself and his visitors. Although the one in the woods is
very pretty, especially at the height of spring, I much prefer the
ancient one. It's set high on an escarpment, exposed to the wildest
of the elements, with the most incredible view. A good spot for
a picnic in the summer...' Voice trailing off, he glanced at her,
then quickly away.

Was he hinting they might go there together? Lucie's heart
soared for a moment before reality struck. Come summer, she
would be long gone. Assuming she actually got some work done
rather than wasting her afternoons mooning over his Lordship.

Needing a bit of distance, as well as to remind herself of what
she was supposed to be doing, Lucie crossed over to the section
of shelving where she'd stacked the personal correspondence and
diaries she'd come across. 'I wonder...'

Flipping through the first pile she scanned and discarded
more than a dozen different notebooks until she came across

one covered in battered, brown leather with the frayed end of a band which would've once kept it secured shut. With care, she eased open the front cover and checked the date at the top of the first page. *1852.* Excited, she put it to one side and scoured the shelves for similar-looking books, knowing she'd seen at least a few similar to this one. After a few moments she turned to face Arthur with more than half a dozen clutched in her hands. 'Thomas's journals! Thank goodness you come from a line of prolific record keepers.'

Arthur rose to join her. Taking the first book from the stack, he flipped through it. 'What are you hoping to find?'

'A clue to what his connection might be to Eudora and JJ, perhaps? I'm not really sure. Hopefully there will be some information about why he became obsessed with a connection to Camelot which we can use to build the Arthurian collection you mentioned.'

'Who's JJ?'

'JJ Viggliorento, he's the artist who might, and I stress might, be the one who made the sketch of Eudora.'

'Wow, even I've heard of him. How amazing would it be to find out he'd been here to the castle?' He gifted her with an excited grin. 'If we could prove a connection to him, maybe we could look at hosting an exhibition of his work. Something like that could be a real draw! And you're hoping to find a clue to that in one of these? You're full of bright ideas.' His excitement waned a little. 'It'll take you ages to wade through all these though.'

'I'll have to abandon poor Isabella.' He gave her a quizzical look. 'Your several-times great grandmother,' she explained. 'I came across a couple of her diaries and they've been my bedtime reading. She's quite funny, newly married to Percy and trying to get used to being stuck out in the wilds of Derbyshire after growing up in London. It's a bit like reading one of those Georgette Heyer romances.' She was a sucker for a good love story—always had been.

'I can't say I know much about her. She would've been Thomas's daughter-in-law, because Percy is surely Percival, the first in the family to get saddled with this ludicrous naming tradition.'

'I quite like it,' Lucie admitted. 'And Arthur isn't too outlandish.'

'True enough. I think after the dreadful teasing my father and Uncle Lancelot had to endure, he tried to find a way to stay true to the tradition without us getting beaten up every day at boarding school.'

The mention of boarding school sent her flashing back to her glory days at Wessingdean. How she'd managed not to flinch when Arthur had mentioned being best man at Henrietta Warner-Mills wedding the other day, was beyond her. They'd been put in the same small dormitory on their first day and had bonded in shared misery over being away from home for the first time in their lives. They'd had huge fun together, and it'd been Henrietta who'd got her interested in horse-riding. There'd even been plans for Lucie to join Henrietta and her family for a period of the summer holidays—until her father's fraud had been discovered.

Arthur shifted next to her, and she realised she'd been lost in her memories for too long. Scrambling for a question that wouldn't reveal any of the turmoil the topic had stirred up, she settled for turning the discussion back to him. 'Did you enjoy boarding school?'

He considered it for a moment before nodding. 'Yes. Well, for the most part, anyway. I still had Tristan to rely on, although I missed Iggy dreadfully. Like I said before, I was very sporty so that made it easy to make friends because I was on so many teams.' His expression clouded. 'It was the best thing for us, even though it meant being separated from our sister for the first time in our lives. Dad couldn't manage the three of us on his own, and we were in danger of becoming quite feral according to Aunt Morgana.'

Wondering if she'd stirred up some bad memories, Lucie winced. 'Sorry, I didn't realise you'd lost your mum as well.'

The sardonic twist of his lips turned his features harsher. 'We didn't lose her, she upped and left when we were barely two years' old.'

'How awful.' Whatever ups and downs she and her mum had along the way, Lucie couldn't imagine being without her; couldn't imagine her mum *wanting* to be without her, and vice versa. And though her dad hadn't wanted to see her, she could understand now that he'd been trying to protect her—even if it had left with her too many unanswered questions and no way to resolve them. 'Do you still see her?'

'Not if we can help it. Not that she's ever shown much interest in us. She called at New Year's, but that was because she wanted... something.' Having clearly caught himself on the edge of confessing more than he wanted to tell her, Arthur made a performance of taking the rest of the journals Lucie was still holding and placed them on her desk.

Taking the hint, she followed him and made herself busy tidying away her tablet, notebooks and the other bits and pieces they'd strewn about the place over the course of the afternoon. When he kept his back to her, Lucie hesitated for a moment before placing a gentle hand on his arm as she circled around to face him. 'I'm sorry for prying.'

'You didn't, just rattled a skeleton or two, that's all.' With a final pat to the journal on the top of the pile, he rested his hip against the edge of the desk, his whole demeanour much more relaxed. 'Let's talk about something nicer. How's *your* mum?'

Just the thought of Constance was enough to bring a smile to Lucie's face. 'She's good. I spoke to her last night, actually. She'd been busy all afternoon planting up her window boxes.'

'Do you miss her? I get the impression the two of you are close.'

'Very. It's been just us since...' It was her turn to hesitate.

134

'Since we lost my father.' When a look of knowing sympathy filled his gaze, her insides began to squirm. He was clearly drawing parallels between his own loss and hers when they couldn't be further apart. From the few times he'd mentioned it, it was obvious Arthur and his siblings were still devastated over losing their father, but his passing had come as something of a relief after a long illness. Whereas her dad dying whilst still in prison had brought nothing but pain and confusion. But what could she say? *I know you miss your father, but mine was a lying, deceitful pig who I was glad to see the back of?*

No. Even on her blackest days, she wouldn't have meant that. Part of her knew she should despise him for all the misery he'd wrought to the people he'd stolen from, but deep down she was still just a little girl who missed her daddy. Even just thinking about him was enough to bring the tears pricking to the backs of her eyes. Better not to mention him at all.

'What are you planning to do over Easter, are you going home to visit her?'

Caught off guard, she stared at him for a few moments. 'I hadn't given it much thought. She knows the initial contract here is for two months, and I haven't made any plans to go back during that time.' And then it struck her. The family would have their own plans for the holiday weekend and likely wouldn't want or expect her to be around. Embarrassed at her lack of foresight, she hurried on. 'I'll check the train timetable later, sort something out.'

Arthur caught her eye for a moment before shifting his gaze to the journals stacked on her desk. 'You're more than welcome to invite her here. If you think she might like a change of scenery, that is.'

Now she was really confused. Did he expect her to work over Easter, or not? 'It would be nice for her to get out of town, and I could keep on top of things here.' She swept an arm towards her desk. 'If you're sure it wouldn't be too much of an imposition?'

Arthur straightened up. 'Not at all, but I don't want you thinking I made the suggestion because I'm trying to keep your nose pressed to the grindstone. Don't think I haven't noticed the hours you've been working.' Folding his arms across his chest, he fixed her with a look that made her want to squirm like a bug under a microscope. 'Iggy said she still hasn't been able to persuade you to join her for that ride yet.'

She felt her cheeks heating. 'There's so much to do, it didn't feel right to take the morning off.'

Poking out his tongue, he made a rude noise to show what he thought of that. 'I hadn't appreciated how big a task this was until we were just going through everything now. The last thing I want is for you to burn yourself out. I'm going to have a word with Tristan and get him to help us.'

'Us? 'What do you mean?'

'If we divide the remaining rooms between us, we can help you pull together a full inventory that much quicker. I appreciate how thorough and conscientious you've been in your approach, and I think it's the way to go. But if it's down to you to document every item in every room you'll be at it for weeks.'

'Once I have these records sorted, I'll be able to spend all day surveying the rooms, which will make it much quicker,' she protested. 'You can't pay me to do a job and then take on half the workload yourself.'

'I'll think you'll find I can do whatever I please.'

There was something very wrong with her that those little flashes of arrogance he showed her had the capacity to melt her brain, her knees and everything else between the two. Angry with herself for being unable to control her reactions to him, she huffed her fringe from her eyes and folded her arms in a mirror to his pose. 'You don't know what you're doing, if you did you wouldn't have had to hire me.'

'I can check off a list of items, take photographs of them and add anything not already recorded to your database. Tristan can do the same. You'll be able to review the images and update the descriptions with whatever additional details you think they need and identify stuff you want to take a look at for yourself.'

Okay, when he put it like that, he had a point, but it still didn't sit right with her. 'You've got your own work to do, and I don't want to take you away from that. Tristan, either.' Although she had no idea what his brother actually did for a living. Being a smartarse couldn't be a full-time profession.

Softening his stance, Arthur placed his hands on her upper arms and squeezed lightly. 'Let us help you with the basic data gathering and then you can get on with the important stuff.'

Her skin tingled where his fingers pressed into her skin, even through the thin wool of her sweater. She was still not convinced he hadn't decided to intervene because he was disappointed with how much progress she was making. 'Okay.'

'Okay.' With one more quick squeeze, he let her go. 'We'll start tomorrow afternoon.'

She opened her mouth only to have him tap the end of her nose, a quirky smile on his face. 'Before you ask why we're not starting first thing, it's because I'm taking you out for a walk. I don't think you've set foot outside these walls since you entered the castle.'

'I've been busy.'

'That doesn't make me feel any better about abusing your work ethic. Besides, it's Saturday tomorrow so you should be off the clock. I'll take you out to see the circle. Bring your tablet to take some photos which you can compare to the paintings, then you can call it research if that makes you feel better.' He checked his watch. 'We'd better get changed for dinner.'

The top of his head was disappearing from view as he climbed down the spiral staircase before she realised she was gaping after him like some slack-jawed idiot. Had she really thought that arrogant streak of his attractive a few moments before? One minute he was telling her he was happy with the way she was

137

doing things, the next he was turning her plans upside down. His Lordship had spoken and there was no more to be said about it, because he'd decreed it so.

Snatching up the stack of Thomas's journals, she tucked them under her arm and stomped down the stairs after Arthur. By the time she'd made it as far as the great hall where she was greeted by the ever-faithful Bella, she knew it wasn't Arthur she was cross with—it was herself. There was nothing wrong with anything he'd suggested. If he and Tristan could help her get through the initial room surveys it could only be a good thing. Taking photos of endless bits of quality, but mostly unexciting furniture wasn't exactly thrilling, and she was sure they were both more than competent enough to do as thorough a job as she'd been doing. They had more invested in this project than she did after all.

No, it was the prospect of spending more time with Arthur that unsettled her. This afternoon had been bad enough, but tomorrow morning, regardless of what he'd said about taking the tablet with her, she wouldn't even have her work to act as a shield between them. And the way he was making her feel, she'd need all the protection she could get.

# CHAPTER THIRTEEN

An afternoon together had shown Arthur his grand plan to keep his mind off Lucie and fixed on his responsibilities wasn't going to cut it. For one thing, he couldn't keep his hands off her, although he'd been careful to keep any contact appropriate. The pain with which she'd spoken about losing her father had struck a deep cord inside him, and it'd been all he could do not to drag her into his arms and hold her close. Not a sexual desire, more a visceral need to offer and receive comfort in their shared misery. There'd been a fragility about her; a way she held herself so tightly together it seemed at any moment she might shatter into pieces under the compression of her emotions.

She was also painfully stubborn, and it'd taken channelling every ounce of command he'd inherited from generations of Ludworths being masters of all they surveyed to overrule her protestations about accepting his assistance. He'd thought it an inspired solution to satisfy his desire to spend more time with Lucie, without having to feel guilty over putting his own needs before those of the family. He'd even roped in his brother to avoid any suspicion over his motives. Although Tristan had given him a knowing look, he'd kept quiet beyond supporting his suggestion the two of them help Lucie out with the survey and had agreed to meet them after lunch in the library.

It wasn't only his brother who was onside with his plans; the day had dawned bright and clear. The old adage about March coming in like a lion and going out like a lamb was holding true, and there was a real sense of spring in the air as he opened the front door and shooed the dogs out onto the gravel to run off their first bit of excitement after being shut in all night. Although Lucie was much better around them, and the love affair between her and Bella was growing from strength to strength, he still didn't want them leaping all over her when she finally decided to join him for their walk.

Resisting the urge to check his watch, he tucked his Barbour jacket under one arm and wandered a few paces to examine the large, circular flowerbed which acted as an unofficial roundabout for any vehicles entering and exiting the sweeping driveway. Iggy and her green fingers had been hard at work from the looks of the rich dark soil scattered amongst the dancing golden heads of daffodils and the delicate little crocuses in shades of pink, lilac and purple turning their faces to the morning sun.

'Am I late?' He turned at Lucie's call, his lips stretching in a smile of anticipation as she jogged across the gravel towards him. Like him, she'd matched jeans with several thin layers on top. Her pale green hooded sweater had been left unzipped to display a crisp white shirt with the outline of a darker green T-shirt showing through. She looked as fresh and bright as the pretty blooms in the flowerbed.

'Not at all.' He glanced down at her feet. 'Are you sure about those? It might be a bit boggy in places.' Under the shade of the trees, the ground in the woods often took longer to dry out.

Lucie lifted a trainer-clad foot and regarded it with a shrug. 'It's these or some slouchy boots, which I know from experience will absorb every drop of water in a five-mile radius. These, at least, are machine washable.'

'You can grab a pair of wellies from the boot room if you want. There's a range of sizes and are intended for anyone who needs them. You'll find some thick socks on one of the shelves, too.'

As he waited for her to return, Arthur raised his head to survey the sky. Other than a few cotton wool clouds, it was blue for as far as the eye could see. Carting his coat around would get tedious. If the wind got up, the trees would provide enough shelter and though thin, his sweater was made of that polar fleece stuff, so he was unlikely to get cold. Returning to the entrance hall, he'd just slung it back onto its usual hook and was fishing a couple of tennis balls from one of the pockets when Lucie emerged from the boot room stamping her feet to ensure they were well secured in the black wellingtons she'd selected. 'All right?'

'I think so. They're a touch big, but the other ones I tried were too tight across the toes. The socks are helping.'

'Let's get going, then.' He tossed her one of the balls. 'You'll need this.'

Raising an eyebrow, she studied the slightly grubby object. 'Thanks, I think.'

He grinned at her lack of conviction. 'Trust me.'

The moment they emerged back out onto the gravel, the dogs swarmed towards them. Without hesitation, Arthur swung his arm back and tossed his tennis ball as far as he could. In a formation on par with a murmuration of starlings soaring across the evening sky, they turned as one and pelted after the ball. 'Now I get it,' Lucie said.

Heading off at right angles to the dogs, Arthur strolled to the edge of the driveway and down the gentle grassy slope which led towards the woods. In a flurry of barking, the dogs returned, a triumphant Nimrod heading the pack with the ball clamped in his jaws. They were a few feet away when Lucie launched her ball into the air, and off the dogs charged again, Nimrod at the back this time as he'd paused to drop his prize at Arthur's feet.

And so they continued, taking it in turns to throw their balls until they entered the bracken and thicker, longer grass that edged the woods. Distracted by myriad scents, the dogs abandoned their game and disappeared off into the undergrowth, noses glued to the ground. Taking the sticky tennis ball from Lucie's hand, Arthur dropped them both on the grass ready to retrieve on their return journey. Grimacing at the blob of drool left behind on his hand, Arthur scrubbed it on the back of his jeans before reaching out to lift a drooping branch obstructing the well-worn path. Lucie ducked under it with a murmur of thanks then turned to wait for him.

A short way ahead, the path split in opposite directions. As he took the left-hand path, Arthur pointed to the right and said, 'That way eventually takes you down towards the lake. It's a nice walk, and you can come back via the ornamental gardens—well, what's left of them. Iggy's doing her best to bring some order back, but they'd been left to grow wild during my grandfather's time and some of the patterns are lost for good, I fear.'

'Such a shame. When I get a chance, I'll have a root through the plans and drawings I've come across in the library. With any luck there might be something there which will help,' Lucie suggested.

'Good idea. Unfortunately, a lot of the old knowledge that was passed down was lost when my great-grandfather laid off most of the staff.' Arthur pursed his lips. 'His own father nearly bankrupted the estate when investments he'd made were declared worthless in a huge UK stock market scandal which helped to trigger the Wall Street crash.' Frustration at his ancestor filled him, even though it was the better part of a century ago. Bending he picked up a fallen stick and began to swipe through the long grass edging the path as he walked. 'I think the estate would've gone under if it wasn't for a couple of foundries we owned which were converted into munitions factories during the Second World War. Profits boomed and my great-grandfather was able to clear the mortgages his father had taken out to try and cover his losses.'

Old guilt tugged at him, knowing their family fortunes had turned for the better on the back of the deaths of thousands. They'd paid for it in blood, though. 'My great-grandfather was one of four. He was excused from the fighting because he was needed to manage the munitions business, but his twin brothers both signed up. They died during the Normandy landings a few weeks shy of their twenty-fifth birthday.'

'Oh, Arthur, that's awful.'

He swished the stick one last time before hurling it far into the trees. 'It's said their father dropped dead in the great hall, still clutching the telegram which delivered the news. My great-grandfather never recovered from the double-blow of losing all three and went into a decline. That's what my grandfather called it, anyway. It was probably a form of PTSD, but they didn't really go in for stuff like that back in those days. It was all stiff-upper-lip and brush it under the carpet. He sold off the foundries, and lost interest in the estate but wouldn't admit to anyone there was a problem. By the time my grandfather inherited in the mid-Seventies things around here had gone to pot and he was too focused on keeping the castle and the farms running to bother trying to restore anything he deemed non-essential.'

'So the gardens were left to go to seed,' Lucie said.

'Exactly.' They wandered along in silence for a few moments as Arthur tried to work out how he'd managed to get onto the subject of his ancestors many failings. 'I'm not sure why I'm telling you all this,' he admitted.

'Perhaps you needed to talk about it. I can't imagine how much pressure you must be under, and it's only natural for stuff like this to play on your mind when you're facing your own crisis.'

Which made perfect sense. 'I still shouldn't be burdening you with it.'

Lucie turned to face him. 'I disagree. I'm going to be digging around in your family's past, and I'm removed enough from the situation that you don't have to worry about upsetting me.' She wrinkled her nose at what she'd just said. 'That didn't come out right.'

Her disgusted expression made him smile, no matter how heavy his heart was right then. 'I know what you mean, thank you. And it is hard to talk about with Iggy or Tristan because in order to finish the story, I have to talk about Dad.' A sudden lump filled his throat forcing him to turn his back until he could get himself under control. Crying over it wouldn't change anything.

'It's still early days, Arthur.' Lucie's soft words were followed by a fleeting touch to the small of his back. 'Give yourself a break.'

'I'm so fucking angry with him.' Covering his face with his hands, he pressed his palms against the burning in his eyes until it subsided. 'Sorry, sorry.' There was a rustle in the grass around him and he suddenly found himself surrounded by the dogs, as though they'd sensed his distress and come to offer comfort. Crouching down, he petted first Nimrod and then Bella, before giving in and sitting on the damp ground to let them all huddle around him. It was hard to stay sad for long in the face of their loyalty and affection and he stroked their fur, letting the familiar rhythm settle him down.

Heedless of the dirt, Lucie knelt on the other side of the wriggling pack and began to tease Bella's ears in the way the greyhound loved. 'Will you tell me what happened?'

It was easier to keep his eyes on Murphy, the little Jack Russell who'd clambered onto his lap, so he kept his head down as he spoke. 'I think he got tired of watching his father struggle and he didn't want us to have to do the same. I can't see any other reason for his actions. He was never a gambler. A flutter on the Grand National, maybe, and the odd trip with Lancelot to the races, but I'd never have thought of him as being a risk-taker.' Bending forward he pressed a kiss to Murphy's head before lifting the dog off his lap and straightening up. 'I suppose the problem was that he didn't think he *was* taking a risk. You must've read the stories in the papers last year about the Masterson scam?'

The way Lucie paled told him she had. 'Your father was one of his investors?'

'Along with lots of other fools, yeah.' Arthur scrubbed at his hair. 'That's not really fair. The policeman who led the enquiry told me it was one of the most sophisticated scams he'd come across in a long time.'

'Cold comfort.' When he looked up at her accurate observation it was to see she had her face buried in Bella's neck. There was something so forlorn about the set of her body that it tugged him out of his own despondency.

'Enough wallowing.' Arthur forced a cheery note into his voice as he pushed to his feet. Lucie nodded, but didn't raise her head. Her shoulders shuddered, and he wondered if she was crying. Crying for him, and the sorry tale of his ancestors' dreadful luck? It was on the tip of his tongue to tell her not to waste her tears, when she gave an audible sniff. Opting for discretion, he decided to give her a little bit of privacy. 'Come on then, boys.' He clapped his hands to draw the dogs with him as he started back down the path.

He walked slowly, so it would be easy enough for Lucy to catch up when she was ready. Finding another stick on the path, he sent it skittering for the dogs to chase, their happy whines and barks filling the air. By the time he'd thrown it twice more it was little more than a stump thanks to some over-enthusiastic chewing, and Lucie had caught back up to him. Other than a little redness around her eyes and a dark streak on one cheek, she looked calm. When she risked a quick glance towards him, he raised his brows in enquiry, but she fixed her eyes hurriedly on the path ahead. 'How much further to the circle?'

Okay. They were not going to talk about whatever had triggered her tears, that much was clear. 'Another ten minutes and we should be there.'

Lucie drew in a deep breath and seemed to shake off whatever lingering melancholy remained as she met his gaze once more and gave him a smile. 'I can't wait to see it in the flesh. Or the stone, would be more appropriate, I guess.'

It was a weak joke, but enough to lift the mood. A companionable silence settled over them as they continued to walk—well, as much silence as was possible with the motley crew bounding back and forth as they tried to draw his or Lucie's attention to whatever latest amazing smell they'd come across. As they neared their destination, Arthur dropped back a couple of paces, and clicked his fingers to draw the dogs to his side. He wanted Lucie to enjoy her first sighting of the circle without any distractions. 'It's just around the next corner.'

Arthur caught Bella's collar to hold her still when she would've padded after her. Hunkering down when Bella whined in protested, he tickled her ears and whispered, 'Shh, pretty, give her a minute.' The dog nuzzled him, settling her slender weight against his hip.

A slow count to one hundred later and he judged it enough time to follow. Turning the corner, he strode through the trees until they vanished at a boundary too neat to be anything other than manmade. Lucie stood a few feet from the nearest stone, hands raised to her mouth. The look in her eyes when she glanced over her shoulder at him was something he'd have paid a small fortune for—if he'd had one.

'It's...' Lost for words, Lucie turned back towards the low ring of stones, and not for the first time Arthur wished his first sighting of the circle could've been as an adult with the full appreciation for its wonder. As kids, it'd just been a place to play. Another treasure in a place full of treasures. Taking a few paces to the side to give himself an unobstructed view, he tried to take it all in with fresh eyes.

An artificial bank and ditch had been created to elevate the stones a couple of feet above the surrounding ground. A carpet of thick mossy grass covered the bank, blending it seamlessly into the environment as though it had always been there. Here and there he could see patches of brown, some of the many burrows created by the rabbits which had transformed the raised platform into a giant warren.

In a larger circle, about a dozen paces from the edge of the ditch, the thick trunks of ancient oaks stood sentry, their boughs stretching like arms to form a natural roof of silvered green leaves through which the blue sky could still be seen. In a couple of months, those leaves would spread to make a shady canopy and the circle would transform into a place of cool shadows and mystery. He could imagine visiting here with Lucie over the year, sharing her joy as each season dressed the circle in a layer of its own personal magic.

As though sensing his thoughts, she turned to him. 'Can we come back here when the bluebells are out?'

'Absolutely. If this warm weather sticks, they might even be out by Easter weekend.' Which reminded him. 'Did you give any more thought to inviting your mum up? It'll be Aunt Morgana's seventy-fifth birthday that weekend which is why Iggy wants to throw a party.'

'I haven't, but I will, if you're sure we wouldn't be imposing?'

Arthur waved off the question. 'Not at all. Tristan thinks we should open it up to the whole village. Get a marquee and put on a big afternoon tea, organise some games for the kids. She's done a lot over the years for people, though you'd never catch her saying as much, so it'd be nice to give them a chance to show their appreciation.'

'And get you all used to the idea of opening the grounds up to members of the public,' Lucie pointed out.

He'd had the same thought, too. It was one thing to accept on an intellectual level the need to use the castle to generate some much-needed income, it was entirely another to surrender the peace and tranquility of the estate to a bunch of strangers. 'It's going to be weird.'

She cocked her head as she began to stroll towards him. 'But not a bad thing? Think of how many people will benefit from having access to somewhere beautiful to bring their children where they can run free in the fresh air without risk from vehicles.'

He groaned. 'Don't mention cars! It occurred to me the other night that I'll need to make provision for a car park somewhere and it kept me up until dawn trying to work out where we can put one without spoiling the views.' Opening up to the public had seemed like such a simple idea—for about the first five minutes, anyway. 'And then there's public liability insurance; welfare provisions; accessibility considerations…the list just goes on and on. Thankfully, Tristan is taking on responsibility for most of that because he has the experience. He was working in corporate hospitality in London before Dad got sick.'

'I was wondering the other day what he did for a living…'

A pang of something uncomfortably like jealousy stabbed at Arthur. Why had she been thinking about Tristan at all?

'…because being cocky will only get him so far in li—*aah*!'

All thoughts of his brother fled as Lucie stumbled and let out a little shriek. Arms windmilling, she tried and failed to steady her balance. Instinct took over, and Arthur found himself in motion, arms outstretched to catch her as she began to fall. His effort to appear heroic ended in abject failure as they went down in a tangle of limbs. A stray elbow caught him just under his ribs, sending the air from his lungs. 'Oof.'

'Sorry, I'm sorry!' Splayed on top of him, hair spilling loose of her ponytail, Lucie raised her head, almost catching him under the chin in the process. As she scrabbled for purchase, her hand connected with the top of his thigh. A couple of inches to the right and he'd be in real trouble. 'I've got my foot caught in something.'

'Hold still before you do me a mischief.' It wasn't only injury he feared. All that squirming around was making certain parts of him pay attention. Arthur grasped her shoulders until she stopped moving. Moss green clashed with hazel, and this close he could see her pupils expand as awareness of their compromising position filtered into her brain. A delicious warmth spread through him. 'This is doing nothing for my good intentions.'

'G…good intentions?' She blinked down at him, and he'd have given anything to know what was going on behind those bright green eyes of hers.

Reaching up, he snagged a twig that was tangled in her hair and gently pulled it free. 'I promise myself I won't think about how pretty you are, and then somehow we end up in a situation like this. If I was a fanciful man, I'd say fate was pushing us together.'

Her breath seemed to catch for a moment before she pressed her hands to his shoulders, pinning him flat. 'Or it could just be a pair of loose wellies and too many rabbit holes.' Her fingers kneaded at the fleece of his sweatshirt as though she wasn't quite sure if she wanted to hold him off or pull him close.

'That's probably more accurate,' he agreed. A large stone was digging into the small of his back, but he didn't dare move a muscle, afraid he'd break the spell between them.

'And you are my boss…' Those fingers were stroking him now, little circular caresses from his collarbone to his shoulder and back.

'Not technically.'

'*Yes*, technically. You are employing me to work here.' Her voice held more than a hint of frustration, and he knew the feeling.

This would have to be her choice, though, because she was right. The power in their current relationship lay firmly with him. If she believed for one moment, he was pressuring her, that remaining at the castle meant he expected anything from him… damn it. 'Sit up, and I'll help you to free your foot.'

She gave him that owlish look of confusion once more, before closing her eyes briefly on a nod. 'Yes. I think that's a good idea.'

A flurry of limbs later and he had her boot free and them both back on their feet. Leaves and twigs tangled in her hair and clung to her jumper and he forced his hands into his pockets before he could be tempted to help her brush herself down. Masking a sigh of disappointment, he dragged his eyes from the pretty flush on her cheeks and whistled to the dogs before starting back through the woods towards home. He heard her boots scuffing and scraping through the leaves behind him and lengthened his stride just a little to keep some distance between them.

Sometimes doing the decent thing really sucked.

# CHAPTER FOURTEEN

With a cry of relief at somehow making it through the rest of the day without spontaneously combusting with embarrassment, jumping Arthur's bones, or a combination of both, Lucie took a flying leap onto her huge bed and buried her face in the pillows. She'd been grateful when Arthur had marched ahead of her as they left woods, and had intended to avoid him for the rest of the day and hide away with the archive records, but he'd had other ideas.

When he and Tristan had appeared after lunch to assist her with the general cataloguing of each room, she'd had no choice but to try and pretend everything between her and Arthur was fine and get on with it. Thankfully, once she'd run through her process, the pair of them had disappeared off together and she'd been able to breathe again.

They'd convened at dinner and she was surprised at just how much progress the three of them had made. At this rate, they'd be finished in no time and she'd be free to concentrate on reviewing their finds, which she'd be able to do well out of Arthur's way.

She flopped over onto her back, throwing an arm across her eyes as though she could shield herself from visions of what had happened in the woods. He'd *wanted* to kiss her. There was no telling herself it was all in her head this time. The heat in his gaze, the tension in his taut body stretched out beneath hers had made it abundantly clear. Her cheeks flamed. Abundantly.

Oh, and she'd wanted to kiss him. She'd wanted it so much her lips had practically ached to be pressed against his. But her stupid conscience had got in the way and she'd started over-thinking it to the nth degree, and then he'd given her that out and like a coward she'd leapt at it, and now here she was, confused, lonely, and wondering if she'd made the very best or the very worst decision of her life.

God, she was going to drive herself mad at this rate!

Sitting up she clutched her head as if that would have any chance at all of stilling the whirring thoughts in her brain. She just needed to be logical about it. Make a list of the reasons it was a bad idea. Starting with the fact he was her employer. Releasing her head, she stared up at the canopy above her bed. There really was no way around that. She was there to do a job, and if she started getting a reputation for dallying with her employer then her career would be over regardless of the outcome of Witherby's investigation.

And if that wasn't bad enough, it transpired the reason the Ludworths were in such dire straits was because their father had been taken in by a conman. A shudder ran through her. Thank goodness she'd not confessed the truth to him when they'd been speaking about both losing their fathers, although perhaps she should've done because nothing was less likely to cool any passion he might feel for her than to know she and her family had prof-ited from a similar kind of fraud.

The Masterson case had been plastered all over the papers for months. At first, Lucie had tried to avoid it, but after a while she'd found herself obsessed with the man behind the case, reading every article about him she could lay her hands on. Almost every story had been accompanied by the same image— Masterson clutching a champagne flute, a broad grin plastered across his too-shiny face. Profile after profile had sought, and failed, to answer the question that had seeded Lucie's obsession—why he'd done it. It didn't take a genius, or the adult therapy sessions she'd never got around to booking to understand she'd been trying to draw a parallel between Masterson and her own father. As if finding out what had made him tick would somehow draw back the veil and help her understand what had driven her dad all those years ago into inflicting the same kind of misery and heartache on so many people, not least his own wife and daughter.

Reaching for her purse on the bedside cabinet, she pulled out the yellowed newspaper clipping she still carried everywhere with her. There wasn't much more than a paragraph beneath the grainy photo, just a bare statement of the facts concluding with the damning words the judge had uttered when passing down her father's sentence: 'There is often a misconception that financial crimes such as yours, Mr Kennington, are victimless, because no physical harm has been caused by your actions. Nothing could be further from the truth. You systematically lied to and betrayed those who had every reason to trust you—your friends and family. They will be counting the cost of your actions for very many years to come.'

Lucie stared at the last picture ever taken of her father and wondered once again why he'd done it. Eyes so like her own stared back at her, revealing nothing new. With a sigh, she carefully refolded the article and tucked it away behind the smiling picture of Lucie and her mum taken on graduation day. Switching her purse for her phone, Lucie pressed the number at the top of her calls list and lay back down on the bed.

A few moments later the familiar soft voice of her mother greeted her. 'Hello, darling, how lovely to hear from you. How's it all going?'

It was on the tip of her tongue to pour everything out—her attraction to Arthur, the ever-present worry over having heard nothing new from Witherby's, the endless questions about her father, but she took a deep breath instead. She was a grown-up now, not a child to keep throwing her worries at her mother's feet and expecting her to pick up the pieces. 'It's going really well, thanks. I think we're making a lot of progress, and you'll never guess what I found yesterday!' As she gushed to her mother about finding the sketch of Eudora Baines and they discussed what it might mean, a sense of calm settled over Lucie. She was there to do a job; everything else was a distraction.

*

By the end of the next week, Lucie was feeling much more like her old self as she tucked herself into a corner of one of the sofas in the family room where everyone had gathered after dinner to relax for an hour before bed. Arthur was present for a change, head bent over a notebook as he scribbled away. He'd thrown himself into his plans to open the castle to the public, spending hours closeted away with Tristan in his study. She hadn't seen him alone since their walk in the woods, and she was grateful he seemed as eager to avoid discussing the matter as she was. Best to let sleeping dogs lie, and all that.

The cataloguing of the rooms was proceeding apace. Arthur and Tristan had covered nearly all the ground floor, assuring her it was as useful for their own plans as it was for her work, because it gave them a chance to discuss which rooms they might want to open. Leaving them to it, Lucie herself had made short work of over half the rooms on the first floor. There was still the top floor to do, but from what Arthur and his brother could remember from exploring up there, quite a number were empty or used as general storage.

The family documents and castle records had now been sorted by type and date. Although she'd only been able to carry out a rudimentary review of the information, she was excited at the prospect of digging deeper into the backstory of the Ludworths. Whether she'd ever get the chance to do that was still very much up in the air, as Arthur had made no mention of extending her time at the castle beyond the original two months she was contracted to work there. Time was flying, and the end of the first of those two months was already looming just beyond the horizon.

Everywhere she looked there were signs the castle was gearing up towards Morgana's big party the following weekend. A marquee had appeared on the large back lawn behind the orangery, thanks to a contact of Tristan's who provided it for free in return for an invitation to bring his wife and kids to stay for the weekend, and it was all hands to the pump in the kitchen. Morgana had treated the arrival of the enormous white tent with a disdainful glare but had otherwise held her own counsel about the plans for her birthday celebrations.

Lucie's mum had been delighted to receive an invitation to stay and would be arriving on Tuesday's train. Being away from her for the past month had been the longest they'd spent apart since Lucie had been at boarding school, and she was very much looking forward to spending a bit of time with her. She'd still heard nothing further from anyone at Witherby's, though her monthly salary had been paid in as normal. Knowing she was being a coward about it, Lucie had decided not to chase for an update into the investigation. Deep down, she knew it was only a temporary relief, but she was determined to make the most of it. The inroads she was making into her current project were starting to repair the dents in her confidence.

Turning her attention back to the journal held in her lap, Lucie browsed through a few more pages, but it wasn't long before the words were swimming before her eyes. Although the weather had remained fine, there was still a distinct chill in the air in the evenings and the heat from the logs crackling in the fireplace was making her drowsy.

She wasn't the only one struggling to keep her eyes open from the duet of snores coming from the opposite sofa where Tristan lay with his feet dangling over one arm, his terrier, Pippin, snoozing on his chest. Nimrod and Bella had curled on the hearthrug, noses resting on each other's flanks.

As though sensing her eyes upon him, Tristan sat abruptly, scrubbing his face. 'God, I'm getting old before my time, with these after-dinner naps.' Rubbing his hands together, he looked expectantly around the room. 'Right, who fancies a nightcap?'

'Nothing for me,' Arthur replied. 'How about you, Lucie?'

Almost jumping in surprise as Arthur very rarely addressed her directly these days, she shook her head. 'I'm okay, thanks.'

'More for me then,' Tristan said, making his way over to the glass-fronted drinks cabinet.

He'd just poured a measure of brandy when the door swung open and Lancelot entered, chafing his hands together. 'Oh, good call, my boy! It's brass monkeys out there.'

Tristan handed his uncle the glass and tipped a similar amount into a second before joining him on the sofa. 'How's the foal?'

Lancelot took a sip of his brandy and slumped back into the deep padding of the sofa with a satisfied sigh. 'He's grand, and the mare too, thank goodness. I've just seen the vet off and Iggy's volunteered to keep an eye on things for an hour or so.'

Arthur shoved his notebook aside and rose. 'We got Betsy to put you something by, shall I fetch you a tray?'

'That'd be smashing, thanks.' Behind the twinkling delight at seeing a new life safely into the world, deep lines of fatigue lined Lancelot's face. 'And then I'll have a hot shower and I'll be right as rain.'

'You're not planning to sit up all night with them, are you?' Tristan frowned. 'Because if you are, you can forget about it.' Draining his glass, he rose. 'I'll turn in now and grab a couple of hours and then I can relieve you around midnight.'

'There's no need for that, my boy,' Lancelot protested, but

Tristan was having none of it and after a brief back and forth he left the room, chin set in a determined line. Shaking his head, Lancelot stared after his retreating back. 'Always trying to look out for everyone else, that one.'

It hadn't occurred to Lucie until he said it, but it was true. Behind his flashy smiles and teasing, Tristan hid a huge heart. Arthur had told her how his brother had put his career on hold to come home when their father fell ill, and stayed on to help Arthur when it became clear how tough things were going to be over the coming months. How hard must it have been to just up and walk away from the life he'd been building for himself, and for no reward other than helping Arthur? There'd be no title in it for Tristan. If they managed to save things, he'd still be the younger son.

And then there was the way he'd thrown himself into helping with Lucie's survey. Every day since Arthur had roped him in, he'd taken himself off with his phone and tablet to spend the morning photographing and recording without so much as a murmur of complaint. He had a bloody good eye, although he'd laughed off her attempts to compliment him on it. Only yesterday, he'd discovered a very fine eighteenth-century mahogany card table half-hidden beneath a lace cloth in one of the drawing rooms and brought it to Lucie's attention when they'd been reviewing his photos over lunch.

She'd need to get a second opinion and hunt through the castle's purchase ledgers to trace the provenance, but it made her pulse race in the right way. If the table could be attributed to a master craftsman from the period, it could realise in excess of twenty thousand pounds. A drop in the ocean of what the family needed, but she had at least a dozen other items on her list with the potential to bring as much, if not more into the coffers. Not that she'd told Arthur any of this yet.

It was stupid, really, given the items she'd valued and handled every day at Witherby's, but it was too important. If she screwed this up, she'd never get another chance again. So, for now at least, she was keeping her cards close to her chest and refusing to be drawn beyond saying they warranted a closer evaluation.

Lancelot leaned forward to pat her knee. 'You're brooding, my dear. Anything an old codger can do to help?'

She couldn't help but chuckle. 'Come on, now. You know you're a silver fox, stop fishing for compliments.'

Throwing back his head, he roared with laughter. 'Damn, you're good for an old man's ego. If you were only twenty years older, I'd sweep you off your feet.'

'Behave yourself!' Arthur exclaimed as he re-entered the room bearing a tray laden with covered plates. 'I can't turn my back for a minute.' Having placed the tray down on a side table his uncle hastily dragged over, he sank down on the sofa next to Lucie close enough their shoulders were almost touching. 'Besides, the only Ludworth she's interested in is Thomas.'

'Ah, yes, good old King Arthur himself,' Lancelot said with a wry smile as he laid his napkin over one knee and removed the cover from a steaming plate of food. 'Damn, this smells good. Perhaps I should run off with Betsy instead.' As the cook had been happily married to her childhood sweetheart for the past thirty years, that seemed highly unlikely.

Arthur wagged a finger at him. 'No poaching any of my staff.'

'Ah, you know me, my boy, too much of a rolling stone to ever settle down.' There was something about the way he said it that struck Lucie deeply, but she made sure to smile when Lancelot caught her eye and winked. He forked up a mouthful of dinner, then paused with it close to his lips. 'So tell me what our Thomas has been up to.'

Flicking back through the journal to find her place, Lucie let her eyes roam over the page. 'Did you know he had an interest in art? He seems to have spent more time at university roaming around galleries than carousing in bars.'

Lancelot glanced over at Arthur. 'Are we sure he's one of us?'

His nephew chuckled. 'I definitely fell into the carousing category.'

Feeling more than a little out of place over her studious tendencies, Lucie joked, 'Not all of us drank our way through our courses. Some of us actually applied ourselves.'

An awkward silence fell, and she wished she'd just kept her mouth shut. She hadn't meant to sound critical, she had nothing but admiration for Arthur's work ethic, something he seemed to share with the whole family. It was his fault for sitting to close to her, unsettling her once again just when she'd convinced herself she was over her silly attraction to him. Shifting in her seat, she tried to make more room between them, but the opposite happened, the cushion beneath her softening until she was all but rested up against Arthur's hip. She froze, not daring to move any more in case it made things worse.

Appearing not to notice, Arthur turned his attention to his uncle. 'If you need me to pull a shift in the stables tonight, you only have to say.'

Lancelot looked up. 'No, no, it's fine. I don't think I really need to be there, I just like to keep an eye on things, you know? Tristan won't be persuaded otherwise, but I won't keep the rest of you up half the night.' Meal finished, he pushed the little table to one side. 'Time for a hot shower. I'll see you two anon.'

'You'll call if you need me, though?' When he received a nod of confirmation as Lancelot left the room, Arthur settled back into the sofa and retrieved his notebook. 'Well, if no one's going to rescue me, I'd better get back to this.' His aggrieved sigh was so loud it caused Nimrod to stir. The greyhound raised his head from the fireside rug to check his master was okay before settling back down.

Curling her feet up beside her to create a barrier of sorts between them, Lucie leaned as far into the arm of the sofa as she could and turned her attention back to Thomas's journal. Having finished at university, he'd moved down to London and seemed hellbent on expanding his mind in as many different directions as possible. She skimmed over several pages where he listed his extensive thoughts on lectures he'd attended on everything from art, to politics, and even to new developments in dentistry. Which was all very interesting, but wasn't getting Lucie anywhere.

A huge yawn caught her off guard, and she smothered it with one hand, the journal slipping from the arm in the process. She grabbed for it, missed and almost toppled over the side of the sofa as she leant forward to grab it. Only Arthur's hand grasping her hip kept her from falling. The journal lay face up, and it was a natural reaction to scan the words as she reached for it. A name caught her eye. 'Oh, my goodness!' Excitement welling, she continued to read, getting lost in Thomas's encounter with a woman on a visit to the newly founded National Portrait Gallery. As she hurriedly turned the page, Arthur squeezed her hip and she realised she was still hanging half-on, half-off the sofa.

Struggling back upright, she waved the journal under his nose. 'He met her! He met Eudora!'

'What? Where?' Notebook forgotten, Arthur huddled close. Squinting at the cramped writing, he was quiet for a few moments before shaking his head. 'I don't know how you can make heads or tails of this.'

'It takes a bit of getting used to.' Lucie pointed to the first mention. 'Look, here it says, "*I had a most fortunate meeting when attending the new National Portrait Gallery with Bertie this morning. As I turned away from the Chandos portrait, I almost collided with the fairest young woman it's ever been my pleasure to lay eyes upon. I swear my heart leapt in recognition of a kindred spirit.*"' Lucie glanced up. 'Thomas is a romantic.'

Arthur rolled his eyes. 'Yeah, yeah, he's amazing.' He nudged her shoulder. 'Go on, what else does he say.'

Lucie found her place once more. '"*Fortune smiled twice, for not only did I see this rare beauty, I was able to gain an introduction as it turned out Bertie is acquainted with her through some cousinly connection. We talked pleasantly for a few minutes, though I fear the pleasantness was all upon her part as my tongue tripped over itself more than once. She did not seem to mind my clumsiness, indeed, she listened most carefully to my thoughts on the Chandos portrait, and was free with her own in a way I found most refreshing. I have already imposed upon Bertie to invite me to their next family gathering, for I must see Eudora again."'*

She closed the journal with a happy sigh. 'Our Thomas is smitten.'

'Certainly sounds like it.' Arthur spoke from so close, his breath stirred a curl of hair on her cheek. His arm was still somehow around her from when he'd helped her back to sitting, unnoticed until now in her excitement. It felt good around her, too good, but she was tired of fighting feelings she longed only to surrender to. Breathless, Lucie lifted her eyes to find him staring down at her, that intense look burning in his hazel gaze. 'I wasn't expecting a love affair, although this has all the hallmarks of one,' she found herself whispering to him, not sure if she was referring to Thomas's situation or their own.'

She wasn't sure if he bent to her, or if she stretched up to him, but as their lips met and her eyelashes fluttered closed at the sheer rightness of it, Arthur murmured across her mouth, 'Yes, it certainly does.'

# CHAPTER FIFTEEN

The next evening, Arthur had some accounts to catch up on, so Lucie joined him in his study after dinner. Running his pen down the column of numbers, he tried to focus on the painful number of outgoings and not on the woman who'd taken over his favourite wing-backed chair by the window. She'd eschewed closing the thick velvet curtains in favour of letting the pale silvery light from the full moon spill in through the pitch-black glass, choosing instead to cover her lap with a thick tartan blanket she'd retrieved from her bedroom. A mug of tea and a plate of shortbread Betsy had sent with it—on account of Miss Lucie skipping dessert according to Maxwell when he'd brought their drinks in—rested on the small, round table at her elbow. In just a few short minutes, she'd made his favourite spot into her own space, and he liked how much she looked at home there.

His head was still spinning from the spectacular kiss they'd shared on the sofa, not to mention the half a dozen he'd stolen from her throughout the day. Although he had some misgivings about the disparity of their situations, he was done fighting his attraction to her. They'd decided to take things slowly, keep whatever this thing between them was on the quiet, until they'd decided whether it was even something worth talking about. Sneaking around didn't sit comfortably with him, but there was a certain frisson to be had from dragging her into dark corners whenever everyone else had their back turned.

Bored with the accounts, he tapped his pen on the blotter in front of him, hoping the noise would be enough to distract her, also. She'd barely spared him a glance in the past half hour, all her attention on the book in her hands. It was ridiculous to be jealous of a dead man, but if Arthur never heard the words 'poor Thomas' from Lucie's lips again, it would be too soon. She'd become obsessed with the man, and his journals, never lifting her nose out of them all day other than to share a brief update on his doomed relationship with Eudora, or to sigh those two bloody words.

'Oh, poor Thomas.' Right. On. Cue.

Ignoring the need to grind his teeth, Arthur laid down his pen and fixed a smile. 'Now what's happened?'

When Lucie raised her head, he was shocked to see tears glistening on the tips of her lashes. 'He's just received a letter telling him his father died, so he's having to drop everything and return to the castle.'

'He had to know it was coming, sooner or later. That's the joy of being the heir.' He hadn't meant to sound quite so bitter about it, but he'd been fighting a growing sense of dread as Lucie had recounted Thomas's efforts to make a name for himself in the artistic community in London. The trouble with having his family history drummed into him as a boy was that Arthur had known the death of the eighth baronet was looming, making the recounting of Thomas's excitement over making friends with members of the Pre-Raphaelite Brotherhood and even securing his first exhibition all the more painful.

Journal abandoned on the table next to the armchair she'd been curled up in, Lucie crossed the floor of Arthur's study in a flash. 'I'm sorry, I didn't think about what I was saying.' Brows drawn down, she touched a gentle finger to his cheek. 'It was crass of me to just blurt it out like that.'

Arthur swivelled his chair enough to make room and tugged her down onto his lap, arms curling around her. His lips found the cool silk of her hair as he drew in the clean scent of her citrus shampoo. 'You didn't upset me. I'm more frustrated with Thomas for pursuing a career which couldn't possibly come to anything. He should've been here with his father learning about how to run the estate not messing around in London with his arty friends.'

'But his art meant everything to him. It leaps off the page, Arthur. When you're driven by something like that it's more than a job, it's a way of life.'

'I suppose so.' God, he sounded like a sulky brat. Settling Lucie more comfortably across his legs, he smoothed her fringe away from her forehead and pressed a kiss to it. 'Ignore me. I'm just feeling really out of sorts.'

'Do you want to talk about it?'

He didn't, because then he'd have to face up to something he'd been avoiding for months. 'Maxwell politely suggested it was time for me to move into the baronet's apartment.' When she raised an eyebrow, he shook his head. 'Not a secret flat I haven't told you about, he's referring to the suite of rooms on the first floor of the west wing.'

Lucie found his hand and squeezed it tight. 'And you don't want to move in there because it was your father's room? I can understand that.'

'That's part of it.' He wasn't sure how to explain the rest without sounding ridiculous. 'It's not a happy place, Lucie. Every time I walk into that room, I can't help but think about all the unhappy memories. People joke about this family being cursed, but it's not entirely without merit. There's too many early deaths, too many unhappy marriages and they all took place in that part of the castle.' Tightening his arms around her, he confessed his final and greatest fear. 'I'm scared that if I move in there something terrible will happen.'

'Arthur…'

164

'I know, it's stupid of me,' he muttered against the top of her head. 'But I can't help it.'

Her lips brushed the underside of his jaw. 'I wasn't going to say that. I was going to say that you're the baronet now so you can create your own traditions. If you're happy where you are, then stay there.'

'With Tristan's room on one side, and Iggy's on the other? It's not exactly private.' When she raised her eyes to meet his, a prickling warmth rose up the back of his neck. 'I don't want them knowing my business.' He cleared his throat, not sure how to phrase it without sounding like a letch. '*Our* business.'

'Oh.' Lucie dropped her head to rest back on his shoulder, her hair falling forward to partially shield her face.

When she didn't say anything for a long time, Arthur cursed himself for bumbling into the topic. It sounded calculated, like he'd been making plans without her, like he was taking advantage of her sympathy to push his luck. 'I'm not trying to rush things...'

'I didn't think you were, I mean you haven't been. You've been a perfect gentleman.' Cheeks glowing, she peeped up at him through her fringe. 'I wouldn't mind if you wanted to be a little less gentlemanly.'

Though her words were hesitant, there was no mistaking the heat in her gaze and it burned through him like a living flame, setting every nerve ending alight. Shifting in his chair to try and conceal his body's instant reaction, he lowered his head until their lips were no more than a breath apart. 'Miss Kennington, are you trying to seduce me?'

Hands curling up to thread through his hair, Lucie coaxed him forward with the softest of pressure. 'Why, Sir Arthur, I do believe I am.'

Her lips tasted of buttery sugar from the shortbread and an indefinable sweetness that was all Lucie. She yielded at the first touch of his tongue and he let himself forget everything in the welcoming warmth of her embrace. He pressed closer, grumbled

165

in frustration at the awkward angle of her side pressing into his chest, wanting as much of their bodies in contact as possible.

Breaking their kiss, he half-lifted her so she could twist around and straddle him. The high-backed leather chair rocked, and he planted one foot firmly on the floor to keep it steady as his mouth sought hers once more. Better, this was so much better, he thought as he pressed his hips up into the heated bliss of her parted thighs.

Lucie made a delicate sound in the back of her throat, an almost whine of need as she locked her arms around his neck and melded their lips together once more. There was no hint of her earlier shyness, just a whole lot of warm, willing woman. Arthur slid one hand up the length of her spine, taking a handful of the soft cotton of her jumper with it. The other he placed flat on the warm skin of her back, his fingers dipping just inside the waistband of her jeans to urge her closer still.

Releasing her hold on him, she wriggled and jiggled on his lap, making the chair rock and his brains scramble as she wrestled first one arm and then the other from the sleeves of her top. He let their mouths part only for the time it took for her to drag the jumper over her head before diving back in to the sweet, addictive taste of her. As her fingers moved to the buttons of his shirt, it vaguely registered they should move somewhere more practical—and more comfortable—but then she had the material parted and as her fingers fluttered down the side of his ribcage he forgot how to breathe, never mind think.

He let his head fall back against the wide headrest, sucking air into his lungs as she leaned back to give her hands room to roam across his chest. A pale pink bra edged in delicately scalloped lace framed her small breasts to perfection.

God, she was beautiful.

Half-naked as she was, the delicacy of her frame stood in stark relief to the muscular bulk of his body. Feeling big and clumsy in comparison, he raised a shaking finger to trace the outline of the lace, aware of the privilege she was granting him, and determined to show her how much he appreciated the trust she was placing in him. Regardless of the need raging through him like a storm, he would treat her with all the care and tenderness she deserved.

He'd just leaned forward to press a kiss to the hollow at the base of her throat when a knock on the door was followed by the sound of his sister's voice. 'Arthur? Lucie? I'm going for a hack around the grounds tomorrow and wondered if Lucie wants to join me.'

Hands on Lucie's hips, Arthur froze with his eyes trained on the doorknob. When it didn't move, he squeezed his hands. 'Answer her,' he muttered.

'Oh! That…that sounds like a great idea, thanks, Iggy.' Lucie slumped against Arthur's shoulder for a second before lifting her flaming face. Their eyes met and he could feel her body shaking as she tried to contain her amusement.

'Great,' Iggy called through the still-closed door. 'I'll catch you at breakfast and we can go out straight after that if you'd like?'

With Lucie kneeling up the way she was, her breasts were in perfect alignment with his mouth. A dark freckle marked the creamy perfection of her skin right at the top of her cleavage, just begging for him to put his lips to it…

'Sounds good…eek!' Lucie's response ended with a squeak as his mouth made contact with her flesh. She squirmed and swatted the top of his head, but Arthur wasn't about to be distracted from his new favourite place.

'As long as you're sure?' Iggy sounded a bit concerned.

'Yes! Yes, very sure!' Lucie said, loudly. 'Looking forward to it.' She buried her face into the top of Arthur's hair. 'Why won't she just leave?' she muttered, breath hitching in a giggle as his hands found a ticklish spot just beneath her ribs.

'Fab!' Iggy replied, in no apparent hurry to end the conversation and for a moment Arthur wondered if she knew exactly what they were up to on their side of the door. 'I thought we could go out first thing and brainstorm a few last-minute ideas for Morgana's party.'

'Sounds good to me-ee!' Lucie's voice climbed an octave as Arthur teased the freckle with the very tip of his tongue. She grabbed a handful of his hair this time, giving it a none-too-gentle tug until he sat back, grinning unrepentantly. 'Beast,' she muttered to him.

'Well, I'll leave you two to it. See you for breakfast at eight-thirty?' Iggy asked.

'Night, Iggy.' Arthur cut in, hoping she'd take the bloody hint and leave them in peace.

'Night!' Her footsteps faded on the wooden floor. *Finally*.

Lucie strained against his hold, sending the swivel chair rocking once more. 'Oh God, what it she'd walked in, she would've seen everything! And what did you think you were doing?' Her accusing eyes met his.

'There was this freckle.' He stroked the curve of her breast with his palm. 'I'm only human, Lucie.'

She arched into his touch for a moment, before wriggling free of his hold and clambering off his lap. 'Beast,' she said again, but her eyes were full of amusement.

He spread his palms in a 'what's a man to do' gesture as she reached for her sweater. When she started to slide her arms into the sleeves, he made a grab for it, but she stepped back out of reach. 'Come back here, things were just getting interesting,' he protested.

Shaking her head, she popped it up through the neck of her top. She tugged the soft fabric down, and he couldn't resist a little pout as she spoiled his beautiful view of her body. 'I'm going to bed, and I'm taking a lesson from that near miss with your sister and locking the door behind me.'

There was no stopping the pang of disappointment as he watched her gather up Thomas's journal and tuck her feet inside the shoes she'd slipped off earlier before curling up in the armchair. Well, damn. It looked like Iggy's ill-timed interruption had broken the mood.

Knowing there'd be no way he'd get to sleep with his head still buzzing with the sensation holding Lucie in his arms, Arthur spun the chair back to face his desk, resigned to a couple more hours of wrestling with the accounts.

'Arthur?' When he glanced up, Lucie was holding out a hand to him, her smile bright with invitation. 'I was rather hoping you'd be on the same side as me when I locked my door.'

The chair was still spinning as they left his study together.

\*

Arthur woke the next morning while it was still dark outside. Still a little disorientated, he wasn't sure what had disturbed him, only that something didn't feel quite right. Mouth dry, he reached for the glass of water he kept habitually beside his bed. Instead of encountering the cool surface of his glass, his fingers brushed against warm skin and he knew what was out of place. *He was.* Not only was he on the wrong side of the bed, he was in the wrong bed. He closed his fingers over Lucie's shoulder. No, definitely not the wrong bed.

She stirred beside him, turning over to snuggle against his side with a contented sigh. Deep contentment filled him. When was the last time he'd slept so well? Not since his father had died, that was for sure. As he eased back onto his pillow, he glanced at the illuminated dial on his watch, and wished he hadn't. It was just before six, and the household would soon be stirring. Though he had no regrets about spending the night with her, he needed to get back to his room.

Being caught doing the walk of shame by one of the staff was not how he wanted to start his day. What he and Lucie had shared last night was special, deeply personal and not the fodder for downstairs gossip. After pressing a kiss to Lucie's cheek, he began to slide slowly out of bed, being careful not to disturb her. As he groped around on the floor beside the bed for his clothes, the soft tap of claws alerted him that he wasn't the only one awake and he paused in the act of tugging on his T-shirt to stroke Nimrod's head. The two greyhounds had followed them up the stairs, and they'd decided to let them in rather than leaving the pair whining on the landing and potentially drawing suspicion.

'Shh, boy, let Lucie sleep.' The dog licked his hand then padded back to the blanket where Bella had remained curled up. 'Lucky thing,' Arthur muttered as he shoved one leg into his jeans.

Once dressed, apart from his shoes which dangled from one hand, he hesitated beside the bed. It didn't seem right to sneak out without saying anything, but he didn't want to wake Lucie when she was sleeping so peacefully. Deciding to let her rest, he crept from the room and closed the door behind him. The corridor outside was empty as Lucie was currently the only occupant of this section of the first floor which was traditionally reserved for guests. The family rooms, including his own, occupied the east wing and not for the first time Arthur wondered at the past tradition by which the baronet's rooms were isolated in the west wing.

Retrieving his phone from his pocket, Arthur tapped out a text to Lucie, wanting her to understand he hadn't crept out for any other reason than to protect her privacy, then continued to make his way to his room. He got as far as the balcony area which overlooked the great hall before his luck ran out. Carrying a tray laden with the makings of breakfast for one, Maxwell was just reaching the top of the staircase.

Not by so much as a shift of his eyebrow did the butler show any hint of surprise at finding the master of the house creeping around barefoot with his shoes in one hand. 'Good morning, Sir Arthur.'

There was nothing to do but brazen it out. 'Good morning, Maxwell. You're up and about early.'

'I'm bringing Miss Morgana her tray.'

As he did every morning at 6 a.m., Arthur recalled about five minutes too late to be useful. 'Yes of course. I woke a bit early, so thought I'd take the dogs out for a walk. Lots to do today.'

'Very good, Sir Arthur.' The butler inclined his head before turning left towards the family quarters which was most definitely not the direction Arthur had just come from.

So much for protecting Lucie's privacy. With no other option, he headed down stairs pausing at the bottom to put on his shoes. With a whistle to the dogs, he grabbed his coat from the cloak-room and trudged out into the still-dark morning. A fine misty drizzle began to settle on his head the moment he cleared the front door. Stuffing his hands deep in his pockets, he set off across the gravel knowing if it weren't for his foolish attempt to do the right thing, he could still be snuggled up in bed with the woman he was coming to adore.

# CHAPTER SIXTEEN

Dressed in her most comfortable leggings and a denim shirt over a long-sleeved pink T-shirt, Lucie flexed her ankle against the restriction of the knee-length riding boots Iggy had lent her, trying to get used to the stiff leather. A couple more rotations of her foot and the boot settled more comfortably. A footstep echoed against the stone flags of the great hall and she turned, expecting to see Iggy, who'd run upstairs to fetch her gilet. Instead, Lucie found herself swept into the cloakroom by a pair of strong arms and before she knew it Arthur was crushing her against him as he planted a kiss firmly on her mouth.

'Good morning,' he said when they finally came up for air. 'I'm sorry I left you to wake up alone.'

Lucie slipped her arms around his waist, her mood improving 100 per cent. Though he'd sent her a very sweet text, when he hadn't appeared at breakfast a little bit of doubt had started gnawing at her. 'It's all right. I appreciated your discretion.'

'For all the good it did me. Maxwell caught me fair and square tiptoeing along the landing.'

She bit her lip, trying not to laugh at the image of the very proper butler catching Arthur in the act. 'Oh, dear.'

'Indeed.'

He snuggled her closer against him, his lips finding the spot where her shoulder met her neck sending heat flashing through her. 'Arthur.'

'Don't say my name like that, or I'll have to drag you back upstairs again,' he murmured against her ear.

'Well, behave yourself then,' she admonished, winding her arms around his neck in a way that told him she wanted him to do anything but behave.

They were still kissing when the sound of boots clattering across the stone floor of the hall was followed by Iggy's voice talking affection nonsense to the dogs. 'Oh, hell.' Lucie tried to wriggle free, but Arthur wouldn't let her go until he'd planted another kiss on her mouth. Grabbing the nearest gilet she could lay her hands on, Lucie all but stumbled out of the boot room. 'Hi Iggy.'

Iggy stopped short, her gaze on the thick hank of hair which had fallen over Lucie's eye. 'Oh, there you are. Are you ready?'

'Yes, I think so.' Apart from the embarrassment she was sure was making her glow like a sunset at almost getting caught by Iggy twice in the past twenty-four hours. A low chuckle came from behind her in the boot room and Lucie quickly thumped her way across to the front door, hoping to cover the sound. 'Let me just sort this out, and I'm all set. She freed her plait from the band holding it together and quickly rewove it as Iggy continued to watch her. 'It gets very slippery when I've washed it,' she added lamely, though the mess had more to do with Arthur's busy fingers than the effects of her shampoo.

'How very annoying for you.'

The dogs, who'd all been crowding around Iggy, suddenly made a beeline for the boot room. In desperation that they'd unearth Arthur and blow their secret, Lucie grabbed the front door and yanked it open. 'Let's make a break for it before they try and come with us.' To her relief, Iggy allowed herself to be ushered out with nothing more than a quizzical glance at Lucie's no-doubt glowing face.

She slammed the door behind them with more force than necessary, although she doubted Arthur would get the message—he was probably too busy congratulating himself for stealing so many kisses, the beast—then hurried after Iggy who was already striding away. Sneaking around with Arthur was proving one thing to Lucie: she would never make a living as a secret agent.

It was only a short walk across the back lawn to the stables. The drizzle she'd noticed on waking had cleared up, leaving tiny shimmering droplets on the grass. As they passed the huge marquee, she paused to marvel at the glistening jewel of a spider's web draped like a diamond necklace between the edge of the marquee and one of the guy ropes holding it in place.

'They're putting the floor matting down today, and the furniture's arriving tomorrow,' Iggy said, 'so we should be able to start decorating inside on Thursday. Tristan's come up trumps with a disco and lights system. Another one of his many contacts from work.'

'I can't imagine your Aunt Morgana getting down on the dancefloor.' Although Lucie was warming to the older woman, she still found her a little bit intimidating.

Iggy laughed as they rounded the corner of a single-storey building built with the same grey stone as the castle. 'You'd be surprised. She wasn't always so severe. When we were little, she used to put on the old record player in her sitting room and teach us how to do the twist, the bump, all those funny Sixties dances.'

'Now that would be something to see. Perhaps we can persuade her to have a bit of dance with us on Saturday after all.'

'We should definitely give it a try. Those kinds of songs are always great at getting people on the floor.' Iggy unhooked one side of the heavy wooden stable door and Lucie gave her hand to swing it back against the wall, securing it in place with an iron hook and eye. 'Right then, let's get you kitted out and these boys saddled up.'

Within about ten minutes, Lucie found herself astride Lightning, a glossy black mare that, Iggy promised her, was the gentlest mount in their stables. 'We'll stick to walking until you tell me otherwise,' Iggy promised, as she turned a much livelier looking bay gelding in a tight circle before urging the horse out of the stable yard with a squeeze of her knees and a click of the tongue. Thankfully, Lightning seemed content to follow in the bay's wake without any real guidance from Lucie leaving her free to concentrate on trying to remember those riding lessons from so many years ago.

Iggy led them along the path Lucie and Arthur had taken to the woods then turned right as they grew close to the trees. She dropped her mount back to walk beside Lucie. 'How are you doing?'

'Okay, I think. She's very easygoing, isn't she?' Feeling confident and much more relaxed as muscle memory took over, Lucie took the reins in one hand and leaned forward a touch to pat Lightning on her thick, sturdy neck.

'She's a proper sweetheart,' Iggy agreed. 'If we follow the tree-line for about a mile, the land will open up and you'll get a good view across towards the dales.'

'Sounds good to me.' Lucie drew in a deep breath. 'I still can't get over how clean and fresh the air is here.'

'Wait until we're up to our knees in snow and the wind tries to knock you down every time you stick your nose out the door, then you'll know the meaning of fresh.' Iggy winked across at her. 'Some people think it's bleak up here in the winter, but I think there's a beauty in the land you don't find anywhere else. I can't imagine not living here.' She sounded so wistful, Lucie's heart went out to her.

'Well, hopefully you won't have to.'

'How's the search going, turned up any masterpieces yet?'

Lucie shook her head. 'Not so far, but there's a lot of very fine pieces here. I've got quite a list of items I want to get a second opinion on when I go back to London.'

Iggy reined in, and Lightning drew to an obedient halt also. 'You're going home?'

'Well, I'll have to at some point. I need to get some proper valuations done once the database is completed, and besides, the contract is only for a couple of months.'

'Yes, of course. Sometimes it feels like you've been with us for much longer, you fit in with everybody so well, it's almost like you're a part of the family.' With a touch of her heels, Iggy urged the bay forward into a quick trot.

Lightning would've followed had Lucie not tightened the reins, and she was doubly grateful she was such an obedient horse when Iggy kicked on again and the bay stretched his muscular flanks into a full-blooded gallop. Lucie patted Lightning once more. 'Leave them to show off, girl, we're quite all right as we are.' The mare nickered in agreement and they ambled along in Iggy's wake, Lucie's brain racing. Had there been something in the way Iggy had looked at her as she'd those words? Did she...*Could* she suspect there was something going on between her and Arthur? No! She was still feeling a bit guilty about nearly being caught earlier, that was all. Not that she and Arthur were doing anything wrong, but perhaps the others wouldn't think so if they found out about it. God, what a muddle. 'Forget Arthur for five minutes, and just enjoy the morning,' she muttered to herself before cautiously urging Lightning into a slightly quicker walk.

When they caught up with her, the gelding was blowing hard, and Iggy's dark curls had half escaped from the loose ponytail she'd dragged it into. 'Sorry about that.'

'We were fine, don't worry about it. If I had a bit more confidence, I might have joined you.'

'You'll get there soon enough. I can see already how much better your seat is. A few more sessions and you'll be charging across the country.'

Lucie couldn't see when she'd have the time to do that, but she didn't want to dampen Iggy's enthusiasm, or get them back to speculating on what her future might or might not be. 'You wanted to talk about the party?'

'Yes. I'm glad we've invited everyone up from the village. Arthur's idea to do a bit of test run before we try and open things up to the general public is a really good idea. I'm just a bit concerned the kids might get bored if we don't have a few things organised for them.'

She had a point, and at the end of the day, the party was supposed to be for Morgana, so keeping the children out from under foot so the adults could relax and celebrate with the guest of honour would be a good idea. 'What do you suggest? Some school sports day style games? A few races, egg and spoon, that kind of thing?'

Iggy nodded. 'I like that. And they wouldn't be hard to organise. There's an old maze that's part of the formal gardens, but it's still in such a state, I'm not sure it's safe enough to let them go wandering around in it.'

'Can we cordon it off, perhaps? A bit of rope should be enough to deter people, especially if there's more fun attractions on offer.'

'I'd like to keep people away from the formal gardens, generally. There's a couple of pools, and a fountain which needs repairing, and a few of the walkways are really overgrown.' Iggy slumped in her saddle. 'It breaks my heart to see them in such a state, they must've been magnificent once upon a time.'

Remembering her conversation with Arthur, Lucie reached out to touch Iggy's arm. 'I've found loads of old maps in the library archive. Once we've got this party out of the way, what say you and I trawl through them and see if we can find anything which might show the original layout.'

Iggy brightened immediately. 'That sounds great.'

'And even if there aren't any, I bet there are loads of designs from the same era online. We could find something that's at least in the spirit of the original, and it would give you something to work with.'

'You're just full of good ideas! I'm going to tell Arthur we have to keep you.'

Lucie laughed. 'I try. If we want to keep people away from the gardens, let's concentrate on keeping them all at the rear. We could open up the orangery for those who are interested in looking around it, set up the games at the bottom of the lawn so they can be supervised by parents from the comfort of the marquee and maybe do a guided walk in the woods. Arthur said the bluebells might be out by then.'

'With any luck, they should be. It's the first time we'll have let anyone other than a professional photographer down there so they should be the star attraction. The paths are straightforward enough to follow, and it wouldn't take much to put a couple of arrows up to point people in the right direction.' Iggy steered her horse in a slow circle and they began to amble back the way they'd come.

As they reached the edge of the woods once more, Lucie ducked over Lightning's neck to peer under the thick branches of the trees. They'd filled out a lot in the past few weeks and as she glanced through the undergrowth beneath the gnarled branches, she could make out a few patches of blue. 'Look!' She pointed, unable to keep the excitement out of her voice.

Iggy ducked down beside her. 'Wait until you get deeper in, the ground will be thick with them.'

'What if we did an Easter egg hunt? We could hide them along the edges of the path and around the stone circle.'

'I love it! It'd certainly give the kids something to do for a couple of hours, and we'd have time on Friday to come out here and set it all up. I have to run into town later to do some errands. There's a retail park on the outskirts that's got a supermarket and a few discount stores, so I'll see what I can pick up.' Iggy beamed at Lucie. 'See, I knew you'd be full of good ideas.' She leaned across and gave Lucie a quick hug.

'Don't forget my mum will be here later, and I'm sure she'll be more than happy to get stuck in with the arrangements, so we'll have an extra pair of hands.'

'Must be nice,' Iggy said, reminding Lucie that the triplets had never had their own mother around to rely on for anything.

'Do you miss her, your mum, I mean?'

'Hardly. You can't miss what you never had, right? Come on, let's get back.' Not quite a slap-down, but it was clear from Iggy's harsh tone the topic was not up for discussion.

They walked on for a few minutes, Lucie feeling worse with every stride of the big mare beneath her. Why hadn't she kept her mouth shut, instead of speaking without thinking and spoiling the happy mood between them? 'I'm sorry. I shouldn't have pried.'

Iggy glanced at her over her shoulder. 'What? Oh, don't worry about it. We're better off without her. Dad gave us everything he could, and what little gaps there were, Aunt Morgana and Lancelot did their very best to fill them. She tried a couple of times over the years, but to be honest it was a relief when she stopped. Some people just aren't capable of putting anyone other than themselves first, and Helena Ludworth-Mills-Wexford-Jones is one of them.'

Lucie goggled at the list of surnames. 'Wow, that's quite a mouthful.'

'That's Mother for you. All she kept of her husbands was their last names and her hand in their pockets.'

They entered the stable yard, the horses' hooves clopping loudly on the cobblestones. Iggy slid easily from the gelding's back before taking hold of Lightning's bit and leading her to the mounting block.

With a groan, Lucie swung her leg free from the stirrup and clambered down. Bending her stiff knees, she winced at the ache in her bottom. 'I'd forgotten how this feels.'

'I've got some muscle soak stuff in my bathroom. Remind me later and I'll get it for you. Make sure you have a hot bath before you go to bed or you'll be sorry in the morning.' Iggy began to lead the two horses back into the stables.

Hobbling down off the block, Lucie did a sort of crab-walk as she tried to catch up. 'I'm already sorry.' When Iggy raised an eyebrow, she laughed. 'My bum is sorry, I should've said. The rest of me is thrilled to bits. It's been wonderful.' And not just because she'd got the chance to be on horseback again. Spending time with Iggy was always easy. On a spur of the moment, she put her arms around Iggy's neck and gave her a quick hug. 'Thank you.'

'My pleasure.' From the way she beamed from ear-to-ear, it was clear Iggy meant it and Lucie was pleased she taken the step towards a closer friendship with her.

They took their time unsaddling the horses, brushing them down and making sure they had a drink. As Iggy did a quick check that the other horses were all happy, Lucie did a few stretches and lunges to keep her lower half from stiffening up. 'I'm sure Arthur will give you a massage later, if you ask him nicely.' Iggy gave her a knowing wink as she secured the last of the stall doors then slung her arm around Lucie's shoulders.

'A...Arthur?' Lucie felt her face flaming.

'Give it rest, Lucie,' Iggy scoffed. 'Anyone can tell you two have the hots for each other. I know he was in the boot room with you earlier.'

'We were going to try and keep things quiet,' Lucie confessed with a grimace. 'Although between you rumbling us and Maxwell catching him sneaking around on the landing this morning, the cat's well and truly out of the bag.'

'Oh, he didn't!' Far from looking upset, Iggy's eyes were dancing with delighted mischief. At least one member of Arthur's family didn't seem in the slightest bit bothered about anything going on between them.

'Apparently so.' Lucie started to giggle. 'Can you imagine it?'

'God!' Iggy was laughing so hard she could barely close the stable door. 'He must've been mortified.'

'Arthur? I think he'll get over it.'

'Not him, Maxwell! I can still remember when Mrs W caught

me sneaking in through the drawing room window. I must've been 17 or 18 and I'd snuck down the village for a most unsuitable liaison with one of the local lads. I'd left the window open a crack and drawn the curtains so no one would notice. Unfortunately, I didn't realise she was in there and scared the daylights out of her when I appeared from nowhere.'

Delighted and appalled in equal measures, Lucie clapped a hand to her mouth to smother her giggle. 'What did she say?'

'What *could* she say? Poor woman was clearing away some glasses after Dad and Lancelot had been making in roads into a bottle of port and nearly dropped them! Thank God they'd gone to bed, or I would've been grounded for a month.'

'They never found out?'

'Nope. She never said a word about it, and the next time I opened my bathroom cabinet there was a box of condoms on the shelf.' Iggy smiled. 'I'd forgotten about that part until just now. So, you see, there was no need to miss Mother, because I had plenty of people looking out for me.'

They were almost at the rear door when Lucie stopped short, a horrifying thought occurring to her. 'Now the staff know Arthur spent the night in my room, you've made me scared to open the cabinet in my bathroom!'

181

# CHAPTER SEVENTEEN

It was easy to spot Lucie's mother as she stepped down onto the platform, and not only because so few people were getting off at the tiny station. Though the russet hair had faded to a lighter auburn scattered through with silver, there was no mistaking the heart-shaped face. It was like looking into a mirror that showed the future, and if Mrs Kennington was any indication, Lucie would age well. 'Here, let me take that for you.' Arthur leaned into the train to lift down the small weekend case. 'You must be Constance. Lucie wanted to come and meet you in person, but she can barely hobble, poor thing.'

Constance Kennington's face crumpled in shock. 'Oh, no! Has she had an accident?'

Kicking himself, Arthur shook his head. 'No, she's fine. She and Iggy went out for a ride this morning and Lucie's a bit saddle-sore.' To say the least. He'd had to all but carry her down from her room earlier. He stuck out his hand. 'I'm Arthur, by the way.'

Constance Kennington took his hand in a cool grip. 'Lucie's told me a lot about you.'

Not everything, he was willing to bet. Though it hadn't surprised him in the least that Iggy had figured out there was something going on, he'd promised Lucie he'd play things cool until she'd had a chance to speak to her mother in private. It might've been easier to let things develop between them without an audience, so to speak, but he had a really good feeling about them. A *really* good feeling. 'All good, I hope. The car's just outside and it's a quick drive up the hill to the castle.'

He held the door open for her, before placing her case in the boot and letting himself into the driver's side. He'd started the engine and was just about to put the car in gear when Constance's cool fingers touched the back of his hand. 'I understand it's you I have to thank for my invitation, and I just wanted to say how much I appreciate your generosity.'

'It's honestly my pleasure. I know Lucie has been missing you.' Worried that sounded a little overfamiliar, he hurried to add, 'She's said as much, and I'm sure you've missed her too.' Hoping Constance hadn't noticed his blunder, he steered the car away from the kerb and started up the hill.

'I have, very much. It's been the two of us for such a long time, I haven't quite known what to do with myself.' Constance let out a soft gasp and twisted in her seat to face him. 'You won't tell her that, will you? It's past time she moved on in her life, the last thing I want is to hold her back because she's worried about me.'

Deciding he liked this small, neat woman who clearly wanted only the very best for her daughter, Arthur took one hand off the steering wheel to make a zipping motion across his mouth. 'Your secret is safe with me.'

They'd reached the top of the hill and the vast curtain wall loomed into view as he crested the rise and followed the single-track road running parallel to it. A hundred metres further and he was turning through the open gates, the gravel of the driveway crunching under the wheels.

Constance leaned forward to peer through the windscreen. 'Oh my goodness. I know Lucie said you live in a castle, but I hadn't realised…'

183

'It's a bit of a monstrosity, but you'll soon find your way around. Mrs W has sorted you out a room in the guest wing, so you'll be near Lucie.' It might put a cramp in his own plans for Lucie, but those could wait for a few days.

'I can't wait to see what it looks like inside, Lucie's sent me a few photos on WhatsApp, but they didn't do justice to the grandeur of the place. Do you really have a replica of the Winchester round table in the great hall?'

Arthur pulled up outside the front door with a nod. 'Yup. I take it Lucie's told you all about my great-great-whatever grandfather and his Arthurian obsession?'

'Oh, yes, and his connection with that Pre-Raphaelite painter, it's all very exciting. I think the idea for an exhibition sounds wonderful. People love that kind of thing, I'm sure they'll be flocking through the gates.' Constance unfastened her belt and Arthur had to be quick off the mark to make it around the car to help her out. 'Thank you.' The shy way she averted her gaze as she took her hand reminded him once more of her daughter.

Speaking of whom... 'Mum! You're here! I'm so sorry I wasn't there to meet you.' Lucie came staggering out the front door, knees akimbo like John Wayne in one of those old cowboy movies his grandfather had loved.

'Lucie, darling, oh come here!'

While the two women embraced on the steps, Arthur busied himself fetching Constance's bag from the boot, not wanting to intrude on their special moment. He followed the two of them into the great hall, smiling to himself as Lucie chattered a mile a minute, trying to cram in an explanation of everything she'd been doing over the past month into a single breath. Well, almost everything. She hadn't mentioned him yet, other than in passing when she was describing how he and Tristan had stepped in to speed up the survey process.

'Your room's right upstairs,' she was saying now as she limped across the hall. 'I can show you where it is, if you'd like? You probably want to freshen up a bit after being stuck on the train all afternoon.'

'Well, I wouldn't mind the chance to change my clothes, and clean my teeth,' Constance replied.

Lucie looked across at him. 'Will you bring Mum's bag up?'

'Yes, of course.'

Their progress was somewhat hampered by Lucie's stiff legs, although she proclaimed it was much easier going up than down. 'Iggy—that's what Igraine prefers to be called by the way, although I wish she wouldn't as her name is so beautiful—she's promised to lend me some kind of miracle bath soak so I'm sure I'll be as right as rain tomorrow,' she assured her mother. 'I thought I'd show you around for a bit in the morning, and then Morgana, has invited us to take afternoon tea with us.'

'That sounds lovely, darling, but you must let me help with the preparations for the party as well.'

'Oh, I've already told Iggy that you would want to be involved, don't worry. There's loads to do.' Lucie linked arms with her mum and leaned into her. They made such a sweet picture as Arthur followed them down the hall. Lucie seemed much younger, much more eager to please, although nothing about Constance struck him as being anything other than delighted just to be close to her daughter again.

'Right, this is you, Mum.' Lucie pushed open the door to a room a couple of doors down and on the opposite side of the corridor to her own. 'And that one's mine.' She pointed to the slightly open door of her own bedroom.

'This is beautiful.' Eyes bright, Constance turned in a slow circle as though trying to take in every detail of her suite. Taking in the shocked expression on her face, Arthur was reminded once again of how different his idea of normal was to almost everybody else. He placed her suitcase on the padded ottoman at the end of the bed, then did his own quick survey of the room. Mrs W would've made sure everything was ready, of course, but this was

Lucie's mother, and he wanted to make the best impression possible.

Although the evening was already drawing in, on any other day the west-facing windows would mean the sitting area beneath them would be a nice sun trap in the afternoon should Constance want a spot to rest in peace and quiet. He wasn't much of an interior designer, but the floral wallpaper gave the room a nice feminine touch, as did the vase of fresh flowers on the bedside cabinet.

Crossing the room, he pushed open the bathroom door and peeked in. Plenty of fresh towels and a whole shelf full of the kind of bottles and jars women seemed to need in abundance. Satisfied, he pulled the door to and turned to Constance. 'I hope you'll be very comfortable in here. Please make sure you let Mrs W know if you need anything at all.'

'I will, thank you. It's so beautiful, like a luxury hotel.' Constance's shoulders were beginning to droop, and Arthur could see the lines of strain not quite hidden by her make-up.

'Right, shall we leave you in peace, Mum? Dinner is usually at seven-thirty, so you've got plenty of time if you want to lie down for a bit.'

'I might do that, if you don't mind?' Constance gave them both a weary smile.

'Not in the least,' he assured her. 'We don't stand on formalities here, so just whatever is comfortable for dinner. Can I send you up a pot of tea?'

'That would be wonderful.'

'If you need anything, I'll be just across the hallway, Mum.'

Having closed the door behind them, Lucie glanced up at Arthur. 'You go and sort out that tea, and I'm going to hunt Iggy down and find that bath soak.' She hobbled towards her bedroom door. 'I'm going to need your help getting me in and out the bath tub.'

'I suppose you'll want me to scrub your back whilst I'm at it?'

186

'But of course.' Lucie paused on the threshold. 'Thank you for being discreet around Mum. I'll have a chat with her later, before we come down to dinner and explain about us.'

He cupped her cheek, using his thumb to soothe the lines of tension pulling at her eye. 'There's no rush. We can drop things until after her visit, if that would make you more comfortable?'

Reaching up, she covered his hand with hers. 'That's sweet of you, and I know we agreed to keep things under wraps, but that might make things awkward when there's no reason for them to be.' A line etched between her brows. 'Unless you've changed your mind?'

'Not in the slightest,' he assured her with a quick kiss on the tip of her nose. When they reached Lucie's room, Arthur pushed her gently towards the door. 'Go and get the water running, I'll get the bath stuff from Iggy and arrange your mum's tea.'

'Okay. Don't be long, I'm going to need you to take my jeans off.'

He waggled his eyebrows at her. 'Are you trying to seduce me, Miss Kennington?'

Her bright laughter filled the air. 'In your dreams, Sir Arthur. In your bloody dreams.'

# CHAPTER EIGHTEEN

Feeling a lot better after her bath—and the full body massage Arthur had insisted on giving her afterwards—Lucie tapped on her mother's bedroom door, waiting until she was summoned before pushing it open. Constance was sitting on a stool before the dressing table, a hand towel draped over the shoulders of her ivory cotton blouse as she added a few touches of make-up. 'How are you, Mum? Better for a rest?'

Smiling at her via her reflection, Constance nodded before turning her attention back to the eye pencil in her hand. 'How about you? You seem to be moving a bit easier than you were earlier.'

Lucie grinned as she eased down on the edge of the bed to watch her mum work. 'Iggy wasn't kidding about that muscle soak, it's miraculous. I feel almost as good as new.'

'You look well.' After returning the pencil to the small make-up bag on the dresser, Constance turned on the stool to face her. 'You look really well, darling, happier than I've seen you in ages.'

'I am.' Knitting her fingers together in her lap, Lucie glanced down at them for a moment before meeting her mother's gaze. 'Arthur and I...'

'Oh.' Constance was quiet for a moment. 'Are you sure that's wise?' When Lucie opened her mouth to protest, her mother held up a hand. 'That's not a criticism, but you must admit that your life is a bit all over the place at the moment. Starting a new relationship, especially when your time here is limited, seems a little hasty.'

Lucie bristled, but only for a moment before her shoulders slumped. 'You're right. I know you're right, but it just sort of happened. I really like him, Mum, and I think he likes me too.'

Crossing to sit beside her, Constance put an arm around her shoulders and pulled her close. 'I didn't mean to upset you, darling, I just don't want you to get hurt.'

'And do you think that's going to happen?' Lucie lifted her head to look up at her mum.

'Don't you? What happens when you have to come back to London? Are you planning on trying to make things work from a distance?'

Lucie blushed. 'We haven't even talked about it.' They hadn't talked about anything very much so caught up were they in this first flush of passion and attraction.

'You can't hide up here forever.' Constance's tone was infinitely gentle. 'Have you heard anything from Witherby's?' Feeling even more miserable, Lucie shook her head. 'Oh, darling, won't you at least tell me what happened?'

'They...they accused me of fraud.'

Constance reeled back as though she'd been slapped. 'You can't be serious?'

Trying not to cry, Lucie blurted out the whole sorry business about the fake Meileau and how she had no idea how it had been substituted for the original. 'They even brought up Dad,' she finished. 'That's the real reason I didn't want to say anything to you about it.'

Constance hugged her tight. 'You mustn't ever worry about that. What your father did had nothing to do with you, do you understand me?'

Lucie nodded against her shoulder, trying to swallow down the tears gathering in her throat.

Drawing back, her mum gazed down at her, concern tugging her eyes tight. 'And you've been carrying this with you for weeks, and didn't tell anyone? You poor thing, does Arthur know?'

'I didn't know how to tell him, and not only because of the non-disclosure agreement.' Lucie knotted her fingers once more. 'Do you remember that case in the papers recently, the big Masterson trial?'

Her mother nodded. 'It was hard to miss.'

She looked so sad, so fragile that Lucie forgot all about her own distress for a moment. This was exactly why she hadn't wanted to tell her about the mess at Witherby's. But she'd come this far, so might as well lay everything out on the table. 'The reason Arthur placed that ad in the paper, the reason why I'm here is because his father lost a fortune in the Masterson scam.'

'Oh, Lucie!' There wasn't any need to say anything more, her mother would understand better than most the terrible position she'd found herself in.

'I'll have to talk to Arthur.' *Somehow.* 'I'll do it after the party. It's so important that everything goes well, I can't afford to be a distraction to him right now.'

Constance didn't look convinced, but she nodded in agreement. 'All right.' Touching Lucie's cheek, she turned her to face her. 'I expect all this has stirred a lot of things up for you. If you need to talk to me...about anything, I'm always here. You must never worry about upsetting me, do you promise?'

'I promise.' Lucie bit her lip. 'I...I miss him. I know I shouldn't after all the awful things he did, but I really do.'

Pulling her close, Constance rocked her. 'There's nothing wrong with that, he was still your father. Oh, darling, why didn't you say something? I didn't want to push you to talk about him, and you seemed to be coping...but I've been protecting myself and my own feelings at the expense of yours. I'm so sorry.'

Dabbing at a tear on her cheek, Lucie leaned closer. 'It's okay, Mum. It's not your fault. I just…' She sighed. 'I just wish I knew why he'd done it.'

They drew apart, and Constance settled herself more comfortably on the edge of the bed before reaching for Lucie's hand. 'I've thought about nothing else for years, but I don't know that I have all the answers. The man I loved, well, I'm not sure he ever really existed. It was like your father created this idealised version of himself and would stop at nothing to maintain that façade. I never met any of his family. He told me he was an orphan, but there was a brother who turned up during the trial. I…I couldn't face him, couldn't face any of it because I should've known something was wrong, but I honestly never suspected a thing!'

It was another thing Lucie had burned to ask her but had never had the courage. She'd heard the whispers, though, and the not-so-whispered comments of their neighbours as they'd watched the sideshow of her father's arrest, the parade of policemen carting box after box of their belongings seized in evidence. 'He lied to you too.'

Her mum nodded. 'Constantly. From the day we first met, I think. That still doesn't excuse my naivety, but things were never great at home for me and when your father swept into my life and promised me everything would be better from then on, I just allowed myself to be carried along with it. I never wanted much—a place to feel safe, to love and be loved, and for a long time that's what I thought I had. All the other stuff, well he told me his business was booming and I had no reason to doubt it.'

The pain and regret etched on her face made her mother look older than Lucie had ever seen before. 'It wasn't your fault.'

Constance pursed her lips. 'Not true, darling, but thank you.' She straightened up, her grip on Lucie's hand tightening. 'Regardless of my own culpability, you are entirely innocent of anything. We were adults, we had choices, you didn't. I'm appalled anyone at Witherby's has tried to tar you with the same brush. You must fight this!'

She was right. 'I've been running away.'

'And no one can blame you for that, darling, but you can't put the world on hold forever.'

Not forever, but perhaps for just a little bit longer... 'Come on, let's wash our faces and go down to dinner, everyone will be wondering where we've got to.'

# CHAPTER NINETEEN

Given the state of her aches and pains, Arthur would've been happy to leave Lucie in peace that night and sleep in his own bed, but she was having none of it. She'd looked a little red-eyed when she and her mother had come down to dinner, but she'd waved off his concerns and assured him everything was fine—which had only proven to him there was something wrong. Fine was Lucie's catch-all for avoiding things. When they'd crawled into bed together, she'd turned into him and clung to his body like she feared he'd slip through her fingers.

He'd woken at one point to her tears wetting his chest, but she'd still been fast asleep, so he'd held her tight and kissed her forehead until she'd settled into a more peaceful slumber. When they'd woken, she'd acted as though she remembered nothing of it, and he hadn't wanted to push, some sixth sense telling him he might not like hearing what she had to say. It was early days, he'd assured himself, it would take time for them to develop a deeper trust between them. When she was ready, she'd share whatever secrets put those shadows beneath her eyes.

Even had he wanted to push her to confide in him, there was scant opportunity to do so. Other than at mealtimes, he didn't see much of her as they were both busy with various preparations for Morgana's party. Arthur also wanted to give Lucie as much quality time with her mum as possible. Whenever he saw the pair of them, they had their heads together, expressions serious and he didn't want to intrude.

*

It was the following Friday afternoon when Lucie came barging into his study, waving one of Thomas's journals. 'Oh my God, Arthur, you won't believe it!' Excitement shone from every pore as she rounded his desk, plopped herself down on his lap and threw her arms around his neck.

'Won't believe what?' he asked after a very welcome, and very enthusiastic kiss.

'You know how I told you last night that some of the Pre-Raphaelite Brotherhood came up to the castle to visit Thomas and Eudora?'

He nodded. From what Lucie had been able to piece together from the journals, it was apparent his ancestor and Eudora had thrown convention to the wind and had been openly cohabiting together since Thomas had been forced to return to the castle after his father's death.

'Well, Thomas has asked Eudora to marry him, and he's talking about commissioning JJ Viggliorento to paint a portrait of the two of them to commemorate it!'

'And you think this is when things are going to go wrong for Thomas and Eudora?' They'd both known it was coming. Lucie had told him that it was on record that JJ and Eudora married in 1859 less than two years after Thomas inherited the baronetcy.

'Well, yes, but sad as that is, that's not really the point.' Lucie grabbed his face in her hands. 'Don't you understand what this means? If such a painting were to exist, it could be worth a lot of money.'

Okay, now he was excited. 'Does it say anything else about it?'

She leaned back, looking sheepish. 'I don't know, as soon as I read that bit, I had to come and tell you.' Her eyes widened in horror. 'Oh, God! What if JJ and Eudora run off together before the painting gets done?' She scrambled off his lap and snatched up the journal she'd abandoned on his desk. 'I need to find out.'

He pointed towards the armchair by the window, trying not to let his excitement get the better of him. 'Get reading.'

*

After the fourth time he'd interrupted Lucie for an update, she'd banished him from the study which was how he'd come to find himself out in the woods with his brother and sister hiding the gaily painted wooden eggs Iggy had found to use for the Easter hunt. The wooden eggs would be exchanged for chocolate treats when the children returned to the marquee. They'd made it clear to people they were welcome to bring their dogs with them, and with the castle's pack roaming around too, they didn't want to risk leaving chocolate eggs out. It also reduced the chances of rubbish spoiling the woods as any missed wooden eggs wouldn't cause any harm and would likely turn up later in the year once the grass died back.

The bluebells were out in all their glory, transforming the clearing where the stone circle sat into a sea of purply-blue. Placing the last egg he'd been given into a hollow created by the roots of an ancient oak, Arthur knuckled the small of his back as he straightened up. 'That's my last one,' he called across to Iggy who was hanging a bright-yellow cardboard arrow from the branches of a tree on the other side of the clearing. 'Those signs are great.'

When he reached Iggy's side, she was studying the arrow with a critical tilt of her head. 'Do you think they'll work?'

'Absolutely, they'll certainly do for this weekend and I'll get some proper ones made up before we open in the summer. The fluorescent colours you've chosen really stand out, so they'll be easy to spot. And we'll be around to make sure people find their way back okay.' He and Tristan had also taken the precaution of tying off any pathways which led in the wrong direction. 'As long as people stick close to the paths, there'll be no problems.'

Iggy hooked her arm around his waist and they strolled back towards the castle, meeting Tristan on the way who'd been in charge of hiding eggs along the main path. 'You done?'

Tristan nodded. 'I reckon so.' He moved to Iggy's other side and took her free hand. 'I can't remember the last time we did something like this, just the three of us.'

'Not since New Year's Eve,' Iggy said in a soft voice.

'Dad would've loved this, wouldn't he?' Arthur swallowed down the lump in his throat. 'Okay, none of that. No one is allowed to be sad.'

'Yes, Sir Arthur. Whatever you say, Sir Arthur.' Tristan put on a broad accent as he tugged his forelock with his free hand.

Arthur aimed a kick at his brother, almost taking the three of them down in the process. 'Stop it, children!' Iggy warned in a mock-stern voice. When they'd settled down and were walking arm in arm once more, she hugged Arthur's elbow with her own. 'Tell us about this great discovery of Lucie's then.'

'We're not sure if it will come to anything yet.' The warning was for himself as much as the others. He'd made the mistake of Googling JJ Viggliorento on his phone and some of the prices his paintings had sold for were mind-blowing. Even some of his preparatory sketches had gone for a hundred grand. With that kind of money, he really would be able to make a go of things.

'But there's a possibility of a painting by this JJ chap?' Tristan asked.

Arthur shrugged. 'Who knows? But at the end of the day, if there is one why hasn't anyone heard of it? The guy's one of the most sought after of the Pre-Raphaelites. There's proper catalogues of all his works and no mention of Thomas anywhere.'

'And surely if it existed, we'd know about it?' He couldn't fault Iggy's logic.

'That's why I'm worried it's just a wild goose chase.' Arthur admitted.

'But if it's not…' Tristan said.

'I know, but we can't let ourselves think about it, not until Lucie's had the chance to do some more research.' No, he wouldn't let himself think about it, but he could hope. God, he could hope…

# CHAPTER TWENTY

With the Easter egg hunt in full swing, the woods around her were bright with the sounds of laughter and excited cries of triumph. Lucie had taken up post about halfway along the path to steer people in the right direction, and to help out any children who'd so far been unlucky in finding an egg for themselves. She watched with a smile as a little girl stomped her foot in frustration while her harassed-looking father tried to placate her. 'Don't worry, Emily, I'm sure we'll find one soon.'

Lower lip wobbling, the little girl shook her head. 'But we've looked *everywhere*!'

Not wanting any tears, Lucie hurried over towards them. She'd had a good scout around earlier so knew where some of the eggs were hiding. 'Look, Emily, what's that over there?' Lucie crouched down beside the little girl and pointed towards a flash of red poking out of the long grass.

The little girl dashed towards her prize, holding the painted egg aloft in both hands. 'I got one, Daddy!'

'Yes, you did. Well done!' Emily's father cast a grateful smile towards Lucie. 'Thanks, you're a lifesaver.'

'You're welcome. We want to make sure everyone gets a prize. There'll be some games up by the marquee in a little bit, and anyone that enters receives something.'

Bending down to gather his daughter up, the man smiled wider. 'We're having a wonderful day, aren't we, sweetheart?'

Emily nodded before suddenly being overcome with an attack of shyness and hiding her face in her father's shoulder.

'We're so pleased everyone's come to help us celebrate. If you follow the path it'll lead you to the circle where I'm sure there are more eggs to find. You'll see the arrows signposting the way back.'

'Thanks again for your help. Say bye-bye, Emily.'

The little girl peeped over her dad's shoulder. 'Bye.'

Lucie sent them off with a wave, then turned to greet the next group of people heading along the path. Recognising, Arthur who was strolling towards her chatting to a couple, her heart skipped a little beat.

'How's it going?' he asked as he bent to kiss her cheek. 'It's mayhem up at the marquee. Iggy can hardly keep up with all the kids clamouring to exchange their wooden eggs for chocolate ones.'

'It's been brilliant, really busy, although it seems to have thinned out now.' She cast a quick glance back up the empty path.

Arthur nodded. 'We reckon just about everyone has come through, so I've come to collect you.' He gestured towards the couple standing off to one side. 'I wanted to introduce you to some friends of mine. This is Joss, and his wife, Henrietta. I think I mentioned them to you when you first arrived. My father was Joss's godfather.'

A wave of nausea ripped through Lucie so fast and hard, she thought she might faint. Though they hadn't seen each other for years, she recognised the heavily-pregnant blonde from their days at school together. From the interested raise of her eyebrow, it was clear that Henrietta remembered her just as clearly. 'Hello, Lucie.'

'Hi, uh, long time no see.' Lucie swallowed the bile in her

throat and turned to the sandy-haired man beside her former friend. 'Hello, Joss, is it? It's good to meet you.'

Apparently unaware of the tension between Lucie and his wife, Joss took her hand and shook it with enthusiasm. 'Hello! I'm delighted to meet you. I couldn't believe it when Arthur told me the other day that he'd finally met a decent girl. About bloody time, too!' He clapped Arthur on the shoulder.

'I didn't know you'd been in contact.' Although why would Arthur feel obligated to give her the details of every person he spoke to?

'I wanted Joss and his folks, and Henrietta, of course, to come and celebrate with us. I'm not sure if I told you, but our fathers were at school together, same as us. We've grown up in and out of each other's homes, so Joss is a bit of a surrogate great-nephew to Morgana.'

'She's in fine form, isn't she?' The way Joss's eyes crinkled as he smiled told her he did a lot of it, and Lucie started to feel a little bit more relaxed in his friendly presence. 'I swear she hasn't aged a day since we were kids.'

'How long have you been here at the castle, Lucie?' The question from Henrietta sent Lucie's nerves skyrocketing once more.

'Umm, just a little over a month, I'm here on a research project.' Feeling panicked by the way Henrietta was scrutinising her, Lucie turned to Arthur. 'Perhaps we should be getting back?'

'There's plenty of time. I thought we could show Henrietta the circle, as this is her first visit here, and we can round up any stragglers along on the way.' He touched a finger to her cheek. 'Are you okay, you're very pale.'

'I'm fine. Just a bit thirsty. I've been out here a couple of hours, and I forgot to bring any water with me. You guys go ahead, and I'll head back and find a drink.'

'Don't worry, we've got you covered.' Joss unslung a small backpack from his shoulder. 'Now Henrietta is in her last few

200

weeks, we've taken to carrying everything but the kitchen sink with us.' He fished a bottle of water out and handed it to her. 'There you go.'

Great. Friendly and helpful, just what she needed.

She tried to refuse it but was assured there was plenty more. Before she knew quite what was happening, she and Arthur were walking hand-in-hand a few paces behind Joss and Henrietta. 'I didn't think you knew each other,' Arthur murmured.

Hating the hot splash of embarrassment rising on her cheeks, Lucie turned her head away, as though admiring the bluebells dancing in the breeze. 'It was a long time ago. We kind of lost touch when I had to leave Wessingdean.'

'I'm sorry. Perhaps I should have mentioned they were coming. Did the two of you have some kind of falling out?'

She should tell him what had happened, about how Henrietta's father was one of the many people who'd fallen victim to her father's fraudulent schemes, but she didn't want to drag it up today of all days. Having already set it in her mind to talk to Arthur about everything, she'd been feeling a bit less guilty. Until now, that was. No. She needed to stick to her plan and wait until after the party, and until after her mum had gone back home. It would be bad enough for Lucie to relive it all, without putting her through it as well. 'It's not that. I don't have anything against Henrietta.' Though that might not be the same case for her. 'I'd just rather not stir up any unhappy memories this weekend, okay? Give me a bit of time, that's all I'm asking.'

Arthur squeezed her hand with his, a comforting gesture that made her feel ten times worse. 'Okay.'

Arthur and Joss kept up an easy stream of conversation as they made their way down around the stone circle and back towards the rear lawns and the marquee. The queue of children claiming their Easter eggs had lessened to a trickle and Lucie could see Tristan and Lancelot setting up for the first of the games—a sack race. Leaving Arthur and Joss to settle Henrietta in a shady spot beneath the marquee, Lucie went to find her mum.

Constance and Mrs W were laughing together as they arranged covered plates of sandwiches, cakes and homemade sausage rolls on a large trestle table set up along the opposite end of the marquee. 'Can I give you a hand?' Lucie asked, not wanting to make a scene in front of the housekeeper.

'I think we're just about there, darling. What do you say, Pauline?' Constance and Mrs W had become firm friends over the past couple of days once she'd insisted on being allowed to help with the party preparations.

'There's just the trifles to bring out, Connie. I'll pop in and give Betsy a hand with them.' The housekeeper departed, leaving the two of them alone.

'Mum...Henrietta's here.'

Constance put her arms around Lucie and drew her into a hug. 'I know. I saw her when she arrived. She's the absolutely spitting image of her mother, so I recognised her instantly.' Putting a finger under Lucie's chin she raised it until their eyes met. 'Did she say something to you?'

Lucie shook her head. 'No, she was very polite, actually. I just felt so awkward and embarrassed.'

Constance clicked her tongue. 'There's nothing to be embarrassed about. You were just a little girl. Like I've already told you, what your father did was nothing to do with you. I feel ridiculous and foolish for letting him dupe me all those years, but there's nothing for you to be ashamed of.'

'I know, it's just...I told Arthur I didn't know her, and now he knows I've lied to him about it.' Lucie hung her head. Only a small lie, but they were building up these lies, and omissions and secrets.

'I'm sure once you explain everything, he'll understand.' Her next words filled Lucie with horror. 'Did you want me to speak to him?'

202

'Goodness me, no!' Talk about taking the coward's way out. No, this was her mess and she would deal with it. *Soon.* 'It's fine, really. I was just a bit shocked to her see her, that's all. Don't worry about it.'

Constance smoothed a stray strand of hair off Lucie's face. 'Well, as long as you're sure?' She didn't look entirely convinced.

'I'm sure.' She caught sight of Mrs W and Betsy making their way from the kitchen doors. 'Look, here come the trifles. I'll go and let Arthur know, so he can make an announcement about the buffet.'

'All right, darling.' As she turned away, Constance stopped her with a hand on her arm. 'Don't leave it too long, Lucie, or he might think you have something to hide. Which you don't, of course.'

Other than she was the daughter of a convicted fraudster who had taken the job here at Bluebell Castle under false pretences. Nothing to hide, at all. Lucie somehow forced her lips into some semblance of a smile. 'I'll talk to him after the party is over.' And hope it didn't mean the end of their own personal party once he understood the full truth.

\*

There was little left of the buffet than a handful of crumbs and those visitors from the village with small children had been slowly trooping back down the hill in dribs and drabs. The sound system was playing some easy listening instrumentals, providing a gentle backdrop to the various conversations at the tables scattered around the marquee. Tristan, had set up some large metal tubs borrowed from the pub and filled them with ice. Bottles of beer and wine, and cans of soft drinks rested in the chilled buckets for anyone who wanted a drink to help themselves. The crowd had thinned out around the central table were Morgana had been set up like a queen surveying her court. Dozens of cards, bouquets of flowers and numerous small gifts covered the table in front of her.

Sitting down beside her, Lucie offered Morgana one of the two glasses of champagne Arthur had pressed upon her. 'Are you having a nice day?'

Morgana, looking stylish as ever in an elegant, emerald green tea-dress with three-quarter length sleeves and a cinched-in waist of enviable trimness accepted the champagne with a smile. 'It's been a wonderful day, my dear, just marvellous. Watching everyone, especially the children, having such a splendid time was a joy.'

They clinked glasses, and both took a sip. 'I'm so pleased you're having a good time, and you've made out like a bandit with all these presents.' Lucie gave her a cheeky grin.

'I did do rather well, didn't I?' Morgana's satisfied expression said she'd received no more than her due. 'And how about you, Lucie? Have you enjoyed playing hostess, today?'

Hostess? Lucie almost choked as the bubbles from the champagne fizzed up her nose. 'I'd hardly call it that. It was a team effort and I just pitched in to help.'

'Nonsense.' Morgana snorted, and even that somehow managed to sound regal. 'Arthur's called you to his side time and again, I've watched him. He's delighted with you, dear, and he's made no bones about showing that to everyone.'

Flustered, Lucie twirled her glass between her fingers. 'We're just having fun together.'

Morgana fixed such a gimlet stare upon her, it was all Lucie could do not to shrink in her seat. 'Well, if all you're after is a bit of fun, girl, I suggest you make it clear to him, and sooner rather than later. The boy's clearly taken with you, and he's had enough upset in his life as it is. If you're playing with his affections, best you stop.'

'That's not what I meant!' Lucie protested. 'Not at all. I like Arthur, very much. It's just early days between us, that's all.'

Morgana pursed her coral-pink lips. 'Take the advice of woman who knows: when you find love, grasp it in both hands and don't ever let it go. Not for anything, or anyone.'

Stunned into silence, Lucie could only stare as Morgana rose from her chair. 'Now where are those nephews of mine, I want to dance.'

As Lucie watched Morgana make her way across to where Tristan and Arthur were laughing over something, her gaze was snagged and held by Henrietta, who was settled quietly in one corner with Joss at her side. Knowing she would have to face the music sooner or later, Lucie made her way over to them. Joss cast a hesitant look between them before rising when his wife nodded. 'Well, I'll leave you to it.'

Taking the chair he'd vacated, Lucie watched as he made his way over to join Arthur who was twisting away on the dancefloor like he'd been born in the Sixties, laughing as he watched Tristan and Morgana twirl through some complicated rock and roll moves. There was so much joy emanating from the three of them, and they were drawing amused and admiring glances from all sides of the marquee.

'They're having a good time,' Lucie said, deciding on something neutral to break the ice.

'Yes.' Henrietta's stilted response forced her to turn away from the fun on the dancefloor and focus on her former friend. Silence stretched between them, and Lucie wished she'd stayed away. Nothing good could come of this, why was she even trying to bridge a gap that had been left open for too long.

'I'm sorry, I'll leave you in peace.' She made to stand, was halfway up when Henrietta spoke.

'Are you? Sorry, that is.'

Lucie sank back down. 'I can never repay your family for what my father did, I wouldn't even know where to begin.'

Henrietta cut her off with a sharp gesture. 'That's not what I'm talking about. No one holds you responsible for that—well, no one with any sense would. I'm talking about us, Lucie. I wrote to you after you had to leave school. I sent cards, I even tried to call but your mum said you weren't up to speaking to anyone. I never heard from you again, it was like you'd dropped off the face of the earth.' She didn't look angry, just sad and disappointed.

'I didn't know what to say.' Even to Lucie's ears it sounded pathetic. 'I was embarrassed and upset. My world turned upside down, and everything was awful. They…they came into my room, Hen, took all my things away. Took my father away and we were left with nothing.'

'Oh, Luce…'

When Henrietta fumbled for her hand, Lucie gripped it hard. 'I'm really sorry,' she whispered. They sat in silence as music and laughter rang around the marquee, but it was like they weren't a part of it. Like the years had rolled back, and they were two lonely girls on their first day at school clinging to each other as they turned a brave face to the rest of the world.

\*

Several hours later, her feet sore from too much dancing, her ribs aching from all the laughter and her head spinning from one too many glasses of champagne, Lucie found herself plastered against Arthur's chest as they swayed to the strains of the last song of the evening. The rich mellow tones of Nat King Cole wove a spell across the mostly empty dancefloor. Henrietta had turned in not long after they'd been sitting together, but not without pressing her phone number on Lucie before she let Joss escort her to bed. Lucie had promised to call her, and she would this time.

'Those two are having a good time,' Arthur whispered against her ear.

Lifting her head from his shoulder, she followed the direction of his inclined head to where her mum and Lancelot were dancing together. There was nothing suggestive about their traditional hold, but the way Lancelot was staring down at her mum sent alarm bells ringing in Lucie's head. 'You don't think they're…'

'Why not? They're both free agents, aren't they?' Arthur nudged her until she met his gaze. 'Look, I know he comes across as a bit of a flirt, but Lancelot's not a bad guy.'

'I know, it's not that. It's just, I've never seen Mum with anyone else, not since Dad.' Which, when she thought about it, was an absolute tragedy. Deciding to mind her own business, she looped her arms around Arthur's neck. 'Have you had a good day?'

He leaned forward to rest his forehead against hers. 'I've had a brilliant day. The food was brilliant, the games, the dancing, everything. And most of all, you were brilliant.'

The affection in his tone warmed Lucie from the inside out. 'I think you're a little bit drunk, Sir Arthur.'

'Not that drunk.' He raised his head to capture her gaze. 'Why do you do that? Why do you deflect when I'm trying to tell you something important?'

Reaching up, she pressed her thumb to the frown line between his brows, stroking until the tensed muscles in his face relaxed. 'I'm sorry, I didn't mean to. Tell me what you wanted to say.'

His lips compressed, and she could tell she'd hurt his feelings. She rose on tiptoe to press her mouth to his, kissing and coaxing in little featherlight touches until he opened to her. Taking control, he kissed her until her head spun from far more than the residual effects of the champagne and she was clinging to him like her life depended upon it. 'Don't go,' he gasped, when they finally surfaced for air.

Confused, she cupped his face in her palms. 'I'm not going anywhere, Arthur, I'm right here.'

'I don't mean now,' he said, then pressed a hard kiss to her lips. 'I mean when the contract's up. Don't go home. Stay here with me. I don't care if there's a painting or not, I want you to stay here and help me build something amazing. Something as strong as the foundations of the castle, itself.'

Sincerity shone from his hazel eyes, and perhaps something else if she looked hard enough. *'But you don't really know me,'* she wanted to say. Not really. He looked and sounded like he was falling for her, the way she was beginning to fall for him and for just a brief moment she wanted to believe the fairy tale. It was too much, too soon, and almost too perfect to be true. What was it Morgana had said to her earlier? *If you find love, grasp it in both hands and don't ever let it go.*

But love could only last if it was built on the truth. Once he knew who she really was, he might change his mind. She was building a life on lies and omissions. It would need to stop, or she'd be as bad as her father. Tomorrow. She would talk to Arthur tomorrow and set him straight.

For tonight, she would let herself believe in the fairy tale.

208

# CHAPTER TWENTY-ONE

After the excitement of the party, things settled down over the next few days. They'd seen Constance safely off on the train back to London, and Lucie had thrown herself into studying Thomas's journals from dawn to dusk. It was like she was on a mission, and nothing and nobody—including Arthur himself—was going to come between her and the answer. By the time they tumbled into bed at the end of the day, she did little more than peck his cheek and turn over, mumbling about being tired.

Although it was tempting to hang around her, waiting for the crucial update that would give them the answer one way or the other, Arthur had decided it would be more helpful to scour the remaining unrecorded rooms and photograph every remaining painting he could find. It wasn't the only reason he wanted to hang around her. Since that night in the marquee, when they'd danced under the stars, he couldn't keep his mind focused for more than five minutes at a stretch. She still hadn't given him an answer as to whether she would stay, and he was worried he'd spooked her by pushing for too much too soon. Why else would she have put this distance between them, other than as a silent warning to back off? Though it was a struggle, he was determined to give her as much space as she needed.

Both Tristan and Iggy had taken confidence from how smoothly the party had gone and were already full of great ideas as to how they could expand upon it to organising regular paying events over the summer. Iggy was gung-ho for his suggestion about holding a huge midsummer festival, her passion for restoring the formal gardens had been reignited after a long afternoon she'd spent walking the overgrown pathways with Constance. The older woman's kind, encouraging presence seemed to have done as much to boost his sister's attitude as it had spending time with someone else who was as obsessed with all things green.

Arthur was pleased for both of them. The guilt he felt over Tristan putting his career on hold to come home and help him out had been weighing ever more heavily on Arthur's shoulders and it was a relief to see Tristan putting his skills to use once more. He'd be able to list any events they organised on his CV which might go some way to appeasing potential employers once Arthur was able to convince his brother to pick up the pieces of his own life once more.

Iggy had always loved being outdoors, and if he could somehow scrape together enough money to keep things going by selling the other items Lucie had identified as being valuable—because he wasn't going to let himself bank on some painting that might not even exist—then helping his sister to restore the gardens was going straight to the top of his priority list.

And as for himself, well it was past time he stopped playing at being the baronet and fully embraced his position, which was why he was standing outside his butler's private office with his knuckles inches from the door. One deep breath and then he knocked. 'Maxwell?'

The door swung open within seconds to reveal the butler straightening the cuffs of his hastily donned jacket. 'Sir Arthur, is there something I can assist you with?'

'Yes, actually, there is.'

*

210

The two of them stood in the centre of the drawing room which separated the baronet's bedroom and the one opposite traditionally occupied by the baronet's wife. Beyond each room lay a pair of en-suite bathrooms and dressing rooms, with a further small study for the baronet, and a private sitting room for his wife. What little furniture remained in the drawing room was hidden beneath dust covers. Arthur grimaced at the flocked wallpaper. 'It's very outdated.'

'It wouldn't take too much effort to bring it up to scratch, sir. We ensured a good lining paper was used when your mother chose this design, so the original walls would be protected.' It was about as close to a criticism Arthur had ever heard from the butler's lips.

'The walls I can live with for now, but I'd like to do something about the furniture at least. Here, and next door.' The baronet's suite was full of dark, heavy pieces that seemed to suck in all the natural light. They also reminded him too much of when his father had occupied the rooms.

Maxwell walked the short distance from the sitting room into the bedroom. 'If we remove the curtains from the bed and swap one or two of the paintings for something a bit less formal, it would improve things no end.' He ran a hand along the carved edge of one of the bedposts. 'Your father never bothered much with things, so everything is long overdue a decent polish. I'm sure that between us Mrs Walters and I can have the suite spick and span within a few days.'

Arthur clapped him on the shoulder. 'There's no immediate rush, Maxwell, so please fit it in around your other duties as and when you can. It just feels like the time is right for me to move in here.'

'Very good, sir.' The butler all but vibrated with happiness. 'And the Lady's suite? Would you like us to make preparations for that to be put to use, also?'

Arthur nodded. 'If you would please. There's a set of four

paintings in the west drawing room showing the stone circle. Would you arrange for those to be hung in the other bedroom?' He knew how much Lucie liked them, and if they reached a point where she was ready to commit to something more serious between them, he wanted her to know he'd been planning this as a space for her as much as for him.

'I'm aware of the ones you mean, sir, I'll make sure they're moved once the room has been thoroughly cleaned and prepared.' He made to leave, then hesitated by the door. 'I do not wish to speak out of turn, but is it to be hoped that Miss Lucie will be staying on with us, sir?'

The affectionate way he said Lucie's name told Arthur he wasn't the only one taken with Lucie. 'All in good time, Maxwell, but it doesn't do any harm to be prepared.'

'Very good, sir.' The butler left, beaming from ear to ear.

*

Arthur managed to stay away from Lucie until shortly before dinner. Having checked both the study and the library and finding them empty, he tapped on her bedroom door. 'Luce?'

'C…come i…in,' she hiccupped.

Slamming open the door, he was shocked to find her curled up on the bed, a pillow clutched in her lap as tears streamed down her face. He rushed over to climb onto the bed and pull her into his arms. 'My God, what is it? Are you hurt?'

'No, I'm f…fine,' she snivelled into the front of his T-shirt, clearly anything but.

Setting her away from him enough so he could see her face, he wiped at the tears wetting her cheeks. 'You're killing me, sweetheart, what's wrong?'

Using the sleeve of her top, she scrubbed at her face and sniffed a couple of times before answering. 'There was definitely a painting, but I think Thomas destroyed it.'

The soar of hope followed immediately by a blast of despair left him breathless for a moment. 'Are you sure?'

'No, but I've just read three pages of almost incoherent ravings about how his true love and his dearest friend have betrayed him and how the portrait is a terrible lie and he can never bring his eyes to fall upon it again.' She pointed to the journal lying on the bed covers beside her.

Arthur retrieved it, then leaned back against the headboard with Lucie curled up against his side. 'Show me where it starts.'

She flipped back a dozen or more pages. 'This is where he talks about the painting in detail. He's calling it *King Arthur greets the Lady Guinevere.*'

Casting his mind over all the paintings he'd photographed in the past couple of days, Arthur shook his head. 'I haven't seen anything that might come close to fitting a description like that.'

'Me either,' she said in a soft, forlorn voice. 'That's why I'm thinking he might have destroyed it.' She flicked over a couple of pages. 'He mentions here sitting for a couple of character studies for JJ to use, and how because he wants Eudora to be the focal point of the portrait that she is sitting for hours. He even compliments her on her patience and ability to remain so still.' She gave a little sniff before turning more pages over. 'It sounds like JJ took over the tower for use as his studio, using the upper chamber for his painting as it had more light, and the lower room as a bedroom.'

Arthur could already see where this was leading. 'So JJ and Eudora were alone for hours at a time in the privacy of the tower?'

'Uh huh. And it's as we suspected. Thomas caught them together one day. He flew into a rage and spent the night locked in his study getting drunk. When he woke the next day, the two of them had fled the castle, leaving only the painting in JJ's studio.' Lucie started sniffling again. 'I know it's stupid when it was over a hundred and fifty years ago, but I feel so sorry for

213

Thomas.' Tears welled in her eyes once more and she brushed them away.

Arthur let his head thud back against the pillows propped behind him. 'Poor bastard. If he did destroy the painting, you could hardly blame him for it.' Taking the journal from Lucie once more, he scanned back over the last few pages, struggling to decipher the flowing script. Thomas had got himself in a right state and most of it was rambling nonsense. He looked further back, read the paragraph describing how Thomas had discovered the couple in flagrante, frowned and read it over again. 'This doesn't make sense.'

Lucie shifted position until she was sitting more upright beside him. 'What doesn't?' She leaned across to read the bit he was pointing to.

'See, here? Thomas talks about following the passage into the tower, but there's no such thing. The only entrance in and out of the tower is external to the castle. Don't you remember, I told you how Tristan and I tried to find one when we were kids?'

Lucie frowned. 'So what does that mean? It's very clear earlier on that JJ was staying in the tower, and that's where Thomas caught the pair of them—in JJ's bed.'

He was still trying to puzzle it out when his mobile started ringing. He pulled it out, and saw Tristan's name on the screen. 'What's up?'

'It's dinner time, that's what's up. Can you put your delectable girlfriend down for five minutes and grace us with your presence? Betsy's done a roast and if her gravy goes lumpy because you've kept everyone waiting, there'll be hell to pay.'

'Damn. We lost track of time. Two minutes.' He ended the call and looked to Lucie. 'Dinner.'

'Oh, hell.' She jumped off the bed and ran into the bathroom. 'God, I look a fright,' she wailed before he heard the sound of the taps running.

When she reappeared a minute later, her whole face was

214

glowing from where she'd washed it. 'Do I look like I've been crying?'

'You look gorgeous.'

'Smooth talker.'

'Come here.' When she stepped into his arms, some of the tightness in his chest eased. Everything between them was fine, she'd just been caught up trying to find an answer in the diaries, nothing more.

\*

They were still discussing the conundrum of the mystery passage as they took their seats in the dining room. 'Sorry we're late.' Arthur addressed his apology to Morgana.

'It's all Thomas's fault,' Lucie added as she laid her napkin across her lap. As Maxwell began to place their plates before them, she gave everyone a brief outline of what they'd found in the journal.

'So there is a bloody painting, I'll be damned!' Tristan grinned and raised his glass towards Arthur as though making a toast.

'There *was* a painting, you mean,' Arthur corrected him. 'I've never seen or heard of anything like it that might fit the description. I know there's quite a few Arthurian-themed paintings around the place, but nothing that would fit that.'

Lancelot paused with his knife halfway through a slice of beef, his face thoughtful. 'No, I'm afraid you're right, my boy, I can't recall seeing it. And as for a tunnel to the tower, your father and I never found one.'

'You mean you looked for it as well?' Arthur asked.

His uncle nodded. 'That's how the pair of you got it into your heads to look for it, after your father told you how much trouble we'd got into trying to find it.'

'If there is such a tunnel, it would have to run from the baronet's apartment somewhere. That's the only part of the castle that shares a wall with the tower.' Morgana paused to thank Maxwell when he placed a glass of sparkling water by her plate. 'Have you heard of such a thing, Maxwell?'

The butler shook his head. 'I heard rumours of hidden passages when I started here as a boy. One of the other under-footmen tried to scare me at the time with a story of a boy my age who'd got lost running an errand in the castle. Said you could sometimes still hear him crying for help in the middle of the night. That must be nearly forty years ago now, and I can't say I've ever heard him, nor come across any kind of hidden passage.'

Arthur hadn't realised Maxwell had worked there for so many years. He'd only ever known him in his present role, and it was hard to picture a time when there were so many staff at the castle for some of them to require the title of *under-footman*, never mind footman. 'If it's a hidden passage, I don't suppose there's any point in look at the old plans in the library, is there?' he mused to Lucie.

Her eyes lit up. 'You never know. I mean if Thomas knew about it, then it can't have been that much of a secret.'

'Well, what are you waiting for, girl?' Morgana asked. 'Go and fetch them!'

*

In all his years, Arthur had never witnessed a scene of chaos in the dining room such as the one before him. The fact it had been instigated at his great-aunt's insistence made it all the more astonishing as he watched the paragon of manners and etiquette shove her half-eaten dinner away in order to more closely study the drawing in front of her. Tristan had lifted his plate from the table and was forking up mouthfuls of roast beef from where he was knelt on the floor with an old blueprint rolled out in front of him. Lancelot and Iggy had another plan stretched between them, while Lucie was sorting and discarding anything dated after

216

Thomas's time reasoning the tunnel, if it existed, would've been built well before then.

Moving to stand beside her, Arthur propped his elbows on the table. 'Any luck?'

'Not so far, although I've found a couple of promising diagrams showing the gardens.'

'Oh, where?' Iggy abandoned the drawing she'd been studying to whip around in her chair on the other side of Lucie.

Lucie smiled and pointed at several rolls she'd tucked on the floor beside her. 'I was saving them for you.'

'Fantastic. You're the best!' She planted a kiss on Lucie's cheek. 'You guys can manage without me, yes?' And without waiting for a response, she scooped up the garden drawings and vanished out the door.

'Well that's the last we'll see of her,' Arthur surmised.

'Hey, I think I've got something.' Scrambling up, Tristan held a large blueprint in both hands.

'Hold on a sec.' Arthur scooped up the dirty plates littering the table and placed them on the sideboard, Lucie and his uncle following suit with glasses, place mats and the large bowl of flowers that stood centrepiece.

Tristan laid the plan flat on the table, turning it upside down to him so it was facing the rest of them in the right direction. 'See, here?' He pointed to what looked like a section of wall to Arthur, and he said as much. 'No, that's what I thought, but if you look over here, this is another section of the same wall that butts up against the tower, but it's only half as wide.'

'That could just be a drafting error by whoever drew this plan,' Lancelot argued. 'They didn't have the same kind of accuracy with these things as they do today.'

'I agree with what you're saying, but this wider section runs along the rear of the baronet's bedroom. Now, if you were going to stick in a secret escape passage into the most highly defendable part of the castle, where would you put it?' Tristan jabbed the blueprint with his finger. 'You'd put it where the most important person had easy access to it!'

Arthur looked from his brother's triumphant grin to Lucie. 'What do you think?'

'It's got to be worth a look, hasn't it?'

# CHAPTER TWENTY-TWO

Morgana had retired to her room, declaring herself content to hear the results of whatever they might find in the morning, but the rest of them had headed straight for the baronet's suite of rooms. The wall Tristan believed the tunnel might be hiding behind was covered from floor to ceiling in sturdy squares of oak panelling. Spreading themselves along the length of the wall, they'd begun to examine the wood for any signs of a seam which might indicate a hidden entrance. It had soon become clear that the panelling was not all of one piece, or age, and that different sections had been removed and replaced from the slight differences in the patina of the wood.

'It's like hunting for a needle in a haystack,' Lancelot grumbled. 'And it doesn't help that the lighting in here is terrible. Why don't we come back in the morning?'

'Where's your sense of adventure?' Tristan grinned from the opposite end of the room. 'Don't you remember how exciting it was doing this as a kid?'

Lancelot laughed. 'I can barely remember what I had for breakfast this morning, never mind what I was doing fifty years ago. I'm off to my bed, and so will you be if you've got any sense.' He left the room after pausing to give Lucie a quick kiss on the cheek. 'Try and talk some sense into them, my girl.'

'Good night, Lancelot. I'm sure we won't be much longer.'

Once he'd left the room, she stepped back to survey the wall, hands on hips. 'I think your uncle has a point. This would be a lot easier in the daylight.' She looked over at Arthur. 'What do you say?'

'You're probably right.' He sounded disappointed but resigned. 'I'm not sure what we're expecting to find anyway. The passage is a distraction, we should be focused on trying to find out what Thomas did with the painting.' He shoved his thick fringe off his forehead only for it to flop back into place as soon as he took his hand away. It was getting really shaggy, the remnants of whatever cut he'd had almost completely outgrown.

Lucie quite liked this unkempt look on him, and it suited the wild nature of the Derbyshire countryside. She could picture him striding across the fells, hair blowing in the wind like Heathcliff, or one of those other old romantic heroes. There must've been something of her thoughts on her face, because he moved to her side, an amused smile ticking up the corner of his mouth. 'What are you thinking about, because it's not the painting.'

Stretching up, she curled her fingers into the tangled strands at the nape of his neck. 'I was having a bit of a *Wuthering Heights* moment.'

Comprehension glinted in his eyes and he swept his arms around her waist to pull her close. 'Why, Miss Kennington, I do believe you're trying to seduce me.'

'For God's sake, go to bed, you two.'

Lucie ducked her head into Arthur's shoulder, having completely forgotten Tristan's presence for a moment. It had felt so good to flirt, to let go for one moment the crushing guilt over still having not been honest with him about everything. She'd reasoned in the end it would be better to discover the truth about the painting, so that even if he was furious with her—and who would blame him if he turned her out on her ear—at least there would be something good to show for it. She would have done the job he had employed her to do, and she would have the comfort of knowing she'd gone a small way in helping to secure the future for the occupants of Bluebell Castle who'd all somehow taken up residence in her heart.

The more she'd thought about it, the more convinced she was that Arthur wouldn't want to see her when all this was over. Even if he could forgive her, a conman's daughter wasn't suitable material for a baronet's wife. Give it a bit of time and he'd get over her and find the right sort of woman to stand by him. Someone born to it, someone like Henrietta or any of the other girls she'd known at Wessingdean.

When she got home, she'd call Hen and see if she could suggest someone. It would be easy enough for her to set up an introduction, perhaps at the christening after Hen and Joss's baby was born. Arthur would likely be invited to be the godfather and carry on the tradition laid down by their own fathers.

There was also the not inconsiderable fear her reputation might cast a shadow over the authentication of the painting, if and when they did find it. Mud stuck, and even though she knew she'd done nothing wrong, just being under investigation by Witherby's could be enough to taint any discovery. Lucie also wasn't sure she'd be able to let it go with the kind of good grace Arthur deserved. She'd become so enmeshed in the tragic story of Thomas, Eudora and JJ it felt almost as if she knew them personally. To spend time working with the painting which was the culmination of their story, only to see it sold off would break something inside her—and if she lost Arthur, too, there wouldn't be very much left of her to put together again.

And so she'd set herself a target: get to the bottom of whether or not there was actually a painting, and then go. Once back in London, she would focus on clearing her name and leave confirming the provenance and authenticity of the painting to someone else. With her mind made up, she'd done her best to keep Arthur at arm's length, without raising undue suspicion. Tonight might be their last night together, so tonight, she'd hold nothing back from him and show him the feelings she could never put voice to.

'Don't do anything crazy, okay?' Arthur warned his brother before taking Lucie's hand.

'As if I would!'

They made their way along the long corridor from the west wing to the central landing above the great hall where Arthur paused to glance down over the bannister. 'I should take the dogs out before bed.'

His innate sense of responsibility was one of the most attractive things about him, and she told him so with a slow, passionate kiss. 'Go,' she said, more than a little breathless. 'I'll be waiting for you.'

'You're killing me, Luce.' Arthur clutched a hand to his chest before jogging down the stairs. With a sharp whistle to the dogs he was out the door without even pausing for his coat.

Lucie forced herself to keep smiling until he disappeared out of sight. She was killing herself, and there was no one else to blame for the dagger in her heart.

*

'Sorry, I'm sorry,' Lucie said as she stifled the third yawn in a row at the breakfast table.

Arthur placed a mug of tea before her, then bent to brush a kiss to her cheek. 'I didn't keep you up that late, did I?'

Avoiding the wicked gleam in his eye, Lucie blushed and shook her head. 'I couldn't sleep afterwards so I turned the light back on and read some more of Thomas's journal, not that it got me anywhere.' She'd read the journal only for long enough to be sure Arthur had been sound asleep before picking up a pen and paper and writing the hardest letter of her life. It was tucked safely beneath her pillow, together with a folded, yellow newspaper cutting.

'I don't remember that.' Which wasn't surprising considering he'd had a pillow over his head and most of the duvet trapped beneath one muscular thigh. She watched as he returned to the sideboard to fix himself a cup of coffee, her eyes following his every movement, her mind recalling all the wonderful things those clever, confident fingers had done to her the night before. The heat rose on her cheeks once more and she was grateful it was just the two of them in the dining room at that moment because if anyone was there to read her thoughts...

The door crashed open to reveal a very dusty-looking Tristan, still dressed in the same clothes he'd been wearing the night before. A dark smudge marred his left cheek and smears of what looked like orange brick dust down the front of his shirt as though he'd wiped his hands on it. 'You have to come and see this!' He vanished before either of them could say anything.

'Did you see the state of him?' Arthur plonked his full coffee cup back down on the sideboard.

Lucie nodded, rising from her seat. 'I don't think he's been to bed.'

'Oh, hell, what's he been up to?' They exchanged a brief, panicked look then dashed towards the door.

Arthur reached the door of the baronet's bedroom a few steps ahead of her and stopped dead, his broad shoulders blocking her view. She nudged him gently in the back, causing him to step into the room and she followed him in. Chaos and mess met her eyes wherever she looked. Several panels had been removed from the wall and rested against the edge of the imposing four-poster bed in a higgledy-piggledy manner.

Dust sheets which had been covering the furniture in the drawing room lay scattered across the carpet, covered in bits of dust and several very dirty footprints. Arthur's focus was all on his brother who stood grinning beside a gaping hole in the wall, the remnants of several red bricks scattered on a dust sheet at his feet. A solid-looking sledgehammer with a wickedly large head rested against the wall next to him.

'What the hell did you do?' Arthur demanded.

'I found the tunnel.' Tristan pointed to the hole, as though that explained everything.

As Lucie surveyed the damage there was something about the scene that was itching at the back of her brain. She looked from the exposed stone at the far end of the room where a couple of panels had been removed to the pile of bricks at Tristan's feet, and back again. Stone. Brick. Stone. Brick. Stone. *Brick*! The structure of the castle was solid grey stone. Bricks hadn't come into popular use until the industrial revolution, well after the original construction of the castle.

'Arthur!' Lucie grabbed his arm. 'I think Tristan is right! Look at the difference in the composition of the wall. It's stone down there, but brick here. Why would they be using brick unless it was for a later alteration?'

He frowned down at her and then across at Tristan who was nodding vigorously. 'That's exactly the conclusion I came to!' He held out a placating hand to his brother. 'Look, I know it looks like a disaster zone in here, but I swear to you I was really careful about removing the panels. The tunnel's here, Arthur, it exists.' His eyes were shining brightly once more.

Arthur chewed on his lower lip for a moment and Lucie could see his emotions flitting through his expressive hazel eyes—anger, frustration, worry, and at the end a brief flash of hope. 'Have you looked inside yet?'

'Not beyond sticking my head through and shining a torch, no, I wanted to wait for you.'

'And it's definitely a tunnel?' Arthur was starting to sound more excited now.

'It stretches the full length of the wall as far as I can tell. Well

224

beyond the beam of the torch.' Tristan rubbed his cheek, the weariness of his sleepless night fully evident on his face. 'Look, I'm sorry if I went overboard, I just got carried away.' He closed the distance to his brother and placed a hand on his shoulder. 'It's here, Arthur. All those hours we spent looking for it, and it's here.'

Arthur gave a slow nod, then lifted his gaze to meet his brother. 'Well, what are we waiting for?'

*

Two hours later, they'd taken down enough panels to fully expose the extent of the bricked area. It was just taller than head-height for Lucie and about twice the width of her body. The rear of several of the panels showed evidence of metal hinges of some kind, but whatever mechanism might have been in place to open them was no longer in existence. Arthur, looking as filthy as his brother, set the last of the removed bricks onto the pile they'd made on one of the dust sheets. Once Tristan had created the initial hole, they'd removed the rest by hand to try and minimise further damage. The initial infill had been a hasty job from what they could tell, the poorly mixed mortar flaking loose as they'd wiggled each brick out of place.

'Are you sure about this?' Lucie asked, suddenly nervous. No one had been inside the tunnel for who knew how long, but if Thomas had been the cause of it being sealed up, then it must have been at least a century and a half.

'We'll be careful, I promise.' Arthur looked his usual, confident self, and she tried to feel reassured by that. 'We won't step inside until we've checked it out, okay.'

'Okay.' Folding her arms across her middle, it was Lucie's turn to pace as Arthur and Tristan took turns to duck inside the entrance hole, their torches shining in every direction.

'It looks solid,' Tristan said. 'No sign of any water damage that

225

I can see.' He took a breath. 'It's a bit musty, but the air doesn't smell bad.'

'I can't sense any damp or rot,' Arthur agreed. He stuck his hand back into the tunnel entrance. 'It's very faint, but there's a breeze which would indicate air flow.'

'You're going in.' It wasn't a question. She could tell from their body language as much as their conversation they were gearing up for it. 'Promise you'll be careful.'

'I'll go in,' Tristan said. 'You should stay here, just in case. You're the baronet, after all.'

Arthur rolled his eyes. 'And as it stands, you're my heir so there's no call for you to take the risk over me.'

Tristan flicked a very pointed look in Lucie's direction. 'And you've got a very big incentive to look after yourself standing right there.'

'Okay, okay, you're right. But no daredevil stuff. You take a couple of paces in and no more.'

Lucie crossed to stand next to Arthur, clutching his hand tight as they watched Tristan bend low and step into the tunnel. As he took his first step forward, Arthur reached out and grabbed the back of his shirt. 'Just in case,' he said, when Tristan laughed.

'I'll be fine, big brother.' His voice echoed from inside the tunnel. 'The walls are still dry as far as I can stretch my fingers. I can't feel any moss or mould, just stone.'

'How do you feel? Any dizziness?'

'Nope, all good. I think I'll go a bit further.'

'Give me your hand, first.' Arthur tucked as much of his body as he could inside the tunnel whilst keeping his head outside.

'You're such a fusspot.' Tristan's voice came fainter as he shuffled further down the tunnel.

'Baronet's prerogative.' Arthur's retort made them all laugh, and Lucie felt the tension begin to seep from her frame. It was a bittersweet moment, and she hugged the simple joy of it close to her heart. A memory to tuck away for later. When she was alone. Arthur winked at her, eyes bright with mischief, and it was all she could do not to cry. Turning back to the hole, he called out to his brother. 'Can you see anything yet?'

When Tristan spoke, he sounded like he was right behind Arthur, making them both jump. 'I think there's a junction further on. I could see a stone wall at the end, but when I shone the torch to the left there was a dark section, like empty space.'

Arthur eased his body out of the gap to let Tristan back into the bedroom. 'You feel okay?'

'I'm absolutely fine, I swear it.'

He looked okay, but that didn't stop Lucie from feeling nervous. 'I think we should fetch the others before you both go in there. If something should happen, I'm not going to be able to get you out on my own.'

Arthur gripped her shoulders. 'I'm not going to let anything happen to us, I promise.' Ah, if only. But the wheels were already in motion, and things were careening out of her control. All she could do was cling on and try to enjoy the final moments of this rollercoaster ride.

While Arthur and Tristan headed out to the stables to find some rope, Lucie hunted down Lancelot in the dining room where he was lingering over a late cup of coffee and Maxwell who was in his office. When she explained what was happening, the butler swapped his suit jacket for a navy-blue cotton overall which he buttoned over his shirt and trousers. 'We have some portable lamps in one of the store cupboards, Miss Lucie. The castle has been known to lose power if we get a severe storm in the area. I'll go and fetch them and join you directly.'

By the time she'd returned to the bedroom, Iggy was there as well, and together with Lancelot she was tying a long length of rope around Tristan, then Arthur, with plenty left coiled on the floor at their feet. It was probably overkill, but Lucie was relieved they were taking sensible precautions. 'Maxwell's bringing some portable lamps.'

The next ten minutes were the longest of Lucie's life as Tristan and Arthur disappeared back into the tunnel each carrying a couple of free-standing electric lanterns. A faint glow could be seen coming from the tunnel, but frustratingly, that was all she could see as Lancelot had stuck his head and shoulders inside to follow their progress.

'Now what's happening?' Iggy demanded for the third time in as many minutes, making Lucie grin. Impatience wasn't gnawing at just her nerves.

'They're coming back,' Lancelot reported a few moments before he backed out of the gap in the wall, Arthur then Tristan following on his heels.

Neither spoke as they untied the rope from around their waists, and then Arthur was holding his hand out to Lucie. 'Come with me.'

'Wait, what did you find?' Iggy demanded, but Tristan stilled her with a hand to her arm and a firm shake of his head.

Anticipation and trepidation warring within her stomach to the point of almost sickness, Lucie let Arthur lead her down the tunnel. The lanterns did their job, illuminating the blank grey stone walls as well as the floor beneath their feet. As Tristan had surmised, the tunnel took a turn to the left where it opened out into a small octagonal shaped area. Arthur's torch swept slowly around the space, and Lucie followed the beam of light. The walls were the same dressed stone as the passage way, apart from a section of red brick mirroring the one they'd removed from the bedroom wall. 'Do you think that leads to the tower?'

'I'm assuming so, but we'll worry about that another day. Look.' The beam from his torch shifted towards the centre of the space, highlighting a small wooden frame covered in a large cloth.'

Knees weak, Lucie clutched at his arm for support, sending the torchlight dancing wildly for a moment before he tensed his muscles to take her weight. 'Is it…?' She wet her dry lips and tried again. 'Did you look underneath?'

Arthur switched the torch to his other hand then lifted his free arm to pull her into his side. 'No. I wanted us to do this together.'

A million thoughts raced through her brain. It could be anything under there, or if it was the painting then it could be damaged either by Thomas's rage or the years it had stood here alone in the dark. It might not be finished, or it could be unsigned…the whirling doubts rolled in an endless loop. 'I can't bear to look,' she whispered.

'But if we don't look, we'll never know. This is it, Lucie, this is the future within our grasp. I can feel it.' The surety with which he spoke was almost enough to drive her to her knees. Fingers trembling, she lifted both corners of the sheet and inched it up. The cloth moved freely and before she knew it, it was a crumpled heap on the floor beneath the easel.

Arthur passed the torch slowly over the surface of the painting, illuminating first the figure of a man dressed in full medieval armour kneeling on the ground his adoring gaze fixed upwards. The beam of light followed that gaze to reveal a woman sitting side-saddle on an ivory-white horse, her brilliant azure gown spilling like a waterfall over the horse's flanks to trail upon the ground. 'She's a redhead, just like you,' Arthur breathed against her ear.

'She's exquisite.' The image wavered before Lucie, tears welling in her eyes until they all but obliterated her vision. 'It's the most beautiful thing I've ever seen.' Overwhelmed, she buried her face into Arthur's chest and began to sob. A tumult of emotions assailed her. They had an original, previously unknown JJ Viggliorento in their possession. Arthur's troubles were over.

And hers were just beginning.

It was a selfish thought, but she couldn't help it. 'We should go.'

'What?' Arthur's incredulous voice echoed from the ceiling.

She tugged on his arm. 'I mean it Arthur. We need to leave

this as it is until an independent expert can come and inspect it.' Digging in, she kept them moving backwards towards the tunnel.

'But you're the expert.' He sounded completely bewildered and looked as much when one of the lanterns illuminated his face. 'You're not making any sense, Lucie.'

She fisted his shirt, trying to get him moving again. Trying to put some distance between her and the painting as though her very presence would somehow taint it. 'I'm not independent though, am I? I'm your girlfriend and the art world is so full of rumours, suspicion and innuendo that if anyone catches wind of my involvement they could claim we cooked the whole thing up. Leave it!'

Desperate now, she tugged until he reluctantly followed her out. 'I don't understand.'

'It's fine, Arthur, everything is fine.' As they made their way back into the bedroom, she couldn't bear to look at him. 'You guys get everything here tidied up and I'll go and make a call to Witherby's. I'm sure they'll be able to send someone up in a day or two and get the ball rolling with authenticating the painting.'

Not waiting for an answer, she fled the room. It was now or never.

# CHAPTER TWENTY-THREE

Stunned by Lucie's swift exit, Arthur could only gape after her until his brother's voice intruded. 'Did you see it?' Tristan demanded.

'It's amazing. More beautiful than I could have imagined,' he replied, still dazzled by the few glimpses he'd seen of the painting.

'I want to see it.' Iggy started towards the tunnel, but Arthur blocked her way.

'No. Nobody can go down there. Lucie said we need to wait for an expert to come and authenticate it.' He held out his arms to cut off the hole in the wall.

'What are you talking about?' Lancelot demanded. 'What's the problem?'

He shrugged. 'I don't know, but Lucie thinks we need to get an independent expert up here to verify it. She's gone to make a call.'

A babble of confusion rose from the others. 'But she's the expert!' came from more than one person.

'But not independent,' he stressed, because that seemed to be important to Lucie. 'Because she and I are together, it might cast doubt on the authenticity of the painting.'

'You can't be serious,' Tristan protested. 'We're all here as witnesses to what happened.'

Arthur shrugged once more. 'That's what she said, and we're going to have to trust her. Come on, let's sort this mess out.'

Ten minutes later, he checked his watch with a frown. How long did it take to make a call? Something wasn't right. From the moment Lucie had laid eyes on the painting, something had been off. Panic gripped him, and he was running from the room before he was fully conscious of moving. As he hurried along the corridor, the dogs sent up a cacophony of noise from the great hall, and he put on a burst of speed.

Running into the hall, he stopped short at the sight of the pack milling around before the closed doors, and his gut twisted again. He waded through the barking mass and dragged open one side of the door just in time to hear the crunch of tyres on gravel. Stumbling out onto the drive, he saw a flash of red as the retreating car touched its brakes before turning out of the gateway and disappearing. *What the hell?*

Leaving the dogs sniffing and snuffling around outside, Arthur was halfway up the stairs when Tristan came thumping into the great hall, the others on his heels. 'Arthur, what's going on?'

'I don't know,' he admitted, before hurrying up the stairs. But he had a very bad feeling about it.

*

'I don't understand,' Iggy said, for what must have been the dozenth time in the past hour. 'How could she just up and leave like that?'

Tristan held up the newspaper clipping he'd retrieved from the carpet after it had fluttered from Arthur's nerveless fingers. 'Do you think this is really her dad? The bloke in this article?'

'Surname's the same, and the dates would fit.' Assuming Lucie had told him the truth about her age, and given she'd apparently lied about everything else, who could tell. Not him, that was for bloody sure. His eyes strayed to the pages of the letter scattered across the bed next to him. It already felt as though every word had burned its way into his brain. Still, it didn't stop him from picking it up to read again.

*My darling Arthur.*

Well, that was a bloody joke for a start, wasn't it?

*I'm so sorry to do this to you, but I wasn't sure how else to try and explain everything to you.*

She could've opened her goddamn mouth and tried. There'd been plenty of time when the two of them had been cuddled up in this bed together. He felt sick just thinking about it. On and on he read as she laid out one excuse after another for not telling him about being put under investigation by Witherby's. How his advert had felt like a lifeline when everything was falling apart—Ha! He knew the bloody feeling. How it was all for the best, that once he'd given it a bit of time he'd understand she was acting in his best interests.

Cold fury settled over him as he scanned the final few lines.

*I fell in love with Thomas and Eudora's story, just like I found myself falling in love with you. And though I know all the reasons why you would have to do it, I couldn't stay and watch you sell the painting. It would break my heart, almost as much as leaving you is going to do.*

*I'm so very sorry, love Lucie.*

Break her heart? Break her fucking heart? A bitter laugh escaped him. She didn't have a heart to break, and she certainly didn't know the first goddamn thing about falling in love. He stared at the telephone number she'd scribbled at the bottom. Not hers, of course, but the details of a contact at Witherby's. A proper expert.

233

He looked from his brother to his sister. They were what was important now. Them and the rest of the family. He was Baronet Ludworth, and he had responsibilities to see to. After tearing the bottom off the letter—the only bit of its contents that were of any use to him—he stood. 'Right, I'd better make a call then.'

*

It was several days later when Tristan knocked at the door of his study before barging right in. 'I told you I was busy,' Arthur said, irritably, as he laid down his pen. He'd sent a photograph of the painting to some bloke named Piers at Witherby's, together with scanned copies of several pages of Thomas's diary and was waiting to hear back. There was nothing more he could do, so he'd thrown himself into planning the midsummer fete. Even if the painting was found to be genuine, he still had the future of this family to secure and had decided to plough ahead with the plans for opening the castle to the public.

Ignoring his glare, Tristan shoved his hands in his pockets as he propped himself up against the wall just inside the door. 'You have to talk about her, Arthur, you can't pretend she never existed.'

Oh, couldn't he? Well, he was going to give it a damn good try. 'There's nothing to talk about.'

'Bollocks! If it wasn't for Lucie, we wouldn't be sitting on a potential goldmine. She was the one who found the sketch of Eudora and understood its significance. She was the one who spent hour after hour ploughing through those diaries and sorting out all the mess in the archives. If it wasn't for her, we'd have never found the plan which led us to the tunnel, and that bloody painting would still be mouldering away in the dark. Forgotten!'

His brother might have a point, but Arthur was damned if he was in the mood to listen to it. 'She lied to me. To all of us.'

Tristan scoffed. 'She didn't lie, she just didn't tell the truth.

234

And who could blame her? No one wants to drag out the worst bits of their life and expose it to the public gaze. I know I wouldn't if I was in her position.'

'But she took the job here under false pretences, she said as much in her bloody letter!'

'She also protested her innocence, most vociferously!'

Arthur's head snapped up. 'You read it?'

'Well, of course I bloody read it, you idiot, what did you expect me to do?' Tristan pushed himself upright and came to stand before Arthur's desk. 'Shall I tell you what that letter said to me?' He didn't wait for Arthur to tell him he couldn't give a shit what it said to him, he just ploughed on. 'It said to me that a young woman who's been branded unfairly by an age-old incident that was nothing to do with her put your needs before her own. Not just yours, the whole bloody family's! She was on the cusp of the discovery of her career and she walked away to make sure that you had the means to save the castle and the rest of us along with it.'

God, why wouldn't he just shut up and leave Arthur alone? Because maybe he had a point, but Arthur wasn't ready to hear it. Lucie had left him, hadn't trusted him with her secrets, and broken his heart in the process. 'She should've told me!'

Tristan banged his fist on the desk, making them both jump. 'Why should she when this is how you reacted?'

No! He was twisting things. If Lucie had stayed and faced the music, had given him the chance to show her he could be trusted, it would've been fine. He would've understood. *Wouldn't he*?

'If you don't get your head out of your arse and stop sulking, I'll never forgive you. Each day you sit in here brooding, you're letting the best thing that's ever happened to you slip through your fingers, Arthur! Dad never fought for Mum when she left and look at how he ended up—miserable and alone for the rest of his life!'

How dare he? How dare Tristan put Lucie and their mother

235

together in the same sentence. 'She's worth a hundred of Mother, a million!'

Tristan slapped his hand to his forehead, as though to say he thought Arthur was an idiot. 'Exactly! Now what are you bloody waiting for?'

# CHAPTER TWENTY-FOUR

It was déjà vu, Lucie thought as she stared at the cracked bedroom wall and ignored the knock of her mother on the door. Leaving Arthur had been the right thing to do, but that hadn't made her feel any better. Hour after hour she'd stared at her silent phone, willing him to call, and yet knowing he wouldn't until she'd turned it off and thrown it into her dressing table drawer.

All the promises she'd made to herself about marching up the front steps at Witherby's and demanding answers had faded to nothing. There didn't seem to be much point in doing anything, not that she could concentrate, which was why she was curled up under her duvet once more. She wasn't just upset this time, she was angry. Angry with Arthur for letting her go, even though it had been the right thing to do, angry at herself for not fighting harder to defend her innocence in the first place. And beneath it all bubbled the bitterest and oldest anger, the one that had simmered inside her since the day her father had betrayed them and turned her life upside down.

The knock came again. 'Go away, Mum, please.'

'There's someone at the door to see you, Lucie. A Mr Hazeltine.'

Lucie sat bolt upright. The head of security from Witherby's had come to her home? This couldn't be good news. Her gut churned.

They'd obviously decided to sack her, and had chosen to do it here rather than summoning her to the auction house. Best to keep the stink of scandal as far away as possible, she thought bitterly.

She glanced down at her rumpled pyjamas. She couldn't face him like this, looking like she'd been wallowing in her own guilt. Self-pity, maybe, but not guilt. 'Tell him I'll be out in fifteen minutes.'

With her wet hair secured at her nape in a neat bun, Lucie eyed the contents of her wardrobe. Her first instinct was to don one of her prim skirt suits, to look every part the Witherby's girl, only she wasn't going to be one of those for much longer, was she? Her gaze landed on the carefully folded garment she'd found in her suitcase and tucked away for safekeeping. Drawing it out, she pressed it to her nose, inhaling the spicy scent of Arthur's cologne still clinging to the fabric.

She was still rolling the sleeves back as she padded into their tiny living room on bare feet. The moment she entered, Mr Hazeltine rose. 'Miss Kennington. It's very good to see you again.'

Good? To see her? 'What are you doing here?'

'I'm here to offer you an apology, and an explanation.' He gestured towards the sofa. 'Perhaps you'd like to sit down?'

Dazed, she could only stare at him. He didn't sound like he'd come to sack her, but why else would he be there? Apparently sensing her confusion, Lucie's mum took the initiative. She pointed at the armchair. 'You sit here, Mr Hazeltine, and Lucie, you take the sofa. I'll make us some tea.'

Lucie waited until the door had closed behind her before she spoke. 'Why are you here?'

The bluff man shifted uncomfortably in his seat for a moment. 'I'm afraid we at Witherby's haven't been square with you, Miss Kennington...Lucie.' He clasped his hands together then braced them firmly on the arms of the chair. 'I'm afraid your suspension was my idea. We've known for some time there's been a problem at the house, and although I had my suspicions, I didn't have enough evidence to act.'

'I don't understand.' The lump in her throat was the size of a golf ball and all she could do was swallow hard and nod at Mr Hazeltine to continue.

'When the incident with the Meileau arose, and forgive me for saying this, your father's unfortunate history was raised, I saw the opportunity I'd been waiting for.' Steepling his fingers, he stared over them at her. 'We've suspected Carl Nelson's involvement with a handful of embarrassing, not to say *costly*, incidences over the past few years.'

Carl? The man who'd taken her under his wing and mentored her from the moment she'd first stepped through the door at Witherby's? She couldn't get her head around it. 'But Carl's been there for years, you can't possibly think he'd have anything to do with this.'

'I'm afraid it's true. He was the one who told me about your father's conviction.' Mr Hazeltine's lips compressed into a straight line. 'He dropped the information in my ear a couple of weeks before the Meileau debacle. I think it was a kind of insurance on his part, setting you up to be the fall guy in case his plan to switch the paintings went wrong.' He raised an eyebrow at her. 'When both you and Piers recognised the copy, he panicked a bit and threw you under the bus as it were. I had no choice but to act immediately and suspend you. If I hadn't, it would've put him on guard that we suspected him.'

She still couldn't believe it. Carl had set her up? 'I don't understand how he thought he could get away with it?'

'Apparently, he was in cahoots with the owner, Mr Richardson. He convinced him to have a copy of the painting made to be displayed on the family's wall at home. Carl then switched the copy out for the original. The plan was for the mix-up over them to be revealed after the launch, forcing Witherby's to quietly withdraw from auctioning the item to hide our embarrassment over putting a faked painting on display.'

'But that doesn't make any sense.'

'Not the smartest of plans, to be sure. Carl was going to drop a rumour to an art critic that Witherby's had dropped the ball and couldn't tell the real painting from the copy, but when you and Piers spotted the fake, he panicked and pointed the blame at you. It wasn't as if he could admit to knowing there was a copy floating around.' Mr Hazeltine continued. 'He'd persuaded Mr Richardson they could sell to a private buyer once the fuss had died down. Carl would handle the entire transaction privately for twelve percent of the selling price. Given this is almost half our commission rate, they both stood to pocket a considerable amount between them. It's not the first time. We've had a number of items unexpectedly withdrawn from sale only to find out they were sold on the private market at a later date.'

Lucie could only stare at him. 'When did you find all this out?'

'I approached Mr Richardson, and to my surprise, he confessed the whole thing. His wife had found out about it and was furious with him, was threatening to expose him if he didn't come clean so I came knocking at just the right time. His statement has been enough for us to take action and Carl Nelson has resigned with immediate effect.'

'Resigned? But where's the justice in that?' Lucie was outraged at the idea.

The security head had the decency to look embarrassed. 'Witherby's has a reputation to protect.'

'But of course.' She couldn't hold in the bitter laugh. 'And where does all this leave me?'

Mr Hazeltine shifted uncomfortably in his chair. 'Well, that's entirely up to you. The board is willing to offer you a full written apology, and you are welcome to commence work again as soon as you wish to do so. Should you find yourself unwilling to return,

I'm authorised to offer you a generous severance package and a glowing letter of recommendation. You shouldn't have any trouble finding work at one of the other London houses. Not that we would wish to lose you.'

Could she go back? Could she walk through that door and act like nothing had happened and pick up the pieces of her life once more? She honestly didn't know. 'Can I think about it?'

As though she'd released him from a trap, Mr Hazeltine bounced up out of the chair. 'Of course, Miss Kennington, of course. Take all the time you need.' He was already halfway to the door before she'd even got up. 'I do hope you'll choose to come back in due course. You might not realise it, but you have a lot of champions there. I can't tell you the number of complaints I received once word got around about your suspension. We had to hold a full staff meeting once Carl resigned.'

'Everyone at work knows everything?' There'd be no slinking back through the door and pretending nothing had happened.

'Everyone knows the truth. Your reputation is fully restored.'

With them maybe, but not with the only person who really counted. 'I'll be in touch in a few days.' Lucie couldn't bring herself to thank him as she showed him out. At the end of the day, he'd used her cruelly to protect the reputation of his employer, and she wasn't sure she could forgive that.

*

Two weeks later, Lucie paused at the bottom of the steps leading to the main entrance of Witherby's and smoothed a hand over her skirt. When the reality of still having bills to pay had set in, she'd found she could forgive Mr Hazeltine after all. Besides, if she let Carl's actions drive her away, she would lose a piece of her self-respect she might never get back. Lucie had done nothing wrong and it was past time to act like it.

As she approached the door, it swung back to reveal the smiling

241

face of James, the doorman. 'Welcome back, Lucie. It's great to see you.'

'Thank you, it's great to be back,' she replied, almost certain she meant it.

'They're waiting for you in the preview room. You know the way.' James beamed from ear to ear like he'd told her something splendid.

Her stomach flip-flopped. Oh, goodness, was there some kind of welcome back party for her? She'd hoped to be able to settle in quietly, track down Piers and a couple of other friends for a bit of moral support before she faced everybody. 'Thanks,' she replied, weakly, and started down the corridor.

As she passed one colleague after another, each greeting her with a smile, a few words of welcome, even a couple of hugs, she grew more and more confused. Maybe there wasn't going to be a big fanfare, after all. Who was waiting for her in the preview room, then?

When she pushed open the double doors, her heart seemed to stop beating for a moment. The room was empty, apart from a very familiar painting nestled on an easel in the centre of the raised dais. Spellbound, she crossed towards it, her eyes roaming over the magnificent image of the woman astride a horse, a knight in full armour knelt in supplication before her. It was even more magnificent than she remembered, from Eudora representing the Lady Guinevere, her stubborn chin raised as though accepting her rightful due, to the love and yearning etched on the face of Thomas as King Arthur. Beautiful. Heartbreaking. A masterpiece.

'I'm furious with you.'

She spun so fast at the low, clipped words, Lucie almost stumbled down the small steps of the dais. Dressed in a smart dark suit and tie, Arthur was even more devasting than in his usual shirtsleeves and jeans. His dark brow glowered, giving proof to his words. Why was he here, what could this possibly mean? He couldn't want her to work on the project to authenticate the painting, could he? To have to deal with him, knowing everything she could've had and let slip through her fingers? It didn't bear thinking about. If she thought leaving Arthur had broken her, she'd been a fool. This would grind her down to dust. He wouldn't be so cruel.

It'd be no more than she deserved, though, given everything she'd put him through. 'You have every right to be. I'm sorry that I lied to you.'

'Is that all you're sorry for?'

The question confused her, what else was there? 'I hope you can at least understand why I did it. A painting like this appearing out of the blue would attract enough suspicion. I couldn't afford to be associated with it in any way.'

'Mr Hazeltine has been good enough to explain the vagaries of the art world to me.' His voice was so stiff, so devoid of warmth. So *Baronet* Ludworth, it cut her to the quick. He clearly couldn't stand the sight of her.

'James—th…the doorman, told me I was wanted in here, but he obviously made a mistake.' She turned towards the door, desperate to escape his cold glare. 'I should go—'

'If you walk out of that door now, I will never forgive you.' Oh, there was no coldness in his tone now, only heat, and anger, and beneath all of that the faintest flicker of something that threatened to turn her knees to jelly. *Need.*

She whirled about once more, expecting to find him glowering still, but instead there was such a look of yearning on his face, it could've been him on his knees in the painting. Hope sent her pulse fluttering. 'And if I stay, is there a chance you might forgive me?'

He took a step towards her, seemed to catch himself and held his ground. 'I shouldn't.'

Oh, he was going to make her work for this. If he wouldn't come to her, she would go to him. Today, and every day for the rest of her life if he would let her. She closed the space between them. 'But you might?' She slipped her hand inside the lapel of his jacket and placed it over his heart, gratified to feel it was pounding as hard as her own.

His lip twitched. 'I might have told the board that Witherby's would only receive my patronage if their *best* expert was put in charge of the project.'

'Me?' It came out as more of a squeak than she'd intended, but she couldn't believe what he was saying. He wasn't making her come to him, he was offering to meet her halfway.

Retrieving the hand she'd placed on his chest, he pressed a kiss to her palm. 'This is your discovery, Lucie. If it hadn't been for you, we might never have known about it. I won't let anyone steal your glory, not now. Not ever.'

The truth of what he'd done for her was staggering. He'd risked everything to rescue her reputation, put her above everything, including the future of Bluebell Castle. Gone against everything she'd warned him about.

She was beyond furious with him. She'd never loved anyone as much as she did him in that moment. 'You're an idiot.' She flung her arms around his neck. 'I love you.'

Arthur laughed as he gathered her close, a rich glorious sound she wanted to hear every day for the rest of her life. 'I love you, too.'

# Acknowledgements

Welcome to *Bluebell Castle*!

Creating a brand new setting has been so much fun, I really hope you enjoy exploring the castle and its surrounds as much as you like the new characters I've introduced you to. I can't wait to explore it with you as the seasons change over the next few months.

If you've read any of my other books, you'll know by now I have a thing for character names and creating a tenuous link from the Ludworth family to the Arthurian legends was just too tempting to resist. Poor Uncle Lancelot got the worst of it, but he seems to be coping admirably!

As ever, though the words on the page are mine, it takes a lot of people to write a book, and I'd like to take a moment to thank just a few of them.

First and foremost, my husband. All my happy endings start and end with you x

My fantastic editor, Charlotte Mursell, without whom I simply couldn't navigate the often-choppy waters of this publishing business. Knowing you have my back means everything.

Everyone at HQ Digital. I say it every time, but without each and every one of you who helps behind the scenes, there would be no book. You're the absolute best x

Special mention to Dushi for weaving her copy-editing magic. You bring the sparkle x

Rachel Bavidge brings my audio books to life. I'm so pleased you're back on board for *Bluebell Castle*.

So many author friends who hold my virtual hand and cheer

me on when I doubt myself. Rachel Burton, Victoria Cooke, Jules Wake, Phillipa Ashley, Darcie Boleyn to name but a few. Getting to know you all has been the biggest joy x

And, saving the very best to last, here's to you, my wonderful readers! Whether this is the first book of mine you've tried, or you've been with me from the start – thank you. If I can give you a few hours of escapism and enjoyment, my work is done.

Thank you for reading!

Thank you so much for taking the time to read this book – we hope you enjoyed it! If you did, we'd be so appreciative if you left a review.

Here at HQ Digital we are dedicated to publishing fiction that will keep you turning the pages into the early hours. We publish a variety of genres, from heartwarming romance, to thrilling crime and sweeping historical fiction.

To find out more about our books, enter competitions and discover exclusive content, please join our community of readers by following us at:

🐦 *@HQDigitalUK*

f *facebook.com/HQDigitalUK*

*Are you a budding writer? We're also looking for authors to join the HQ Digital family! Please submit your manuscript to:*

*HQDigital@harpercollins.co.uk.*

*Hope to hear from you soon!*

Turn the page for an exclusive extract from *Sunrise at Butterfly Cove*, the first novel in the enchanting Butterfly Cove series...

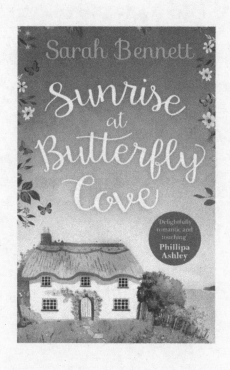

# Prologue

'And the winner of the 2014 Martindale Prize for Best New Artist is…'

Daniel Fitzwilliams lounged back in his chair and took another sip from the never-emptying glass of champagne. His bow tie hung loose around his neck, and the first two buttons of his wing-collar shirt had been unfastened since just after the main course had been served. The room temperature hovered somewhere around the fifth circle of hell and he wondered how much longer he would have to endure the fake smiles and shoulder pats from strangers passing his table.

The MC made a big performance of rustling the large silver envelope in his hand. 'Get on with it, mate,' Daniel muttered. His agent, Nigel, gave him a smile and gulped at the contents of his own glass. His nomination had been a huge surprise and no one expected him to win, Daniel least of all.

'Well, well.' The MC adjusted his glasses and peered at the card he'd finally wrestled free. 'I am delighted to announce that the winner of the Martindale Prize is Fitz, for his series "Interactions".'

A roar of noise from the rest of his tablemates covered the choking sounds of Nigel inhaling half a glass of champagne. Daniel's own glass slipped from his limp fingers and rolled harmlessly under the table. 'Bugger me.'

'Go on, mate. Get up there!' His best friend, Aaron, rounded the table and tugged Daniel to his feet. 'I told you, I bloody told you, but you wouldn't believe me.'

Daniel wove his way through the other tables towards the stage, accepting handshakes and kisses from all sides. Will Spector, the bookies' favourite and the art crowd's latest darling, raised a glass in toast and Daniel nodded to acknowledge his gracious gesture. Flashbulbs popped from all sides as he mounted the stairs to shake hands with the MC. He raised the sinuous glass trophy and blinked out at the clapping, cheering crowd of his peers.

The great and the good were out in force. The Martindale attracted a lot of press coverage and the red-carpet winners and losers would be paraded across the inside pages for people to gawk at over their morning cereal. His mum had always loved to see the celebrities in their posh frocks. He just wished she'd survived long enough to see her boy come good. Daniel swallowed around the lump in his throat. *Fuck cancer.* Dad had at least made it to Daniel's first exhibition, before his heart failed and he'd followed his beloved Nancy to the grave.

Daniel adjusted the microphone in front of him and waited for the cheers to subside. The biggest night of his life, and he'd never felt lonelier.

\*\*\*

Mia Sutherland resisted the urge to check her watch and tried to focus on the flickering television screen. The latest episode of *The Watcher* would normally have no trouble in holding her attention—it was her and Jamie's new favourite show. She glanced at the empty space on the sofa beside her. Even with the filthy weather outside, he should have been home before now. Winter had hit earlier than usual, and she'd found herself turning the lights on mid-afternoon to try and dispel the gloom caused by the raging storm outside.

The ad break flashed upon the screen and she popped into the kitchen to give the pot of stew a quick stir. She'd given up waiting, and eaten her portion at 8.30, but there was plenty left for Jamie. He always said she cooked for an army rather than just the two of them.

A rattle of sleet struck the kitchen window and Mia peered through the Venetian blind covering it; he'd be glad of a hot meal after being stuck in the traffic for so long. A quick tap of the wooden spoon against the side of the pot, and then she slipped the cast-iron lid back on. The pot was part of the *Le Creuset* set Jamie's parents had given them as a wedding gift and the matching pans hung from a wooden rack above the centre of the kitchen worktop. She slid the pot back into the oven and adjusted the temperature down a notch.

*Ding-dong.*

At last! Mia hurried down the hall to the front door and tugged it open with a laugh. 'Did you forget your keys—' A shiver of fear ran down her back at the sight of the stern-looking policemen standing on the step. Rain dripped from the brims of their caps and darkened the shoulders of their waterproof jackets.

'Mrs Sutherland?'

*No, no, no, no.* Mia looked away from the sympathetic expressions and into the darkness beyond them for the familiar flash of Jamie's headlights turning onto their small driveway.

'Perhaps we could come in, Mrs Sutherland?' The younger of the pair spoke this time.

*Go away. Go away.* She'd seen this scene played out enough on the television to know what was coming next. 'Please, come in.' Her voice sounded strange, high-pitched and brittle to her ears. She stepped back to let the two men enter. 'Would you like a cup of tea?'

The younger officer took off his cap and shrugged out of his jacket. 'Why don't you point me in the direction of the kettle and you and Sergeant Stone can make yourselves comfortable in the front room?'

Mia stared at the Sergeant's grim-set features. *What a horrible job he has, poor man.* 'Yes, of course. Come on through.'

She stared at the skin forming on the surface of her now-cold tea. She hadn't dared to lift the cup for fear they would see how badly she was shaking. 'Is there someone you'd like us to call?' PC Taylor asked, startling her. The way he phrased the question made her wonder how many times he'd asked before she'd heard him. *I'd like you to call my husband.*

Mia bit her lip against the pointless words, and ran through a quick inventory in her head. Her parents would be useless; it was too far past cocktail hour for her mother to be coherent and her dad didn't do emotions well at the best of times.

Her middle sister, Kiki, had enough on her hands with the new baby and Matty determined to live up to every horror story ever told about the terrible twos. Had it only been last week she and Jamie had babysat Matty because the baby had been sick? An image of Jamie holding their sleeping nephew in his lap rose unbidden and she shook her head sharply to dispel it. She couldn't think about things like that. Not right then.

The youngest of her siblings, Nee, was neck-deep in her final year at art school in London. Too young and too far away to be shouldering the burden of her eldest sister's grief. The only person she wanted to talk to was Jamie and that would never happen again. Bile burned in her throat and a whooping sob escaped before she could swallow it back.

'S-sorry.' She screwed her eyes tight and stuffed everything down as far as she could. There would be time enough for tears.

Opening her stinging eyes, she looked at Sergeant Stone. 'Do Bill and Pat know?'

'Your in-laws? They're next on our list. I'm so very sorry, pet. Would you like us to take you over there?'

Unable to speak past the knot in her throat, Mia nodded.

# Chapter One

*February 2016*

Daniel rested his head on the dirty train window and stared unseeing at the landscape as it flashed past. He didn't know where he was going. Away. That was the word that rattled around his head. Anywhere, nowhere. Just away from London. Away from the booze, birds and fakery of his so-called celebrity lifestyle. Twenty-nine felt too young to be a has-been.

He'd hit town with a portfolio, a bundle of glowing recommendations and an ill-placed confidence in his own ability to keep his feet on the ground. Within eighteen months, he was *the next big thing* in photography and everyone who was anyone clamoured for an original Fitz image on their wall. Well-received exhibitions had led to private commissions and more money than he knew what to do with. And if it hadn't been for Aaron's investment advice, his bank account would be as drained as his artistic talent.

The parties had been fun at first, and he couldn't put his finger on when the booze had stopped being a buzz and started being a crutch. Girls had come and gone. Pretty, cynical women who liked being seen on his arm in the gossip columns, and didn't seem to mind being in his bed.

Giselle had been one such girl, and without any active consent on his part, she'd installed herself as a permanent fixture. The bitter smell of the French cigarettes she lived on in lieu of a decent meal filled his memory, forcing Daniel to swallow convulsively against the bile in his throat. That smell signified everything he hated about his life, about himself. Curls of rank smoke had hung like fog over the sprawled bodies, spilled bottles and overflowing ashtrays littering his flat when he'd woven a path through them that morning.

The cold glass of the train window eased the worst of his thumping hangover, although no amount of water seemed able to ease the parched feeling in his throat. The carriage had filled, emptied and filled again, the ebb and flow of humanity reaching their individual destinations.

Daniel envied their purpose. He swigged again from the large bottle of water he'd paid a small fortune for at Paddington Station as he'd perused the departures board. The taxi driver he'd flagged down near his flat had told him Paddington would take him west, a part of England that he knew very little about, which suited him perfectly.

His first instinct had been to head for King's Cross, but that would have taken him north. Too many memories, too tempting to visit old haunts his mam and dad had taken him to. It would be sacrilege to their memory to tread on the pebbled beaches of his youth, knowing how far he'd fallen from being the man his father had dreamed he would become.

He'd settled upon Exeter as a first destination. Bristol and Swindon seemed too industrial, too much like the urban sprawl he wanted to escape. And now he was on a local branch line train to Orcombe Sands. Sands meant the sea. The moment he'd seen the name, he knew it was where he needed to be. Air he could breathe, the wind on his face, nothing on the horizon but white-caps and seagulls.

The train slowed and drew to a stop as it had done numerous

times previously. Daniel didn't stir; the cold window felt too good against his clammy forehead. He was half aware of a small woman rustling an enormous collection of department store carrier bags as she carted her shopping haul past his seat, heading towards the exit. She took a couple of steps past him before she paused and spoke.

'This is the end of the line, you know?' Her voice carried a warm undertone of concern and Daniel roused. The thump in his head increased, making him frown as he regarded the speaker. She was an older lady, around the age his mam would've been had she still been alive.

Her grey hair was styled in a short, modern crop and she was dressed in that effortlessly casual, yet stylish look some women had. A soft camel jumper over dark indigo jeans with funky bright red trainers on her feet. A padded pea jacket and a large handbag worn cross body, keeping her hands free to manage her shopping bags. She smiled brightly at Daniel and tilted her head towards the carriage doors, which were standing stubbornly open.

'This is Orcombe Sands. Pensioner jail. Do not pass go, do not collect two hundred pounds.' She laughed at her own joke and Daniel finally realised what she was telling him. He had to get off the train; this was his destination. She was still watching him expectantly, so he cleared his throat.

'Oh, thanks. Sorry I was miles away.' He rose as he spoke, unfurling his full height as the small woman stepped back to give him room to stand and tug his large duffel bag from the rack above his seat. Seemingly content that Daniel was on the move, the woman gave him a cheery farewell and disappeared off the train.

Adjusting the bag on his shoulder as he looked around, Daniel perused the layout of the station for the first time. The panoramic sweep of his surroundings didn't take long. The tiny waiting room needed a lick of paint, but the platform was clean of the rubbish and detritus that had littered the Central London station he'd

258

started his journey at several hours previously. A hand-painted, slightly lopsided *Exit* sign pointed his way and Daniel moved in the only direction available to him, hoping to find some signs of life and a taxi rank.

He stopped short in what he supposed was the main street and regarded the handful of houses and a pub, which was closed up tight on the other side of the road. He looked to his right and regarded a small area of hardstanding with a handful of cars strewn haphazardly around.

The February wind tugged hard at his coat and he flipped the collar up, hunching slightly to keep his ears warm.

Daniel started to regret his spur-of-the-moment decision to leave town. He'd been feeling stale for a while, completely lacking in inspiration. Every image he framed in his mind's eye seemed either trite or derivative. All he'd ever wanted to do was take photographs. From the moment his parents had given him his first disposable camera to capture his holiday snaps, Daniel had wanted to capture the world he saw through his viewfinder.

An engine grumbled to life and the noise turned Daniel's thoughts outwards again as a dirty estate car crawled out of the car park and stopped in front of him. The side window lowered and the woman from the train leaned across from the driver's side to speak to him.

'You all right there? Is someone coming to pick you up?' Daniel shuffled his feet slightly under the blatantly interested gaze of the older woman.

His face warmed as he realised he would have to confess his predicament to the woman. He had no idea where he was or what his next move should be. He could tell from the way she was regarding him that she would not leave until she knew he was going to be all right.

'My trip was a bit spur-of-the-moment. Do you happen to know if there is a B&B nearby?' he said, trying to keep his voice light, as though heading off into the middle of nowhere on a freezing winter's day was a completely rational, normal thing to do.

The older woman widened her eyes slightly. 'Not much call for that this time of year. Just about everywhere that offers accommodation is seasonal and won't be open until Easter time.'

Daniel started to feel like an even bigger fool as the older woman continued to ponder his problem, her index finger tapping against her lip. The finger paused as a sly smile curled one corner of her lip and Daniel wondered if he should be afraid of whatever thought had occurred to cause that expression.

He took a backwards step as the woman suddenly released her seat belt and climbed out of the car in a determined manner. He was not intimidated by someone a foot shorter than him. *He wasn't.*

'What's your name?' she asked as she flipped open the boot of the car and started transferring her shopping bags onto the back seat.

'Fitz…' He paused. That name belonged in London, along with everything else he wanted to leave behind. 'Daniel. Daniel Fitzwilliams.'

'Pleased to meet you. I'm Madeline although my friends call me Mads and I have a feeling we will be great friends. Stick your bag in the boot, there's a good lad. I know the perfect place. Run by a friend of mine. I'm sure you'll be very happy there.'

Daniel did as bid, his eyes widening in shock as *unbelievable!* Madeline propelled him in the right direction with a slap on the arse and a loud laugh.

'Bounce a coin on those cheeks, Daniel! I do so like a man who takes care of himself.' With another laugh, Madeline disappeared into the front seat of the car and the engine gave a slightly startled whine as she turned the key.

Gritting his teeth, he placed his bag in the boot before moving around to the front of the car and eyeing the grubby interior of the estate, which appeared to be mainly held together with mud and rust. He folded his frame into the seat, which had been hiked forward almost as far as it could. With his knees up around his ears, Daniel fumbled under the front of the seat until he found the adjuster and carefully edged the seat back until he felt less like a sardine.

'Belt up, there's a good boy,' Madeline trilled as she patted his knee and threw the old car into first. They lurched away from the kerb. Deciding that a death grip was the only way to survive, Daniel quickly snapped his seat belt closed, scrabbled for the aptly named *oh shit!* handle above the window and tried to decide whether the journey would be worse with his eyes open or closed.

Madeline barrelled the car blithely around the narrow country lanes, barely glancing at the road as far as Daniel could tell as she sang along to the latest pop tunes pouring from the car radio. He tried not to whimper at the thought of where he was going to end up. What the hell was this place going to be like if it was run by a friend of Madeline's? If there was a woman in a rocking chair at the window, he'd be in deep shit.

The car abruptly swung off to the left and continued along what appeared to be a footpath rather than any kind of road. A huge building loomed to the left and Daniel caught his breath. Rather than the Bates Motel, it was more of a Grand Lady in her declining years. In its heyday, it must have been a magnificent structure. The peeling paint, filthy windows and rotting porch did their best to hide the beauty, together with the overgrown gardens.

His palms itched and for the first time in forever, Daniel felt excited. He wanted his camera. Head twisting and turning, he tried to take everything in. A group of outbuildings and a large barn lay to the right of where Madeline pulled to a stop on the gravel driveway.

Giving a jaunty toot on the car's horn, she wound down her window to wave and call across the yard to what appeared to be a midget yeti in the most moth-eaten dressing gown Daniel had ever seen. *Not good, not good, oh so not good…*

Don't miss *Sunshine over Bluebell Castle*, the next book from Sarah Bennett, coming later this year!

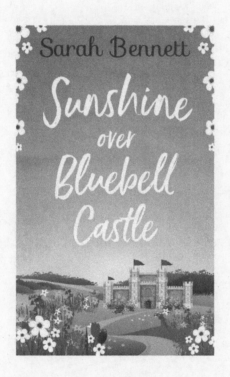

Don't miss Something over Bluebell Castle, the next book from Sarah Bennett, coming later this year!

DIGITAL HQ

If you enjoyed *Spring Skies Over Bluebell Castle*, then why not try another delightfully uplifting romance from HQ Digital?